AF230096

Also, check out these other offerings from the Author KR Bankston available via krbankstononline.com, and these fine online retailers: Amazon.com, BN.com,.

THE GIANNI LEGACY:
A Deadly Encounter (eBook/paperback)
Sins of the Father (eBook/paperback)
Smoke & Mirrors (eBook/paperback)
Life After Death (eBook/paperback)

THIN ICE – THE SERIAL (eBook)
Thin Ice
Thin Ice 2- Hide & Seek
Thin Ice 3 – Armageddon
Thin Ice 4- Resurrections
Thin Ice 5 – Checkmate
Thin Ice 6 – Hangman & Socrates
Thin Ice 7 – Echoes of Reckoning
Thin Ice 8 – Separazione Finale
Thin Ice 9 – Epiphany
Thin Ice 10 – Ambition
Thin Ice 11 – Homecoming
Thin Ice 12 – Siren Song

NOIR FROST SERIES: (eBook)
Shattered
Evolutions
Darker Shades of Light
Crosshairs
Reawakening

<u>**ORIGIN SERIES:**</u> (eBook)
X-Mafia: The Rise of Pirate & Creeper
Unholy Empire (pt1 & 2)
Christian
Atomic

<u>**OTHER BOOKS:**</u>
Three The Hard Way (eBook/paperback)
Crossroads: An Anthology (eBook/paperback)
Crossroads 2 (eBook/paperback)
Now You're A Star (erotic)
The Agency (eBook/Audiobook)
The Master Orchestrator (eBook/Audiobook)
King of the Game (eBook)
Unraveled: A Short Story Collective (eBook)
Interception (eBook)
Ace High (eBook)

<u>ABOUT THE AUTHOR:</u>

KR BANKSTON is a Fiction Novelist, Publishing Consultant, Public Speaker, and Mentor.
She hails from Tallahassee, FL and now resides in Jonesboro, GA. Having written various works of fiction including short stories for most of her adult life, Bankston entered the world of commercial publishing in 2008 with her first novel, A Deadly Encounter. She has since gone on to write and publish to date some 30+ novels, including two anthologies and two novellas. Even with accolades coming from varying lovers and consumers of Urban Fiction, KR is a nonconformist novelist who writes in a multitude of genres.

Contact the Author:
www.krbankstononline.com
kirabaco@gmail.com
http:/www.patreon.com/KRBankston
http://twitter.com/KRBankston
http://www.facebook.com/KRBankston
http://www.youtube.com/user/KRBTheAuthor

Cover Design info: missDEEsigner@urbanizdskillz.net

**Liberation is not a gift bestowed upon us
from our oppressor.
It is taken and owned by the decision that
NO ONE can keep them from it.**

For too long we've watched silently as we've been violated by our government at every turn. The rights and needs of the poor, minorities, and women have been ignored and trampled upon. It's time to stand up and say no. You have the power to make a difference and it is as simple as casting a ballot in your local, state, and federal elections.

If you haven't registered to vote, you may do so in the following ways:

- Contact your Secretary of State and request a voter registration form by mail
- Register at your Public Library
- Register at the DMV when you renew your license
- Register when you renew your TANF/Food Stamp benefits

Registering to vote doesn't automatically sentence you to jury duty. If you get a jury summons, don't avoid it! We need rational voices to keep our men and women from behind bars! **Convicted felons are not barred from registering!** States such as Rhode Island, South Carolina and Utah automatically restore your voting rights upon completion of your sentence. Check your state laws for complete information on restoring your voting rights if you've been convicted of a felony.

To Report Voter Issues: call the Civil Rights Division toll-free at (800) 253-3931, or contact them by mail at:
Chief, Voting Section
Civil Rights Division Room 7254 – NWB
Department of Justice
950 Pennsylvania Ave., N.W.
Washington, DC 20530

Your right to vote was secured through blood, sweat, and tears. Exercise it to the fullest without relenting. Social change and justice for people of color is not optional: it is mandatory. Make them know this by registering your voting voice today!

Even when all I can see is darkness, there is still light.
I need only take one step after another until the place
that I am in, becomes the place of once was.
KR Bankston

COLLIDING WORLDS

Peace Allah, Allah you justice, oh oh oh," the sound rang again and again until Tatiana finally rose from bed and sighed deeply. Glancing at the clock she sucked her teeth in disgust, peering out of her bedroom window to the plaza below. Tatiana didn't want to yell down and tell them to be quiet. There were certainly far worse things the group of teenagers could be doing on a Friday night. She could have done without the disruption in her sleep tonight though. Hearing a train whiz by she once again glanced outside.

Tatiana lived in an apartment complex called Londen Plaza, found on the street of the same name, between Elbert Lane and Lankton Avenue. There were five surrounding buildings elevated above the train yard below the complex. Each of the five buildings shared long ramps and stairs that led up onto the plaza area where the singing teens were now. Tatiana lived on the tenth floor, apartment 10E. She loved leaving her windows open in the evening, enjoying the cooler air of the late-night hours. She didn't worry about anyone breaking in, not through the window anyway. No one in their right mind was going to scale the side of the building up ten floors.

Heading into her kitchen Tatiana grabbed her tea kettle filling it with water and placing it on the eye. Igniting it, she turned and left the kitchen headed back to her bedroom to grab her robe and book. With the kids outside beginning to pick up volume and stamina, Tatiana knew sleep was gone for her until they finished.

Boy I tell you these folks and their religions, cults, and crap. She headed back into the kitchen as her tea kettle signaled its readiness. Pouring the steaming hot water on the cranberry apple teabag, she inhaled deeply the rich aroma rising from the cup.

After adding a touch of honey, Tatiana headed into her living room, tumbling into her favorite easy chair. Big and overstuffed you could shrink into it and imagine yourself invisible from the world. The medium forest green sofa and loveseat, complete with the matching multicolor pillows, meshed well with the woodsy rustic oasis. Tatiana opened the book finding the marker left earlier and began to read.

*****

Saturday morning found Tatiana still resting in her easy chair. Stretching and pouring herself from the comfortable cocoon she headed into the shower. Exiting moments later, she dressed to begin her day. Standing in the hallway, Tatiana mumbled under her breath growing more and more irritated with each second that passed waiting on the antiquated elevator. Listening to the gears as they ground against each other, she wondered if taking the stairs would not be a far safer risk at this point. The contraption finally made its way to the tenth floor where she stood. The doors laboriously opened.

Stepping inside Tatiana immediately frowned again. Inhaling the foul stench of too many souls and their cargo, assaulted her senses. Emerging lastly into the beautiful sunlit morning, Tatiana inhaled the welcomed fresh air. Her senses berated her lungs for the putrid hell they endured on her ten-floor descent in the elevator.

Naimah greeted her as she passed the bench where the young woman sat.

"Hey Miss Reynolds."

She and several other young ladies were listening intently once again to the four or five young men that were speaking to them.

"Hi Naimah."

One of the young men also addressed her.

"Peace Miss Reynolds."

"Hello," Tatiana smiled somewhat.

"My name is Sharif. Perhaps you would like to sit in and be enlightened by Today's mathematics?"

Tatiana regarded the young man silently for a few moments before finally opening her mouth.

"Thank you, Sharif."

Naimah lowered her head. She already knew what was going to come out of her neighbor's mouth. Tatiana held the reputation for being an atheist who didn't take very kindly to anyone trying to talk to her about anything religious.

"But I think I'll pass."

Not wanting to hurt the young man's feelings, she remained calm.

Sharif opened his mouth about to say something else when he was interrupted.

"So, you're not interested in truth?"

The rich masculine utterance startled her. Turning she took in the man standing in front of her.

"And you are?"

Smiling a tad, the man introduced himself.

"I'm Infinite Knowledge."

"Mmhm, I see. What is your legal, given name?"

Her eyes freely roamed the presentation before her, pleased with the nature inspired work of art.

"Jaden," he never took his gaze away from hers. "Jaden Paine. And yours?"

"Tatiana Reynolds."

"It's a pleasure to meet you. Why don't you join us, I think you'll find it very enlightening."

Tatiana chuckled.

"Oh, I'm sure you do think that."

Sarcasm dripped from the words as she prepared to walk away.

"What do you have against the truth?"

Jaden baited the query, not wanting her to leave just yet.

"Nothing, I just find that most times the truth is a very gray area with cults like yours."

"We are not a cult Tatiana. Please, sit down. Listen for a few moments and decide for yourself."

Jaden gained eye contact with her once more.

"Or are you afraid?"

Giving him a defiant look, Tatiana sat down, crossed her legs and folded her arms.

"Let's hear what you're working with then, hotshot."

The young people gasped quietly and turned their attention to their mentor. Amazement held them that he would allow such a blatant disrespect. Smiling somewhat Jaden turned his attention to the young people waiting.

"Peace gods. Peace earths."

They all returned his greeting and continued giving him their undivided attention.

"Today's mathematics, Wisdom and Understanding."

Tatiana allowed her mind to wander looking him over again as he talked. She took in the sexy frame, toned and muscular, with ample sized feet. Beautiful, deep, probing almost ebony brown eyes seemed to swallow her whole. All the sizzling attributes were complimented by an exquisitely toothy smile and full, desirable, lips. *He would be perfect if he wasn't into this craziness.* Tatiana reeled her thoughts in finally paying attention as Jaden continued to talk.

"Understanding is that which shows and proves the completion of Knowledge and Wisdom."

Tatiana took in his audience. The teens were paying rapt attention, hanging on his every word. She smiled marginally seeing the romantic school girl crushes some of the young women displayed watching their mentor, stars in their eyes.

"It is the Original child which is the star. The highest form of Understanding is Love, the bond between Man and Woman, or Knowledge and Wisdom."

Jaden finished up the lesson looking directly into Tatiana's eyes as he spoke. He held her gaze until one of the teens broke the connection asking a question and Jaden launched into yet another explanation.

Having heard more than enough, Tatiana rose as Jaden talked and made her way from the group headed out to find a taxi and begin her day of shopping and errands.

Jaden continued to talk to the group as he watched the woman leave. He admired every inch of her sexy frame as she walked. *She is a challenge.* Tatiana was a firebrand. She challenged him to be better in his thoughts and he loved that. She was also stunning. Sensual legs, manicured toes and hands, infectious smile, biting wit, and soft caramel melt eyes. Her hair was cut short and tapered in the back. He didn't care for that much, but even so Jaden would find a way to deal. *Hafta figure out how to get her attention again.* He wondered if any of the earths or gods knew her personally. Wrapping up the discussion finally, Jaden began systematically weeding out the answers to his questions. The gold strike landed once he began talking to Naimah, finally gleaning the information he sought, making plans to secure his own Earth.

CHAPTER 1

FICKLE ATTRACTIONS

Rushing, Tatiana headed for her office and another long Monday. She stopped and grabbed herself a cup of coffee, a bagel, and the morning paper before heading to the subway. She boarded a crowded car, thankfully found a seat and began perusing her paper.

"Good morning."

Jaden gazed directly into her eyes once she looked up.

Surprised to see him, the smile spilled into her face before she could stop it.

"Good morning."

Jaden smiled internally before addressing her again as they disembarked at their stop.

"Are you still angry with me about Saturday?"

Tatiana regarded him for a moment, sipped her coffee before she casually answered.

"Not at all."

"That's good to know."

"How did you get all mixed up in that whole Islam stuff?"

Jaden smiled a tad once more.

"It's not really a part of the Nation, Tatiana. And again, we aren't a cult either."

She continued to soundlessly regard him.

"Will you let me explain it to you more? Maybe over dinner?"

Tatiana thought about his request, trying hard to deny the curiosity and deep arousal felt in his presence.

"I guess we could do that."

She sounded a lot cooler than she actually felt.
She couldn't explain it. There was something about Jaden that turned her on deeper than lust. She wanted to explore every inch of this man physically and emotionally. Jaden smiled, and Tatiana felt her heart race.
"Great, can I get your number?"
Tatiana managed to give him the information, as well as retrieve his own.
"Have a great day, Tatiana."
That man is dangerous, Tatiana wickedly surmised watching his back as he left. She prided herself on being tough and holding her own, but Jaden already made her feel vulnerable and helpless when he was around. *What the hell?* Finally arriving at her desk, she tried desperately to push away what she felt developing for this man.

*****

"Hey Jaden," Nakida greeted him as he arrived. Jaden gave a small upturn of his lips and returned her greeting, not wanting to get started early this morning. He realized for some time Nakida held a huge crush on him. Now she started subtlety letting him know as well.
"How was your weekend?"
Nakida pressed him as she walked with him to his area. Taking him in once more, Nakida was even more determined that Jaden Paine not get away from her. He was a rare breed. A sexy brother with a good job, good credit, respect for his Nubian sisters, straight, and single. She just had nil clue what to do to get through to him.
Jaden was always pleasant, but he would never discuss his personal life, ever.
"Weekend was good. Went too fast, but good."
Chuckling he sat down at his desk.

"I can totally understand that."

Nakida remained in his presence trying to work up the nerve to ask him what she really wanted to know.

"Hey Jaden," another co-worker threw out as they passed by.

Jaden smiled and returned the greeting before turning to his computer booting it up.

Nakida ventured nervously into the deep clearing her throat, as he returned his attention to her.

"Jaden?"

"Yes?"

"I was wondering if maybe we could go out for lunch?"

Jaden watched her wordlessly. Sighing quietly, he gathered his thought before speaking.

"I don't think that would be a good idea, Nakida."

"Oh, I see."

Crushed by his rejection, she fought to keep her expression neutral.

"I'll let you get to work then."

She turned hurrying away before Jaden could speak. Exhaling deeply, he returned to his computer, hating that he hurt her feelings, but knowing he didn't return them.

His thought immediately went to Tatiana and their meeting this morning, bringing a true smile to his face. *She is going to be quite a challenge.* Normally he wouldn't have given her a second thought. Especially after the way she disrespected him in front of the gods and earths. Something told his heart that she was the one. Jaden was looking for his life mate. The woman who would bring compliment to his life. *What if she doesn't come around?* Could he be with a woman who didn't share his beliefs? What about children they would have? There was so much up in the air right now. Jaden wrestled on the inside before dismissing it and promising himself to take it one day at a time. Tonight, at dinner he would feel her out. There was a way to get inside Miss Tatiana's heart and spirit. He was going to find it. Once he found it, he would slowly help her find her way to awakening. They would become just what he sought, perfection together.

******

Nakida returned to her desk after a quick trip to the ladies' room to calm her nerves. She just didn't get Jaden at all. No matter what she did, Nakida just could not seem to find a way to pique his interest. *I only asked him to lunch, not an orgy!* Opening a folder on her desk she began her day. As she sorted the paperwork contained, Nakida had a distasteful thought. *What if he's gay?*

"That would be so messed up."

She prayed it wasn't true.

Rahshaun threw out a greeting as he walked by her cube.

"Wassup Kida."

Looking up she sucked her teeth softly and chose not to speak. She couldn't stand Rahshaun. He was a complete dog, always trying to get into every pair of panties inside the office and out.

"Stop being so damned evil. Maybe you could get a man."

He coolly headed toward Jaden's desk, leaving Nakida fuming.

"Bastard."

The phone on her desk rang and she blocked out all other thoughts, answering it.

****

Rahshaun greeted his friend smiling.

"Hey Jaden."

"Wassup man"

Rahshaun sat down in the cube across from his.

"Your girlfriend been over here this morning?"

Jaden sighed deeply at the jibe.

"Yeah, she came to say good morning."

Rahshaun chuckled again.

"She is trying hard to get that dick man."

Jaden frowned faintly at the crude statement.

"She's not my type."

Rahshaun continued to laugh.

"Man, you're too picky. If a trick wants to give it to me, I'm definitely going to take it."

Jaden again exhaled noisily.

"To each his own man."

Turning his attention once more to his computer screen, he went back to work.

Rahshaun calmed himself and began to start on his own work for the day. His mind remained on Nakida and her continual rejection. Truthfully, he was extremely attracted to her, even if she were just a gold digger in his mind. *She thinks to fucking much of herself.* He asked her out on at least three occasions. She turned him down flat each time. *Not like the bitch ain't passing it out like lifesavers.* Rahshaun felt himself slipping, immediately shifting his focus elsewhere. Nakida wasn't the only bitch in the sea.

Making up his mind to not think about or pursue her anymore, Rahshaun sent Tisha an email asking her to lunch. She worked with them, and she was seriously fine in Rahshaun's mind. *Cannot wait to get up in them guts.* He smiled receiving her answer, asking what time.

CHAPTER 2

SHE'S NOT READY YET

Tatiana internally admitted she was very leery when Jaden suggested she come to his place for dinner. *Another snake trying to screw me,* she recalled thinking. Now however, she silently apologized for the thought. Jaden remained the consummate gentleman since her arrival. The fung-shui of his gorgeous apartment worked for him. The furnishings contained deep earth tones, varying colors thrown in through paintings, artifacts and pillows. Jaden was also an excellent cook. Tatiana was delightedly stuffed from the Lobster bisque made from scratch, salad, and stuffed flounder. Jaden returned to the room with the hot tea requested, as well as his own after dinner drink. He sat down next to her on the plush sofa. Handing her the tea, Jaden began to speak.

"Tell me what you really know about the movement."

Tatiana sipped her tea and loosed a small breath before telling him the things she learned from Google, various opinions, and hearsay.

"So frankly, it sounds very much like a religious cult."

Jaden's mind raced. There was a lot of hurt there he could tell from her statement. Something or someone turned Tatiana's world upside down. She held religion solely responsible. He needed to tread lightly, or he would lose her. That was a price too high for Jaden right now.

"Well, I guess it would, considering how it was presented to you."

Tatiana listened wordlessly. He went on to tell her more about the movement, making it more personal for her. He described some of the people and organizational goals, contributions to the community, as a whole.

"We don't condemn people to hellfire and brimstone for being human."

Tatiana smiled slightly.

"And you really believe all this?"

Tatiana once again maintained eye contact.

"Yes."

Tatiana didn't comment. She couldn't. Jaden's tone completely unnerved her, especially with the way he gazed at her. *You need to go home now.* Jaden reached over and gently stroked her face. His voice quietly soothing, he addressed her anew.

"Tatiana, sometimes we have to come to a place in our lives when we realize we really don't have any control over destiny."

Tatiana smiled a tad and sipped her tea again. She didn't want to admit anything like that. To admit she held no control would put her right back in the prison she fought so hard to escape all those years ago. Maybe for Jaden it worked to trust some invisible, supernatural being to guide his direction, but for Tatiana, the only person she could trust and depend on was self.

"Enough of that for now."

Jaden seeing that she struggled internally, moved on. He already knew it was going to be a process and patience remained his long suit.

"Tell me about Tatiana, and what makes her tick?"

Tatiana chuckled and answered his question. She harbored a couple of her own after enlightening him of her own status.

"Why are you still single?"

This time Jaden tittered before answering her question.

"She's not ready yet."

The answer once again shook Tatiana's core. She looked away, silent, without further interrogation. Jaden reached out and pulled her to him. Holding her in his arms, they enjoyed the soft jazz. He didn't think anything else needed to be said right now. *She wants to love you.* Jaden's mind knew there was a huge wall keeping Tatiana forever on the defensive. Closing his eyes as he held her, he began to pray silently. He asked for insight and direction on demolishing the block to make Tatiana his. Opening his eyes moments later, he saw that she too had her eyes closed enjoying the moment. Jaden kissed her softly on the forehead and continued to hold her, relishing her presence.

*****

"You're being disobedient," Sharif told Naimah angrily.

"But I'm not ready!"

She continued to cry. Sharif badgered her to have sex for the last month or so. Naimah was scared to death. She wasn't sure she was ready for the responsibility sex brought. She witnessed too many of her friends hurt after they had sex, soon finding themselves abandoned or talked about.

Sharif tried again, kissing her on the lips.

"You're my earth, Naimah, let me be your god."

Voice hoarse with lustful desire, his hands roamed her body.

"I can't."

Pushing him away, Naimah gathered herself.

They were meeting in the basement of their building, both their homes too crowded with bodies for privacy.

"So, you're going to defy me and be disobedient?!"

Naimah pleaded, seeing his anger.

"Please Sharif, its not like that."

He slapped her hard the first time.

"Who have you been with then?"

His jealousy bloomed fully, thinking she was denying him because there was someone else.

"Sharif, I told you. I'm not having sex with anyone. I'm still a virgin."

"Hmph, that ain't what I heard."

Naimah began to cry harder.

"I swear Sharif."

He grabbed her, pushing her into the wall, by her stomach. Naimah struggled to breathe.

"Be still!"

His hand went under her skirt and inside her underwear, fingers invading her.

"I can tell you know."

Naimah began to cry again. Removing the hand seconds later, he stepped closer, nose to nose.

"You better be glad. I'm not going to put up with you disobeying me too much longer. Either you're going to let me be your god, in every way, or I will find myself a new earth, and make sure you get put out."

Naimah sniffled miserably.

"I'll see you tomorrow."

She nodded understanding. He kissed her quickly and left her alone.

Naimah sank to the floor after he left and sobbed deeply. She dated Sharif for the last six months, his temper progressively worsening. *You need to leave him alone.* Naimah cried harder. She genuinely cared for Sharif, and honestly the group was all she had. Her home life was terrible. Her mom worked like a slave just to keep them afloat. Her father hit or miss, most times miss. Naimah and her two younger brothers shared their small three-bedroom apartment with her aunt and her three kids. Being with Sharif and the rest of the Percenters made her feel loved and wanted. *Would it be the end of the world to have sex with him?*

Naimah exhaled seriously. She might not have possessed much, but she completely believed Infinite Knowledge when he told them their bodies were temples. They should take great care with them. What they put in, what they allowed to flourish in their temple was what they would become. Naimah wanted to have sex just like any other young woman, but she wanted it to be right. A serious love, not just a high school fling.

Finally managing to gather herself, Naimah dragged up the ten flights of stairs. Taking her own time, allowed the distance to clear her mind and help her see her path unmistakably once more. *Maybe I could talk to Infinite Knowledge.* She quickly dismissed the idea, knowing if Sharif ever found out, there would be hell to pay. Arriving finally, Naimah pushed every conscious thought aside and shut her emotions down, entering the house vowing to make it through one more night.

*****

"Girl, sounds like quite the challenge."

Tiffany held court with Nakida, stuffing another forkful of pasta in her mouth. Tiffany and Nakida were best friends. She knew all about her feelings for Jaden.

"I mean, damn. What's lunch?"

Nakida sighed profoundly.

"That's what I said too girl."

"Do you know where he lives, works out, hangs, or anything?"

"I'm working on finding out. He only talks to a couple people at work and neither of them are people I talk too."

Tiffany commiserated a moment before picking up her glass of iced tea.

"I mean Jaden's cute and all, but…"

Nakida gave her a look. Immediatley surrendering, Tiffany spoke again.

"OK, I am just saying."

She and Nakida were friends since grade school. Once her sights were set, they were set.

"I'm thinking about going to the after-work meet-n-greet Friday."

Tiffany again nodded her understanding still devouring her dinner.

"Is he going to be there?"

"Yeah, he normally goes. He never stays long, per the couple of people who would give me information. I'm thinking if we're outside of the office, maybe he will loosen up and not be so standoffish."

"Might work," Tiffany voiced her agreement. "Are you sure he is single?"

"I did my homework. Trust me, he's single."
Nakida took another sip of her tea before completing her thought.
"He's in this group or something called the Percenters."
Tiffany immediately frowned.
"Girl, they are Muslims!"
Tiffany was not trying to get caught up with that movement. Wrapping her head up, wearing long sleeves and long skirts. She didn't want her friend caught up in it either.
"Well, I don't know much about it. Hell, I just want him to give me the time of day. After that everything else can be worked out."
Nakida chuckled nervously after the declaration. Tiffany laughed with her before speaking another time.
"True that girl, true that."

*****

"Thank you for a wonderful evening," Tatiana told Jaden as she rose to leave.
"Tatiana, it's late, please, stay here."
Jaden didn't want her out alone after 1:00 AM.
Tatiana's defenses were immediately up again.
"Umm…"
Seeing the distrust in her eyes, Jaden moved to immediately disarm her.
"Tatiana, I have a spare bedroom. I'm not trying to have sex with you. I just don't want you out alone this late at night."
Tatiana released a silent breath.
"I'm sorry. Sure, I can stay."
"Don't worry about it. No harm done."

He showed her to his second bedroom and left her alone after offering her a T-Shirt. Alone Tatiana began to think about the evening, about Jaden, the things he said to her and the feelings she held concerning him.

The soft knock broke her thought as she called out come in and the door opened.

"Here we go," Jaden told her amiably, handing her the T-shirt.

"Thanks."

"You are more than welcome. Good night and sweet dreams."

"The same to you, good night."

Sitting on the bed once the door was closed, Tatiana fought the tears wanting to come. Jaden was so perfect. How could she keep him at bay? How could she fight the love forming in her heart for him? She was terrified. Scared of being hurt again, misused and abused all over again. Her mind immediately went back to the answer of his availability. It was obvious she was the woman he was talking about, but what did he mean she wasn't ready? Tatiana breathed acutely and undressed. Putting on the T-Shirt she climbed into the queen bed. Pulling up the comforter and closing her eyes, Tatiana for now shut out the world as she relaxed, sleep immediately finding her.

CHAPTER 3

SILLY LOVE GAMES

"TGIF," Rahshaun chuckled as he stopped at Jaden's desk.

"Wassup man?"

"Nothing, just glad it is Friday and glad it is 4:57."

Both men laughed after the declaration.

"You coming over to Porter's," Rahshaun asked.

Some of their co-workers got together for after work happy hour and to shoot the breeze with each other at the popular establishment.

"Yeah, I will stop in for a quick minute, but I have a meeting tonight."

Rahshaun nodded thoughtfully.

"Man, you still hanging with that movement thing?"

"Yes, I am."

"Well, hey, that's cool."

He and Jaden were cool at work and occasionally hung out over some weekends, but Rahshaun loved women, sex, and clubbing. All in that order. He was not trying to hear anything that would even minutely slow or deter him from them. Still he found Jaden to be a straight-up brutha and he appreciated that.

"It's 5:00!"

Rahshaun loudly declared this fact as Jaden laughed again and shut down his computer.

Grabbing his briefcase, he began walking with Rahshaun headed to the elevator laughing and joking along the way.

Nakida saw the two of them get onto the elevator. Smiling she headed to the ladies' room. She brought a change of clothes. Tonight she was going to make sure Jaden Paine got a good look at what he was missing. Arriving, Nakida immediately entered the large handicap stall and took off her business suit. Replacing it were a pair of skintight, form fitting jeans and a deep plunge, sleeveless top. The push up bra she bought along did its job showcasing both her girls sitting at full attention. *Now let's see him brush me off wearing this.* After refreshing her makeup and lipstick, Nakida also headed to the elevator and over to Porter's.

The walk was short, since the bar was only a couple of blocks away. When she entered everyone was already having a good time. Spotting a couple of friends from her department sitting with Tiffany, Nakida headed over.

Trenice, her co-worker, remarked one her appearance, sipping her martini.

"Damn girl, whose attention are you tryna get?"

Nakida smiled, returning an answer to the observation.

"I just wanted to be comfortable."

Tiffany smirked as she and Nakida exchanged looks. She slyly nodded toward Jaden and Rahshaun. They were sitting only a couple tables away, shooting the breeze with some of the other guys from the department. Jaden continued smiling and talking. Nakida took in every nuance wanting very much to feel his lips on hers as he undressed her and made love to her. Trenice and her other co-worker excused themselves leaving Tiffany and Nakida alone.

"So, what are you going to do?"

Nakida's answer was swift and confident.

"I'm going over and say hello to everyone."

Tiffany shrugged.

"Go ahead then."

Rahshaun noticed her first and immediately knew what was up. He was secretly glad that the man paid her no attention. *Bitch thinks she is all that.* Taking in her outfit he wanted very much to screw her presently.

"Hi guys."

Nakida's eyes found Jaden's and held his stare.

"Hey, wassup," one of the men greeted her.

"Hey Nakida," Jaden replied calmly.

He was repulsed by her attire. Jaden didn't fancy himself a prude, but he did have standards. She was being way too obvious for him.

"You're looking ready for the pole girl," Rahshaun threw out half-jokingly.

Nakida fought hard not to frown at the veiled insult. She knew why Rahshaun was being nasty to her. On a mission, she ignored him.

"You mind if I join you?"

Rahshaun threw out an answer before Jaden could speak.

"Yeah. We're talking man talk, but I mean hey, if you wanna add a woman's view on ass and tits, be my guest."

Nakida was about ten seconds from slapping the hell out of Rahshaun but continued to ignore him as she waited on Jaden to speak.

"Actually Nakida, I'm leaving, but maybe the others won't mind."

Nakida frowned somewhat as Jaden rose and paid for his soda.

"Mind if I walk outside with you?"

Jaden took a deep breath.

"Sure, that's fine."

They both exited the bar.

"Jaden, I hope I am not being too forward, but.."

Jaden steeled himself.

"I think you are such an attractive man, and I would really like a chance to hang out with you."

Jaden slowly let go the breath he held and tried to weigh his words.

"Nakida, I think you are a very pretty woman…"

Nakida smiled slightly.

"But I'm already seeing someone."

He hoped that would be the end of it.

Nakida was floored. *This had to happen within the last week!* She did her homework keeping as close a tab on Jaden as she could. Last week he was single. She knew that for a fact.

"Wow, really? Did that happen recently?"

"Yes, we just hooked up."

Nakida began to see red. *Who is this bitch and what makes her so damned special?!*

"I'm sorry, Jaden. I didn't know."

Jaden smiled a tad.

"It is all right, Nakida, no harm done."

Offering a small hug, he bid her goodnight, turning and walking away.

Nakida was trying to slow her breathing and regain her composure. She needed to find out who this chick was and hurriedly remove her from Jaden's life. *That one is mine and I am not taking no for an answer.* She returned to the bar resolve on one-hundred she not fail. Enlightening Tiffany of the new developments, her friend suggested heading to the club for a night of partying and strategizing.

*****

Tatiana readied herself to relax and read her latest novel when the phone rang. Sighing deeply, she grudgingly rose. Seeing the caller I.D. she answered amiably.

"Hi."

"You sound relaxed."

Jaden loved the resonance of her voice.

Tatiana giggled.

"I was just about to curl up with a good book."

"That sounds like a great night."

He was pleased she wasn't headed for some club or other.

"I hope so. This author is new to me, not sure how good the writing will be. What are you up to?"

"Heading for a meeting."

"Oh okay, are you speaking?"

"No, not tonight; maybe soon I will be able to talk you into coming with me one of these nights, hmm?"

Tatiana chuckled again.

"I don't know about all that, but stranger things have happened I guess."

Jaden grunted in response. He wasn't deterred. Coming from Tatiana, that was as good as a yes in his mind.

"I'm going to let you go and enjoy your book."

"OK, thanks. Enjoy your meeting."

"Sweet dreams."

The tender words made Tatiana's heart begin that marathon again.

"Thanks, Jaden. Goodnight."

Sitting back in her chair, Tatiana again closed her eyes and asked herself what she was going to do about this man. They saw each other four times already this week. She gave him credit. Jaden didn't push. He took what she gave him in terms of time and even affection. They only kissed once and even then, he didn't try to take it any further. Tatiana chuckled silently thinking how disappointed she was. Jaden was dead sexy. She wanted to see his lovemaking skills in action. *Enjoy getting to know the man.* Tatiana knew that moving too fast killed many a relationship, a couple of hers included. Jaden was by far the most unique man she met in a long time. *What about all this cult stuff?* Tatiana chose to not ponder that at the moment, instead opening her book and beginning to read.

Her cell went off again just as she got to page ten, irritating her.

"Hello?"

The slight edge made its way to her voice.

"Hello Tatiana," Virginia greeted her.

Tatiana frowned profoundly hearing the voice. Virginia Reynolds was her mother, but their relationship was far from loving.

"Hey ma."

"You didn't call this past weekend."

Tatiana respired heavily. She normally called her mother every Saturday. It kept her from calling Tatiana.

"I'm sorry ma, I got tied up," Tatiana tried, hoping that would be the end of the conversation.

"Hmph," Virginia returned. "Well anyway, your daddy is in the hospital again."

Tatiana wanted to blurt out how much she didn't care. How she hoped he wouldn't come home. As usual she didn't.

"I'm sorry to hear that."

"I doubt that," Virginia threw back acidly. "But he is still your daddy, so you could at least come see about him."

Tatiana felt the walls closing in on her again.

"OK Ma."

Getting all the particulars about her father's confinement, Tatiana moved to end the conversation.

"I will be there tomorrow."

Gratefully, Virginia finally acquiesced and disconnected.

Before she knew it, the nausea hit her. Tatiana raced to the bathroom. Barely making it, the hot bile left her stomach and bolted out of her mouth. She continued to throw up until there was nothing left except air. Tatiana fell to her knees the sobs coming and racking her body, visibly shaking it. She cried long and hard until she was exhausted and her voice ragged. Even then she couldn't drag herself from the bathroom.

Tatiana curled up in a corner next to the tub and laid her head on the side of it trying desperately to stop the throbbing of her head and the screaming from her soul. *Please, why can it not ever be over?* Tatiana miserably questioned the torment as tears once again began to stream down her face. The blessed darkness finally descended as she passed out.

Jaden continued to mull over the message given tonight by one of his close friends. Infinite Wisdom, a.k.a., Wiz. The teaching entailed the day to day battle they faced with the mainstream thinking the Nation of gods and earths was a gang. That they condoned and participated in gang activities, like extortion and black supremacy as a form a subtle extermination of other races. Pondering quietly Jaden considered how true Wiz's words were. Everyone seemed to think they were this group of self-serving egomaniacs looking for attention. Something as simple as the phrase, word is bond, had been reported as a term used by snipers before they were sent to kill a target or targets.

His mind went back to the encouragement Wiz gave them as he admonished them to continue their efforts to bring truth and awakening to all our people. *Regain your status as Nubian Kings and Queens. Throw out all your old ways of thinking and begin that journey back home today. I keep stressing the importance of our initiative because time waits for none of us. The children need something positive to draw from. Positive education always corrects errors of the past.* Jaden hoped everyone was listening. The work of the movement was filled with challenges but also filled with hope and enlightenment. He sincerely wished the few bad apples didn't ruin the entire crop. Jaden shuddered to think how he would be, or where he would be, right now if he never met Wiz and joined the movement. He was headed for nowhere fast. Running the streets and smoking dope. Thankfully the graduation to crime eluded him, but that couldn't have been far down the road. After joining the movement and gaining invaluable knowledge, he was able to get himself on track, finish school, go to college and make his life worth living.

He was by all accounts successful, but in his mind, there was always that one thing missing. Jaden's parents were good people. Still stuck in their old fashioned religious ways, but good people. They shared a wonderful marriage and of course just like any, they possessed issues. They persevered and stayed together. His mother stood by his father's side, as he did hers, through thick and thin, good times and bad. Jaden wanted the same for his own life. He was ready to settle down with the right woman, love her and raise a family. *I've found her.*

Jaden finally arrived home letting himself in. *Now I have to help her find her freedom.* Turning off his thoughts, he turned on the computer. He needed to make notes for his meeting tomorrow morning. He went to speak to the young gods and earths at the apartment complex every weekend. *I'll stop in and check on Tatiana too.* He felt something amiss for some reason concerning her. There was nothing he could put his finger right on, just a feeling. The screen finally came up. Jaden put everything else out of his mind as he concentrated on the notes in front of him.

CHAPTER 4

NO ESCAPE

Tatiana arrived at North Central Bronx hospital and took a deep breath as she entered the sterile edifice. *Why do I keep letting them push me around?* Tatiana headed toward the information desk. The elevator bank directly adjacent to it. She made her way toward the huge metal doors pushing the up button. *You are not a child anymore, tell them how you feel and keep it moving.* Sighing gently, Tatiana knew she wouldn't. For as long as she could remember her parents ran every aspect of her life, terrorizing her in the process. Even now, her mother still tried to dictate what she did and didn't do. Her thoughts were once again interrupted as the doors opened and several people spilled out into the hallway where she waited.

Tatiana allowed everyone to exit the elevator, before finally entering and pushing the fifth-floor button, watching the doors once again close. The trip was short; much too short for her liking. Tatiana found herself standing outside of her father's closed door. *Just go in and get through it.* Shoring up her resolve, she pushed the door open. Her mother saw her first, shooting a condescending look, taking in the form fitting jeans and V-neck sweater. Tatiana exhaled slowly, trying hard not to get angry. Virginia always criticized Tatiana's choice of clothing, telling her she dressed cheap and looked like a tramp.

"Hi mama."
"Good morning," Virginia returned brusquely.
Her husband stirred.
"Hey Chip."
Garlan Reynolds greeted his daughter looking directly into her eyes.
"Hi daddy."
The lump in her throat grew. Chip was her nickname, from her love of chocolate chip cookies as a child. No one other than her father called her that for years. Tatiana fought hard not to let the darkness she felt approaching enter as she sat in the chair next to his bed. Garlan never took his eyes off the young woman as she questioned his condition and made small talk. He could see the hurt still in her eyes, the fear, and the angst. Loosing a small breath Garlan wanted nothing more than to hug Tatiana tightly and tell her he loved her. He couldn't though, not yet. Not until Tatiana realized the error of her ways and apologized. Then they could be close like they used to be. Before the demon took over and changed all their lives forever.
"When are they letting you go home?"
       She just wanted to get through the visit and leave. Sitting this close to her father and mother was making her physically ill. Though they both seemed completely oblivious to her plight however. They continued to chat pleasantly and regard her as a relative absent far too long, yet not long enough. *They are still in total denial.* Virginia chattered away about nothing. Tatiana regarded her, thinking how very much she loathed the woman who gave birth to her. All her life, all she ever received from Virginia were continual lectures

about how much of a disappointment she was to both herself and Garlan.

"Did you hear me Tatiana?"

Virginia's sharp tone once again brought her back to the present.

"No, I'm sorry."

The one thing Tatiana definitely didn't want was for her mother to start in on another one of her berating tirades.

"I said, Let's pray before you leave."

Virginia took a deep breath for emphasis of her disgust at having to repeat herself.

This was basically her dismissal from their presence but not without punishing her once again. Taking a deep breath and swallowing hard, Tatiana opened her mouth.

"I don't pray anymore, mama."

Virginia smirked.

"You know that."

Tatiana waited for hell to break loose.

Sucking her teeth noisily Virginia again regarded her daughter.

"Who are you that you are too good to pray now?"

Garlan regarded Tatiana silently. *That demon is still there I see.*

"I'm leaving," Tatiana said simply, rising from her chair.

"Sit your behind down, Tatiana Elizabeth Reynolds! I am still your mother, and in this room, you will respect me!"

Tatiana felt the tears come.

"You don't have to say anything. Just be in the presence."

Garlan's eyes pleaded with her.

Taking another full inhalation, Tatiana shrugged. Garlan smiled marginally. Virginia rolled her eyes at her daughter and went to her husband's bedside.

"Come over here!"

Tatiana obediently complied.

Taking a few deep breaths to calm herself, Virginia took Garlan's hand, closed her eyes and began to pray. Garlan watched his daughter as his wife prayed. He saw her jaw clench at the mention of God and Jesus, the anger and hatred raw in her face. *Let go of my daughter,* Garlan prayed as he continued to watch her, his heart wrenching in pain. *Please God, take her back from that demon. I know she has been disobedient, I know she has cursed you, but please, please God, help her.* He ended his prayer just as Virginia finished up and pressed everyone to say Amen in unison.

"I will talk to you both later this weekend when I call."

Tatiana punctually headed to the door and opened it.

"Thank you for coming to see me Chip."

Tatiana smiled a tad. The love he felt floating through the words.

"Yes, thank you," Virginia threw out sarcastically.

Garlan sighed intensely.

Tatiana left, allowing the door to close behind her.

*****

Jaden was a bit disappointed that Tatiana wasn't at home this morning. She texted him an immediate response when he contacted her earlier about stopping by and them having breakfast. *Wonder what the errand was?* Jaden was giving serious thought to his and Tatiana's budding relationship, deciding it was time for him to get in deeper. There were so many things he didn't know about her or her past. Jaden needed her to be transparent so he would know how to reach her. How to help her, how to love her. His thoughts were interrupted as the gods and earths began to arrive at the bench area where they normally met.

Jaden noticed Naimah and Sharif, immediately picking up on the underlying tension between them as they interacted. *What is going on with these two?* He knew they were romantically involved. He hoped it wasn't serious or life altering. His mind catalogued his suspicions making a mental note to talk to one or both of them after the meeting.

"Greetings gods, Greetings earths."

The young people responded almost simultaneously.

"Greetings, Infinite Knowledge," Sharif returned brightly.

He was excitedly looking forward to talking to his mentor after the meeting. He was ready to move up in the ranks and he needed guidance on the how of it. *That's why Naimah won't sleep with me.* Sharif reasoned if he were more important and held more responsibility, Naimah would want to be with him to elevate her own position within the movement. Satisfied that this was the answer, Sharif reeled his mind in paying rapt attention as Jaden continued to speak.

Naimah's mind raced. She was leaving New York unbeknownst to Sharif. Her father finally convinced her mother to follow him to Birmingham, Alabama where his family still lived. Truthfully Naimah was scared to tell Sharif. He was extremely volatile these days, having threatened her again just this morning. Her mind went back to the conversation as her mentor continued to teach. *"I'm tired of playing with you Naimah," Sharif told her angrily as he twisted her arm. "Tonight," he hissed again, close to her face as she fought desperately to hold her tears and endure the pain of him holding her arm. "We are going to be together like we're supposed to be, or I'll make you sorry you said no again," Sharif told her as a final thought, twisting her arm even harder. Naimah heard her joint pop. Sharif let go of her arm and pushed her against the wall as he forcefully kissed and groped her once again. "Wear a skirt tonight," he told her in her ear, breathing hard as he continued to grind against her, his erection evident. "If we didn't have meeting this morning," Sharif mumbled as he rubbed her behind under her skirt, his hands in her underwear. "We should go, Sharif," Naimah tried; terrified he would take what he wanted from her right here in the building hallway. Breathing loudly Sharif continued to lean against her, kissing her neck. "Don't do anything stupid when we get to the meeting, Naimah," Sharif told her finally pulling away and looking into her eyes. She knew exactly what he meant, nodding her head quickly. Sharif grunted his approval and took her hand to walk outside into the common with her.*

"Naimah," Jaden addressed her. "Are you all right?"

She remained so deeply in thought he ended the meeting and almost everyone was gone from the area.

"I'm sorry, Infinite Knowledge. I guess I just got caught up."

"Is something wrong?"

Jaden watched the young woman closely. She looked completely disconcerted. Respiring heavily Naimah regarded the man in front of her, wanting desperately to tell him about Sharif and her fear. Instead she put on her best smile and told him she was fine. She felt eyes on her and turned to find Sharif watching her, the dark expression on his face, scaring the hell out of her.

"If you're sure…"

"Yeah, I am fine," Naimah lied another time.

Jaden sighed quietly.

"Okay, if you're sure."

He left her, turning toward the bench where Sharif remained and was now looking at their mentor, smiling. Naimah shuddered at the Jekyll and Hyde transformation before reminding herself she would never have to see Sharif again after today. *He is in for a big surprise.* Naimah smirked at the sweet revenge of it all.

*****

Tatiana was glad to be out of her father's room and her parent's presence. Sighing intensely, she thought about their relationship and how everything went so terribly wrong. Tatiana believed that if her mother wasn't around, she and her father would be able to work out their differences, maintain some sort of closeness. She knew Garlan loved her, but he wouldn't allow himself to believe that his wife was capable of the kind of evil that Tatiana tried to tell him about all those years ago. Pushing the thoughts out of her mind, Tatiana instead thought about Jaden. He texted her earlier and asked about spending time today. Thinking of him brought an immediate smile to her face. Jaden was the most wonderful thing that happened to her life in a long time. Tatiana was still smiling somewhat when the elevator doors opened. She looked into the face of hell once more.

"Hi Tatiana," Sylvia Conklin greeted calmly, never losing eye contact.

"Hello."

"How is your father?"

Sylvia knew that was the reason for Tatiana's visit.

"He seems to be feeling better today."

Tatiana wanted very much to leave the woman's presence, knowing her husband could not be too far behind. Tatiana never wanted to see Reverend Samuel Conklin again.

"Hmph, well, it would be nice to see you at service sometime."

"It was good seeing you."

The words from Tatiana dismissed Sylvia, desperately wanting to get out of the woman's presence.

Sylvia smiled before turning to walk down the hallway

"You too."

She's still blind as hell I see. The elevator doors opened once more.

Stepping to the side to allow the other passengers to disembark, Tatiana entered the elevator her back remaining toward the open door. She never saw him or noticed that he re-entered the elevator once she got on. Finally straightening up and turning around, she caught her breath.

Samuel addressed her, never taking his eyes off her.

"Hello Tatiana."

Swallowing hard, Tatiana fought to find her voice.

"Hello."

Shrinking into the corner of the elevator, she prayed it hurriedly reached the lobby.

Samuel continued to watch her in silence, taking in every inch of her, his desire and arousal growing. She was still beautiful.

"How is your father?"

Samuel made her talk to him.

"He's okay."

Tatiana pressed her nails into the palm of her hand to stay conscious.

Samuel began to walk across the elevator as Tatiana shrank further into the corner.

"I have really missed you."

Samuel's voice nearly inaudible standing close enough to touch her.

"Please, just leave me alone."

The first tear spilled down her cheek.

"Tatiana...."

Samuel reaced out to touch her as she pushed him forcefully.

The elevator doors mercifully opened at that exact moment. Several other people boarded the car. Tatiana took the opportunity to slip out. Unfortunately, she wasn't quick enough getting to the stairwell.

"Stop, Tatiana!"

Samuel forcefully pushed her into the stairwell, hurrying in after her and holding her against the wall.

"Do you remember what I told you?"

Samuel leaned in kissing Tatiana's lips.

Her tears were flowing like a river.

"Please…"

Samuel smiled and kissed her once more, forcing her mouth open and his tongue inside it.

The darkness approached speedily, but Tatiana knew she had to hold on and get away from this man before he took what she didn't want to give. Samuel was a big man. Tall and well built, he was good looking with seductive eyes and a convincing smile. That explained why no one saw him as a monster except her. Finally pulling away he exhaled noisily as he held her tightly.

"Tatiana, you can't ever escape me. I have let you run for long enough."

Tatiana began to lose the fight. Her body began to go limp.

"That's right baby."

Samuel spoke softly as his hands slid effortlessly under her sweater, caressing her breast.

His touch shocked Tatiana out of her cocoon and she fought back, pushing him hard enough to knock him off balance. She took the opportunity to run out of the stairwell into the semi crowded hospital hallway. Looking nervously over her shoulder, Tatiana finally saw Samuel emerge from the stairwell. He spotted her as she stepped onto the elevator. The doors began to close, and Tatiana began to feel a sense of relief, until she looked up and saw the deadly look on Samuel's face. The doors finally met, and Tatiana made her way to the hospital lobby.

CHAPTER 5

MOTIVES & SECRETS

Nakida smiled internally not believing how fortunate she was, spotting Jaden as she walked toward J.R.'s, a popular street café here in the city. Making her way toward him, Nakida put on her best smile and approached his table. Jaden sat deeply engrossed in the book lying on the surface in front of him.

"Hi there."

Jaden looked up, startled by the voice and somewhat annoyed by the interruption.

"Hi Nakida. What are you doing here?"

He was being polite but wanting to get back to his book.

"I was just out enjoying the weekend, doing a little window shopping."

She was a bit taken aback Jaden had not invited her to join him.

"What are you so engrossed in?"

The smile accompanied the query once more taking in the book.

Jaden smiled a tad before answering, sighing as he finally invited her to sit down. He really didn't want company, but he wouldn't be rude.

"It's a book by Michael Muhammad Knight."

Nakida nodded. The waitress returned and Nakida ordered an herbal tea. She was still giddy with excitement sitting across from this sexy man as she continued to take Jaden in. Deciding she needed to get a little more information on her competition, Nakida began to strategically ask questions.

"Your girl lets you hang out alone like this?"

Jaden smiled faintly.

"She has nothing to worry about."

Mildly deflated, Nakida took a sip of her tea. She regrouped and tried again.

"So, who is this woman that has managed to capture your attention?"

Jaden regarded her a few moments more in silence as his mind processed her true motives. Obviously their conversation and his telling her he was now attached didn't slow her roll a bit.

"She's my compliment."

Nakida fought hard not to frown at his response. She wasn't getting anywhere with her questions and frankly was jealous as hell that this mystery woman captured Jaden's heart and affection so completely.

"It's nice to find that."

Nakida's gazed never wavered, her voice soft and resonant.

Jaden decided he wasn't going to get any more reading done with Nakida there. If he didn't leave, she would continue to try and seduce him, embarrassing them both. Rising, Jaden addressed her anew.

"It was good seeing you Nakida. I have to leave now though."

Jaden hoped Tatiana was finished with her errands. He really needed to spend some time with her. The calm she brought when they were together was something Jaden relished.

"I didn't mean to offend you, Jaden."

Nakida didn't want him to leave.

"You didn't, Nakida," Jaden offered, smiling at her. "I really do have to leave."

Nakida fumed as she watched him walk away. Her cell rang. She answered without looking at the I.D.

"Struck out again I see."

Rahshaun's voice chuckled in her ear.

Nakida frowned acutely looking around, finally spotting him across the street waving at her.

"Are you stalking me or what?"

The embarrassment landed heavily that he witnessed her encounter with Jaden.

"Why the fuck I gotta stalk you?"

He honestly only stumbled on them as he headed to his latest flings apartment. Nakida sucked her teeth and again asked him why he was calling her.

"You should give up. Jaden is not interested."

Nakida rolled her eyes at him, now that he was standing directly in front of her. He turned his phone off and put it in his pocket, sitting down without invitation.

"You should stop tripping and go ahead and give a brutha a chance," Rahshaun tried again, ordering a cup of coffee.

Nakida grumbled under her breath and gave him a look.

"Why? You're not getting enough to keep you satisfied?"

Rahshaun smiled before regarding her again.

"It's not always about that, Nakida."

She was slightly unnerved by what she saw in Rahshaun's eyes. There was something just a bit dangerous about him right now.

Nakida rose and grabbed her tea.

"I'll see you Monday, Rahshaun."

Paying her own tab, she turned to leave. She felt Rahshaun's hand on her arm but didn't turn around. He stood close enough for her to feel his body heat.

"I could make you really happy if you let me, Nakida." Rahshaun spoke tenderly, kissing the nape of her neck, before releasing her arm and letting her walk away.

Nakida walked straight ahead her mind racing thinking about the thing Rahshaun said to her and the intense feeling of fear it raised.

*****

Tatiana scarcely made it inside before she began to vomit again. She threw up twice on the way home. Every time she thought about Samuel touching her, kissing her, Tatiana fell physically ill. Gagging with nothing left to throw up, Tatiana collapsed onto the bathroom floor and began to cry again. The nightmare she escaped almost seven years ago was once again threatening to destroy her. She was terrified of Samuel Conklin. He was dangerous, but no one believed her when she tried to tell them that. Pastor Conklin, as he was known, was their family pastor. They attended the large family-oriented church, Christian Cathedral, ever since Tatiana could remember.

Samuel became the pastor after her fifteenth birthday. That is when everything began to go horribly wrong in Tatiana's life. Her cell rang just as her mind attempted to take flight. Grateful for the intrusion, Tatiana answered.

"Hi," Jaden greeted her sweetly.

Despite the hell she just endured, Tatiana smiled at the sound of his voice and returned his greeting. She needed to see Jaden, to spend time with him, and feel safe. To enjoy his touch as he held her and be enclosed in his essence as he kissed her.

"Did you finish your errands?"

"Yes."

She intentionally told Jaden nothing about her father's confinement or her tumultuous past.

"Good," Jaden replied, chortling. "Can we meet up?"

"I would much rather stay in. Come over instead, I will cook for us."

"Sounds great. I'll bring the wine. See you in about an hour, okay?"

Disconnecting Tatiana stripped and jumped into the shower. She wanted to wash away all the filth of Samuel Conklin. To push this afternoon out of her memory and enjoy her evening. Emerging moment's later feeling completely refreshed, Tatiana headed into the kitchen and began pulling out various ingredients for dinner. She turned on the CD player and sang along as No More Drama by Mary J. Blige floated from the speakers. By the time Jaden arrived and she heard the soft knock on the door, Tatiana was in a far greater frame of mind. Smiling she opened the door and invited him in.

Jaden hugged Tatiana tightly, loving the feel of her soft, warm, flesh in his arms.

"You smell really good."

Taking the opportunity after the hug he kissed her. Tatiana returned his kiss and thanked him for the compliment. Taking the wine from him, she put it in the fridge to chill and invited him to take a seat.

"Dinner should be ready in a few minutes."

Jaden reached out and pulled her down on the couch next to him.

"I am really glad to see you."

He kissed her once more.

Tatiana smiled as she looked into his eyes. Jaden had to be the most honest and real person she met in a long time. She couldn't let her past destroy what she saw as her future. Tatiana made a vow she would do whatever she must to make sure it never did.

"What did you do with yourself today?"

She made conversation trying to get Jaden to stop looking into her eyes.

He chuckled and recounted his day after the morning meeting with the earths and gods.

"Do you talk to Naimah?"

Recalling the girl's demeanor this morning Jaden waited for her to answer.

"Occasionally, why?"

"She just seemed kinda out of it this morning, and I was a little concerned."

Tatiana smiled at him.

"What?"

"It's sweet how much you care for those kids."

Jaden smiled.

"I genuinely love helping kids. I'll be the same way with ours."

Tatiana blushed as Jaden hugged her close. She sat up to go check dinner, when Jaden pulled her back to him kissing her deeply and passionately. Tatiana was blown. He never kissed her like that.

"I want to define us," Jaden told her, never taking his eyes from hers.

Tatiana swallowed hard.

"Okay, what do you want to define us as?"

Jaden smiled fully, kissed her again deeply, before answering.

"I am your man, and you are my one and only woman."

Tatiana smiled.

"I like your definition."

*****

Samuel was sitting at the table as his wife served his dinner.

"I'm surprised you didn't run into her."

Samuel grunted and said nothing, eating his dinner as she continued to chatter.

He wasn't really listening. His mind was on Tatiana and their meeting at the hospital. Samuel lied to his wife when she asked if he saw the young woman. He didn't see the need to involve her in his personal business, and trust, the business with Tatiana was intensely personal. Samuel internally exhaled recalling her scent and the softness of her lips as he kissed her. *She is so perfect.* He continued to fantasize about the young woman. She always was; since the first day he laid eyes on her.

"Samuel?"

"Yes, honey."

Samuel finally returned his attention to his wife.

"I said you're going to be late for your counseling session."

"Oh okay."

Samuel rose grabbing his suit jacket.

"I'll be back around 10:00."

"Alright, be careful."

Sylvia lovingly bid him goodnight. Samuel smiled back.

"I will."

He walked out of the door and to his vehicle. Sliding effortlessly inside the black SL560, he headed for his destination. *Make a small pit stop first.* Turning down Elberton Lane, he sat outside the Londen Plaza gazing up at the 10th floor.

Samuel saw the large shadow pass the window and immediately knew it was a man. He grew furious, instinctively reaching for the .9mm he kept beside his seat. Calming himself Samuel put the gun back and took another deep breath. *All in due time.* He continued to strategize reuniting with Tatiana. Smiling Samuel glanced at the shiny object and started his car once more continuing on to his destination. His mind worked ahead to his divorce from Sylvia and making Tatiana his new wife. He was still smiling when he reached Prospect Park. There weren't a lot of people who ventured out here anymore. Dangerous activity and drug dealing saw to that.

"Wassup Sam?"

Gordon sauntered over to the car, climbing into the passenger seat.

"How is it going Gordon?"

Samuel and Gordon were friends since grade school. He moved with them from Philly when things got too hot to handle there.

"You got the paper?"

Gordon handed him a wad of cash in response.

Samuel greedily counted the money before giving Gordon the new supply of dope.

The two sold dope for years using Samuel's cover as a trusted and respected pastor to stay under police radar.

"We still on for Saturday?"

"Yes, already gave Sylvia the spiel about a conference this weekend."

He laughed silently at how trustingly stupid Sylvia was.

"They both gonna be in place?"

Gordon laughed at his expression.

"Relax, the pussy is gonna be there, you just bring your condoms."

Samuel laughed with him. They got together at least once a month and held a sex party. Gordon would find two young and willing girls to have sex with them for a small profit, some cheap jewelry and of course dope. Samuel licked his lips in anticipation.

"I'll see you Saturday."

Gordon got out of the car after the statement.

Taking a deep breath Samuel's mind immediately went back to Tatiana. *Look at the shit you are making me do.* Samuel touched his erection. Stroking it he pictured Tatiana and her beautiful body.

CHAPTER 6

STORM WINDS

Sharif was finishing the first 40-ounce and feeling no pain. He was smoking weed now as well. Almost two months passed since Naimah left him. The deception still angered him.

Shandi walked inside the abandoned apartment where they met.

"Hey Sharif."

He regarded her momentarily before returning her hello. Shandi was another of the young women in the movement. Sharif picked up on her attraction right after he found out Naimah was gone, and immediately exploited it. He slept with her the same night Naimah left, continuing their affair since. Sharif slept with a lot of girls these days. Infinite Knowledge chastised him about his promiscuity telling him he needed to slow down. *What the fuck does he know?* Sharif was in pain. The alcohol, drugs, and sex were the best numbing agents he knew.

"Did you hear me, Sharif?"

She was on the receiving end of at least four or five ass whippings when Sharif was angry. Still she always came back, and always forgave him. Sharif looked at the girl again taking in how cute she was. He knew if he truly allowed himself he could fall for Shandi. They would have a great relationship, but he couldn't. His heart still belonged completely to Naimah.

She hurt him beyond measure sneaking away like she did. Granted he knew she was forced to move, she could have at least told him. They could have worked out something. Made a way to see each other, keep in touch, continue their relationship. *I bet she has given it to someone else already.* Sharif's fury rose thinking of another man touching Naimah.

"What do you want now Shandi?"

Sharif answered her finally, trying to clear his mind and push the anger away.

Shandi steeled herself to speak once more.

"I missed my period."

She prayed Sharif didn't flip out on her.

"So you're pregnant?"

Déjà vu. He just held this exact conversation with Amanda. His other girl, unknown to Shandi.

"I think so."

Shandi cautiously tried to gauge his mood.

"Hmph. You need to tell whatever dude you got it from then."

Shandi felt the tears sting. She also felt the anger rise at his insinuation.

"I am telling the dude."

The smart retort earned her an open hand slap from Sharif.

Shandi tried to rise from the floor where they sat as Sharif grabbed her. Hitting her head hard on the unyielding surface, he slammed her back down.

"Don't be getting smart with me!"

Sharif slapped her again.

"You're mine now Shandi!"

"Leave me alone Sharif!"

She cried trying to pull away.

"You better do everything I tell you to do, and you better not let nothing happen to my seed!"

He kissed her hard after the admonishment. Shandi kissed him back as his hands began to roam her body.

"I love you so much, Sharif."

He said nothing, removing her panties instead.

"You're my earth, Shandi."

Sharif unzipped his pants and freed his erection.

"Mm, Sharif."

I knew he loved me.

Foolishly she surrendered to the fantasy, as Sharif continued to have sex with her.

"It's so good."

Seeing Naimah in his mind, the words were murmured in her ear. Each stroke brought him closer and closer to orgasm.

Amanda lost it seeing them together.

"What the hell is this?!"

She came over to talk to Sharif again about their baby and what they were going to do. Sharif jumped at the sound of her voice just as he reached orgasm. He removed himself from Shandi as Amanda fumed. She eyed them both murderously.

"Relax!"

Amanda calmly gave him a incredulous look.

Shandi, having gathered herself by now, also questioned what was going on.

"Nothing is going on."

Sharif plainly spoke the words, unmoved by either of their presence.

Amanda reacted first.

"I walk in and see my baby's father with his dick in some braud and you're telling me nothing is going on?!"

Shandi's eyes grew big as she heard the words baby father, turning on Sharif now.

"What is she talking about?!"

"Y'all both about to get on my nerves."

Amanda another time spoke up.

"I'm Sharif's earth, the mother of his seed."

Scoffing, Shandi regarded her classmate before speaking.

"Oh yeah? I'm Sharif's earth, and I'm the one truly carrying his seed."

Amanda's eyes narrowed.

"Everybody at school knows you are a whore."

Amanda began walking toward Shandi.

"That baby could be anybody's!"

Amanda slapped her hard having taken enough insults. The two began to fight.

Sharif regarded the two women and enjoyed the melee for a while before finally separating them.

"Stop all this stupid shit!"

They continued to eye each other hatefully.

"Then tell this silly tramp the truth!"

Shandi implored Sharif to speak up and defend her. Amanda sucked her teeth and tried to get to Shandi again.

"Look, y'all both carrying my seed."

The two women's mouths dropped.

"Squash this drama, deal with it."

Done with the conversation, he picked up the new 40-ounce bottle, opened it and began to drink.

Shandi began to cry as the reality of the situation dawned on her. Amanda was absolutely furious, unafraid to let her words fly.

"So you were screwing both of us, at the same time?!"

Sharif shrugged and said nothing.

"You trifling dog!"

She spit at him as she turned to leave.

"You can have his nasty ass! All I care about is my child support."

Reaching the door, opening it, Amanda went about her way. Shandi took a moment to gather herself. The hurt she felt took her breath away.

"I thought you really loved me Sharif."

He gave her a scathing look, drinking more of the malt liquor.

"Grow up."

Shandi's eyes narrowed.

"Let's see how grown up Infinite Knowledge thinks this stunt is!"

She walked out of the room, just as Sharif hurled the beer bottle at the door and it shattered.

******

Naimah found the south very pleasurable to her. She adjusted quickly excelling at school and sports. She joined the track team upon her arrival at her cousin's insistence. Tabitha, or Tabby as everyone called her, was Naimah's first cousin. They clicked like sisters. Her best-friend Sheila however was another matter. For whatever reason the girl just never seemed to warm up to Naimah. She was sitting in Trigonometry trying hard to concentrate. Math was her worst subject even though she managed to keep a B average. She had to work extremely hard at it. The bell rang finally and Naimah rose headed to her history class, literally bumping into Denzel Padgett.

"How you doing miss?"

Denzel smiled once recognition took place.

"I'm good Denzel. Sorry about bumping into you."

Denzel continued to watch her and smile. Naimah was faintly unsettled by his constant gaze. Denzel Padgett was the local pastor's son and by all accounts a complete hellion. He was incessantly trying to talk to her on a romantic level for the last month. Naimah thought he was an attractive enough guy, but she didn't like him that way.

"Are you going to make it up to me?"

Using the incident as an angle to spend time with her, he baited her. He found Naimah extremely attractive and her pushing him away was beginning to annoy him. Denzel was positively spoiled being an only child, and his father's only son. No was not a word he heard often, and even when he did, it always translated to not right now.

"Excuse me?"

Denzel chuckled noting her confusion.

"Well you did bump into me, rather hard, I might add," Denzel teased. "So, I'm thinking going with me to the movies tonight should show me how sorry you are."

Exhaling casually Naimah finally gave in and told him okay. Denzel smiled as he told her what time he would pick her up. As a final point he walked away letting her continue to class. Naimah thought about him as the teacher gave the assignment. Denzel was tall, medium build, with very nice eyes. He was way too full of himself for her tastes. The thing that bothered her most about him was his attitude. He reminded her very much of Sharif. The way he could turn his emotions on and off at will bothered her. Naimah recalled the scene a couple of Sunday's ago when she accompanied Tabby to church. *Naimah was looking for the restroom when she took a wrong turn and instead ended up outside one of the choir rooms. She heard the raised voices, recognizing Denzel's immediately. Whoever he was talking to, he was giving a royal tongue lashing. Then Naimah heard the sound of flesh meeting flesh as the door flew open and Denzel was standing right in front of her.*

"I was looking for the restroom." The scowl left his face and a huge fake smile replaced it. He cheerfully escorted her to the restroom and left her alone. The bell once again rang shaking Naimah from her thoughts as she headed for her bus to go home. *It is just a movie, get through it and go home.* Getting on and finding Tabby, she sat down beside her, mind still racing.

******

Enjoying her day, Tatiana basked in the sunshine as she walked toward home, mind filled with thoughts of Jaden. Their relationship was moving along wonderfully. She found out so many new and exciting things about him. Jaden was indeed a very deep and intelligent man. He treated her like a queen and went out of his way to make her happy. *He is definitely taking his time.* Tatiana chuckled regarding their lack of lovemaking. Jaden kissed her on a regular basis, but he never tried to touch her or make any moves toward the bedroom. At times Tatiana admitted it frustrated her. Other times it made her feel more confident in her decision to be with him. She sighed heavily unlocking her door making a mental note to call her mother. She promised to call twice a week now, since her visit to the hospital. Her father asked about her more frequently. Tatiana smiled marginally thinking of her father. She and Garlan made a few tentative strides toward co-existence. She was more than sure her mother knew nothing of it though. Virginia seemed hell-bent on keeping the two of them at odds.

Walking inside the apartment, Tatiana threw her purse into the chair. Headed into her kitchen, she grabbed a bottle of water from the fridge. She ventured into her bedroom, straight to the bathroom. Finishing up and washing her hands, Tatiana walked back into her bedroom, stopping in her tracks.
"Hi baby."
Tatiana was stunned. *What the hell?!* She blinked rapidly, praying this was a dream and she would wake up.
"What, how?"
Samuel continued to watch her a little longer before answering.
"I have a key."
Showing her the metal instrument, he placed it back in his pocket.
Tatiana frowned quizzically completely at a loss.
"Your mother thought it would be a good idea for me to check on you."
It all became clear to Tatiana. Virginia was once again helping this man destroy her.

Taking a deep breath, Tatiana stepped back closer to her bathroom door, intending to run inside and lock it.

Samuel took the gun from his pocket laying it on her TV.

"Don't."

She swallowed hard too terrified to move.

"What do you want?"

Why wouldn't he leave her alone, let her live her life. Tatiana fretted as Samuel began walking toward her.

"Why are you so afraid of me baby?"

Samuel reached out stroking Tatiana's face.

"I've never hurt you."

Looking into her eyes, the fear endured.

"Please, just leave me alone."

Samuel sighed, taking her hand and pulling her into the room.

"Baby, we have talked about this."

"Please, I don't want any part of this."

Tatiana's tears flowed. She needed him out of her house. Her mind was already racing thinking of who to call to change her locks.

"Tatiana, do you remember our first time together?"

Samuel speaking reeled her mind back in.

Tatiana did indeed remember their first time and it still scared the hell out of her.

"That was wrong."

Samuel sighed again.

"Baby, I explained that to you."

He hated how she kept blaming herself and holding onto guilt that was not hers to carry.

"You were my pastor."

Tatiana tried to buy time and clear her head.

"I loved you," Samuel replied. "I still love you."

Turning her face to his, he kissed her soulfully.

Tatiana almost pushed him away before remembering the gun and how deadly sinister Samuel Conklin could be.

"Tatiana, we are only 12 years apart."

She was still lying on the bed where he pushed her as they kissed. He was propped on his elbow, the gun within his reach.

"You're married."

Samuel kissed her again.

"I'm divorcing her."

He casually touched her breast.

"You and I are going to be married, and everything will be all right."

His cell went off making Tatiana jump. Samuel exhaled tiredly and pulled it from his pocket. Answering, he signaled Tatiana to remain mute. She listened as he talked praying whoever was on the other end would make him leave her house. After he ended the call, Tatiana's wish was granted.

"I have an emergency."

Samuel rose and pulled her up into his arms.

"Don't do anything stupid this time."

Tatiana swallowed hard and closed her eyes, the words floating into her ear. She wouldn't tell anyone. Who would believe her anyway? Her past was replaying in her minds eye as Samuel pulled away and looked into her face.

"I am your destiny."

Samuel kissed her yet another time.

"It was sealed seven years ago when you and I met."

The tear again trickled down her cheek.

Samuel kissed her for the last time before turning without a word and leaving her apartment. Tatiana broke hearing the door close behind him as the darkness consumed her and she passed out.

*****

Samuel thought as he drove. Sometimes this Pastor gig really got in the way of his life. Still he would play the role and keep making his money on the side. Tatiana was so beautiful. He loved touching and kissing her. Making his way toward the hospital once more, he tabled the desires. One of his other members was in an accident. They wanted him to come and pray with the family for recovery. Samuel reflected on his tenure at Community Christian. He fought hard to become the pastor after learning of the opening from another of his friends in the ministry. It was a hard sell considering he was only twenty-seven years old at the time. He and Sylvia had been married three years with no children. The congregation consisted mostly of young and middle-aged families. Samuel used that to his advantage that he could relate to them, increase the membership, and overall quality of the church.

The strategy paid off and he was installed some six months later. He enjoyed the people at the church and the demands on his time were not enough to keep him from all his other pursuits. Samuel recalled seeing Tatiana like it was yesterday. She came to church with her parents the second Sunday after his installation. She was stunning, even young like Samuel knew that she was. He made it his business to meet her after church. Her parents cheerfully introduced them. Samuel immediately began making plans to have Tatiana in his life. She was the one and he knew it. He married Sylvia at the insistence of his family and his pastor. She was the perfect church girl and would make him the perfect Pastor's wife. Samuel blew a long breath thinking that she was also the perfect prude. True she had sex whenever he wanted; there was never any fire in it. She obediently did what he asked, let him get his, and left him alone. Samuel was always careful however. He didn't want children with Sylvia and he took every precaution to insure it.

He chuckled thinking how gullible she was when he told her it was God's mandate that they not have children of their own right now. *Not when I marry Tatiana.* He planned to have her pregnant on their wedding night. Sighing severely, he thought about the fear in her eyes today when he was with her. *Why is she so afraid of me?* He never hit her, or intentionally hurt her. All he ever wanted was to love her in peace. *Maybe it was the loss.* Seeing that he reached the hospital he gathered himself. Samuel put on his game face heading for the elevator and the members of his flock.

*****

Jaden was disturbed with all the drama he was handling now. Sharif went completely off the deep end. Both girls, Amanda and Shandi confided their pregnancies to him as well as Sharif being the father. Sharif managed to get locked up for fighting in public. Jaden was on his way to the jail to pay the small fifty-dollar bond set. Concerned, he hoped this short time in lockup convinced Sharif he didn't want to go back. There was also the matter of the two girls having children from him. He was going to have to man up and quick, so he could provide for his offspring and be a good father. These were the life lessons that the movement was trying to teach the young men and women who became a part of their family.

His cell went off and Jaden answered amiably seeing Wiz's name on the I.D.

"as-Salamu alaikum."

"wa alaikum assalam," Wiz returned. "What is going on with your sector?"

Jaden took a breath. He gave his friend a quick general rundown of the events taken and taking place with the earths and gods.

"Way too much turmoil."

Jaden readily agreed.

"Well keep on counseling," Wiz advised. "We can only do what they allow and hope they listen."

"I agree, but it is still distressing to see them spiraling like this."

"Let's hope this time of confinement turns on lights for brother Sharif."

Wiz's words, iterated Jaden's earlier thoughts.

"I will keep you up to speed."

Jaden went on to talk about other business concerning the movement. After conversing for the next thirty minutes, Wiz told Jaden he was going to let him go. Jaden thanked him again for his advice before disconnecting.

His cell rang almost immediately after he disconnected, and he looked at the I.D. again. Smiling, Jaden cheerfully answered.

"Hey baby."

"Hi."

"Are you okay?"

Jaden frowned with concern, picking up the tone.

"I just needed to hear your voice."

"Baby, what's wrong?"

Jaden spoke again before she could return a response.

"I'm on my way."

"Jaden, no, you don't---."

"I'm on my way."

What is going on with her? Jaden grabbed his wallet and locked his front door, heading over to Tatiana's. Thinking as he rode, he realized anew how much about Tatiana was still a mystery to him. *That changes tonight.* Finally arriving at his stop, he headed up out of the subway station toward her apartment.

CHAPTER 7

INTENSITY

Girl you need to tell him to back off."

Tabby gave Naimah advice as they talked about Denzel. Since taking her to the movies two weeks ago, He was unbearable. Calling her constantly. Making everyone think they were a couple at school. Using his parents to make sure they served on the same committees at church.

"He just doesn't seem to get it."

Tabby nodded and sipped more of her tea. She offered up a warning to her cousin.

"Just be careful. I heard he likes to put his hands on girls and stuff."

Naimah sighed aloud.

"If he does anything crazy like that, you better tell me!"

Naimah knew her cousins, Jason and Jasper, Tabby's twin brothers, would take care of Denzel for her. They were eighteen having graduated last year, both earning scholarships to the University of Alabama where they played linebacker and fullback on the football team.

"Tabby, take Ruben something to drink."

Naimah chuckled hearing her aunt's directive and told Tabby she would do it. Auntie Bettie made their lives very comfortable since they arrived. Naimah still spent far more time here than at their own house. They moved a month after getting here.

"I'll go with you."

Tabby smiled internally, plotting.

They headed outside where the young man was working on their shed, replacing the roof.

"Ruben!"

He stuck his head over the side of the building when Tabby called out.

"I brought you some lemonade."

He smiled and climbed down off the roof.

"Here."

Ruben took the lemonade and began to drink before he noticed Naimah, stopping mid swallow.

"This is my cousin, Naimah."

Ruben swallowed his mouthful finally.

"Hello."

"Hi. You want some more?"

"Yeah, that would be great."

Ruben held the glass out.

Tabby took the time to slip away, leaving them alone, and she hoped, time to connect.

"You're the one that moved from New York, right?"

As she smiled and answered his question, Ruben took the opportunity to look her over. Naimah was stunning; deep sable complexion with flawlessly smooth skin. The mid-length wavy hair accentuated her bright brown eyes and soft kissable lips. Finally shaking himself out of his thought he struck up conversation anew.

"So how do you like Alabama?"

Naimah smiled another time and Ruben's heart began to once again race. *I have to date her.*

"I'll let you get back to work now."

Naimah gathered the glass and pitcher, preparing to leave.

"Um, Naimah…"

"Hm?"

"I don't know if you are seeing anyone yet, but I'd like to take you out."

Naimah smiled a tiny bit.

"I would like that."

She was already smitten with this fine, handsome man in front of her.

"How about Friday?"

"Friday's good."

After giving him her phone number, Naimah finally left the yard to find Tabby waiting for her in the den.

"You set me up!"

Her eyes twinkled as she teased her cousin. Tabby burst into laughter.

"Ruben is good people."

Naimah told her about their pending date.

"So why didn't you date him?"

Tabby laughed aloud.

"He's DonJuan's best friend."

Naimah chuckled at the revelation. DonJuan was Tabby's boyfriend.

"Oh, okay then."

Tabby left her for a moment headed into the kitchen.

Naimah thought about Ruben as she sat alone and how nice he seemed. He was fine. The huge biceps bulged every time he flexed his arm to drink from his glass. He was graced with beautiful dimples and soft brown eyes. His complexion was far lighter than she normally liked her men, but she dismissed it deciding to give the man a real chance. Tabby returned moments later and they began to talk about school, friends and gossip, making Ruben for the moment, a fleeting thought.

*****

Tatiana was tossing and turning as the nightmare played in her minds eye. *"Daddy, I swear," she pleaded as Garlan regarded her. "I am not lying," Tatiana screamed again as Virginia entered the room. "Don't listen to this nonsense, Garlan," she told him calmly, giving Tatiana a look. "Pastor Conklin told us this would happen," she added as Garlan sighed audibly still watching his daughter narrowly. "Daddy, please, believe me," Tatiana cried. "Garlan, don't be fooled again," Virginia threw out, giving him a side look. Tatiana knew she was alluding to the dope and condoms they found in her room and the lies she told them. Tatiana didn't do drugs and she was still very much a virgin. The items belonged to her best friend Candice. She didn't tell though, knowing Candice's parents and their ultra-strict conservative views. They would have killed her friend or shipped her off to some boarding school or other. So Tatiana lied, thinking it would get her a couple months of grounding as punishment. She was terribly wrong. Instead Virginia told their Pastor and he immediately suggested one on one counseling.*

"Daddy, he touched me," Tatiana screamed as Virginia walked over and slapped her hard. "Don't you dare lie on a fine man of God like Pastor Conklin!" Tatiana recoiled from the slap and cried even harder. "Go to your room, Chip," Garlan told her finally. "Pray and ask God to deliver you from this lying demon you have." Tatiana grudgingly made her way to her feet and did as she was told. She cried for hours until the house grew quiet and she gingerly made her way downstairs to the kitchen. "He doesn't believe her," Virginia was whispering as Tatiana got close enough to hear. "Yes, of

course, I totally understand," she continued to talk quietly as Tatiana wondered who was on the other end. "He promised to keep our secret as long as she continued counseling," Virginia told them. "Let me go before Garlan wakes up looking for me," she whispered once more. "I love you too, Richard," she whispered and disconnected.

Tatiana quickly ducked behind the dining room table, crouching out of sight as her mother stealthily made her way back upstairs. "That tramp," Tatiana mumbled having discovered her mother's secret. Now she understood why Virginia insisted on taking her to counseling every week. Thinking about Pastor Conklin made Tatiana shudder involuntarily. "He is going to hurt me one of these days," she spoke again aloud before heading back upstairs praying she could talk to her father alone and he would believe what she told him.

Tatiana awoke from the dream bathed in sweat, her heart racing as she looked around the room trying to gather her bearings. She had to get some help, some counseling or something. These nightmares and memories were going to drive her over the edge. Everything was fine until Samuel came back into her life. Tatiana shuddered anew thinking about his visit. Thankfully he didn't return. She immediately changed her locks. Still Tatiana was terrified every time she walked by a darkened area, expecting him to jump out. *He is crazy.* His declaration of love and his plans that they marry solidified his insanity. Tatiana endured hell and back with this man. Now it seemed no matter how hard she tried, she just could not get away from him. Her thoughts shifted to Jaden. They talked well into the wee hours of the morning that night after Samuel's visit.

Tatiana broke and told him some things about her childhood and her strained relationship with her parents now, but she would never, ever, tell him the things that happened between her and Samuel Conklin. *He would leave me in a heartbeat.* Realizing sleep was over for her for now; Tatiana rose and headed into the kitchen making a cup of tea. Sitting down she began to sip it as her cell rang. The number was unknown, so she sent it to voicemail. As soon as the instrument stopped ringing, it began again; once more the unknown number. Tatiana again sent it to voicemail. It stopped and remained silent as she turned her attention back to her tea.

The sharp knock on her door scared her, making Tatiana jump and spill some of her tea. *What the hell? They must have the wrong apartment.* She ignored it sipping the hot mixture again. Tatiana heard sounds like metal scraping metal. She turned toward her door just as the deadbolt flipped and unlocked. She held her breath. The door opened. Samuel walked inside gun in hand, dark expression on his face.

"Where is he?"

Closing the door, he locked it once more.

Tatiana was stunned.

"How did you get in my house?"

Samuel smiled before showing her the small burglary kit he carried.

"Cheap lock."

The smile evaporated with his question repeated.

"There's no one here."

Samuel looked at her silently for a little while longer. Tatiana's dread grew.

"Then why didn't you answer the phone?"

Tatiana panted a bit.

"I don't answer calls without caller I.D."

Satisfied she was telling the truth, Samuel put the gun away and walked over to her. Taking her in his arms he hugged her tightly.

"What are you doing up this late anyway?"

"I had a nightmare."

Adoringly he stroked her face, looking into her eyes.

"I'm here now."

Tatiana held her tongue.

"Come on, let's go lay down."

Samuel began pulling her toward the bedroom.

"Don't you have to go home?"

He removed her robe, pulling back the covers for her to get in. Samuel smiled at her question, standing and undressing, joining her in bed before answering.

"I'm still at my conference."

Question answered, he began kissing Tatiana fervently.

What am I going to do now? She knew what he wanted and that he had the means to take it from her.

"Baby.."

Treading very carefully, looking into her eyes and seeing fear once more, he framed his query.

"Listen, tell me why you are so afraid of me. I've never touched you hurtfully."

Tatiana swallowed dryly.

"Tell me."

His eyes never left hers as he waited for a response.

*****

Jaden and Wiz were walking together talking and shooting the breeze. They just left a gathering of the Percenters.

"How are things with the group now?"
Wiz referred to all the turmoil of late.
"As well as can be expected."
Wiz nodded.
"The girls are both having the babies and keeping them."
"We need to step up and be as available as possible. These are future kings and queens coming into the world," Wiz told Jaden as he nodded attentively.
"If Brother Sharif is not going to be around, then we must be."
The three shadowy figures jumped out of the alley they were passing.
"Gimme your wallet!"
Brandishing a gun, he waved it at the two men. The other two also brandished weapons but said nothing. Wiz spoke up.
"Young brutha, what are you doing?"
"Shut up! Just give me the money!"
"Let me school you to some knowledge," Wiz began again.
"Man, save that bullshit, give me your money or I will shoot your ass!"
Jaden calmly pulled his wallet from his pocket opening it and giving them the money, hoping they would let him keep all his identification. The second young man reached out to take the cash Jaden held when Wiz grabbed his arm and his hood fell back off his face.
"Sharif!"
Jaden gasped as the first robber got nervous and fired hitting Wiz in the chest.

The trio ran off as Jaden pulled his cell from his pocket and dialed 9-1-1 requesting an ambulance for his friend. Wiz was breathing erratically bleeding profusely from the wound. Jaden put his hands on it, applying as much pressure as possible to stop the bleeding. He heard the ambulance screaming in the distance and prayed they would make it to them in time.

"What happened sir?"

The police officer was taking his statement as they worked on Wiz. Jaden told them about the three youths robbing them and shooting Wiz. He didn't however enlighten the officers to the identity of the one man he recognized. Glancing over the officer's shoulder, Jaden saw the paramedic shake his head as the other one handed him a sheet and covered Wiz's body. Jaden's knees were threatening to buckle under him. Not only did he just witness his mentor's murder, he was shaken at how easily the body lying under that sheet could have been his own. *Sharif is dangerous*. Jaden still could not bring himself to turn the young man in. After all it wasn't Sharif who fired the fatal shot. *He knows who did though*. The officer called for the coroner and Jaden began answering their questions all over again.

******

Naimah grimaced as she held her cell phone and Denzel talked.

"Denzel, I can't be there Friday."

"Why not?"

Denzel had plans for Friday night when he and Naimah would finally become an official couple.

"Because I have something to do."

Naimah was really tired of having to explain her comings and goings to a man she wasn't even involved with.

"Okay, then Saturday."

Naimah sighed aloud.

"Is it for the anniversary program?"

"Yes," Denzel lied.

"Yeah, okay fine."

Denzel cheerfully told her that was cool before moving on to a new subject.

"So, am I your boyfriend now or what?"

Naimah again rolled her eyes.

"Denzel, we have covered this before."

She took another breath trying to be patient and not lose her cool.

Honestly Naimah had Ruben on the brain right now. She was looking excitedly forward to Friday night and their date. Tabby confided to her that Ruben was eighteen already having graduated early. Naimah asked if he knew she was sixteen and Tabby told her he did, but that he also knew she would be seventeen in a couple of weeks. Naimah smiled thinking of him, before reeling her mind back in and listening to Denzel who was once again complaining that she kept pushing him away.

"There are at least four girls I can think of right off hand that like you Denzel."

"I want you, Naimah. I would be really good to you, and you know I got it going on."

Denzel often bragged on his car and the money he carried. Naimah stayed unimpressed with both.

"I have to go."

"OK, I'll see you tomorrow," Denzel told her good-naturedly.

"Sweet dreams Mrs. Padgett."

He disconnected before Naimah could respond. Sucking her teeth once more Naimah dismissed it heading to the shower hoping to wash away her cares.

******

Ruben was hanging out with DonJuan shooting the breeze and talking as the subject of Tabby and Naimah came up.

"She is definitely a cute girl," DonJuan told him of Naimah. "You know preacher boy been all over her."

Ruben's jaw clenched. He really couldn't stand Denzel Padgett.

"Spoiled brat."

DonJuan chuckled and concurred.

"Does she like him?"

DonJuan laughed again.

"Nah, but his stupid ass doesn't seem to get it."

Ruben grunted yet again. He really liked Naimah and planned to show her the time of her life Friday night. Fortunately, it seemed she was yet unaffected by the gossip from the rest of the clucking hens, as Ruben liked to call them, with their lies and stories about him. He also prayed she wasn't one of these material chicks.

Ruben drove his beat-up Chevy truck because he liked it. He was more than capable of buying and paying for a new car if that were his desire. No, Ruben did what he did because he was smart. He saved his money for important things, like a nice home and a stable future for the woman he would eventually marry.

"She's younger than Tabby."

DonJuan grunted.

"Only a few months."

He gave Ruben a look.

"You gonna leave her alone because of that?"

Ruben smiled.

"No, just making conversation."

"From what I can tell, she's good people," DonJuan told him. "Ain't nobody been in the panties."

Ruben nodded thoughtfully.

"Ever."

Ruben's head snapped up.

"Really?"

"That's the skinny I got from Tabby. She might just be what you say you have been looking for all these months."

DonJuan grabbed another beer tossing one to Ruben.

"She just might."

His mind worked at warp speed as he opened the beer and tried to quell his excitement.

CHAPTER 8

MIND GAMES

Tatiana tried to find the words to answer Samuel's query as he patiently waited.

"I, um, I just…"

Samuel stroked her cheek, kissing her again.

"You can talk to me baby."

The hurt and anger came full circle.

"I was fifteen years old Samuel. You had sex with me, and I was fifteen years old!"

She began to cry with the declaration.

Samuel took a deep breath, pulling her close and holding her in his arms.

"Tatiana…"

She quieted and endured, hoping he wouldn't hurt her again like he did all those years ago.

"I know you were young honey, but I loved you, and you loved me too."

Tatiana pulled away from him.

"That's not true."

Sighing seriously once more, Samuel began to talk to her another time.

"I told you I loved you, and you said you loved me too. It was the day of the baptism celebration."

Tatiana recalled the words. That fury returned.

"I was saying I loved you as my Pastor! Not as my boyfriend, or my lover!"

Samuel sat up beside her.

"Tatiana, you don't have to feel guilty anymore baby. Do you remember when we made love?"

Tatiana tried to block out the memory.

"You wanted it. You were wet with desire; you told me you wanted me."

"No..."

"Baby, stop. I know you felt guilty, but it's okay."

"I was confused Samuel. You knew that. I was fifteen years old for christ's sake, you were a married, twenty-seven-year-old, pastor!"

He another time pulled her to him and held her.

"Don't be ashamed of what you felt for me Tatiana."

Samuel stroked her body once more.

"I loved you too baby. Tatiana, we made beautiful love, and created a beautiful child."

Tatiana broke, sobbing mournfully.

She forced herself not to think about the pregnancy or child she lost for years.

"Shh baby, it's okay. I know the miscarriage wasn't your fault."

Tatiana continued to cry, the pain unbearable.

"She pushed me."

Samuel sighed again. He knew all about Virginia's jealousy of Tatiana's pregnancy and her pushing the young woman down the stairs. Virginia was a complete bitch. Once he and Tatiana were married he was going to deal with her.

"Samuel can't you see what happened between us was wrong?"

He must be completely unbalanced if he didn't see anything wrong with a grown man having sex with a child.

"Tatiana, my father was twenty years older than my mother."

The kisses came again.

"Our age doesn't matter."

Drying her tears, he laid her gently back into bed.

"Samuel, no, please don't."

He began kissing her all over again. His hands ventured between her legs.

Another loud sharp rap on her door startled them both. Samuel's cell went off immediately afterward. Snatching it from his pants pocket he sucked his teeth and answered.

"Man what the hell?!"

Disconnecting, he began dressing much to Tatiana's relief. Fully dressed, Samuel walked over to her side of the bed and sat down, stroking her face again, eyes welded to her own.

"Tatiana, it's almost time. You need to stop seeing him, and start getting yourself ready for our life together."

Tatiana could see the danger in his eyes.

"I'll give you one month."

Checking the gun once more, he put it back into his pocket.

"One month."

Leaning down he kissed her wispily before telling her goodnight and leaving her apartment.

Tatiana jumped from bed, locked her door and pushed her chair and loveseat behind it. Shaking violently, she returned to her bedroom closing and locking the door pushing the dresser behind it. *What the hell am I going to do?* Samuel wasn't kidding.

******

Samuel was still irritated when he reached the parking lot, finding Gordon waiting for him.

"Man, what the hell?"

The annoyance showed on his face.

Gordon exhaled noisily and lit his cigarette before answering.

"Relax fool. I just saved your ass."

Samuel gave him a quizzical look.

"Seems your old lady ain't as stupid as you think."

"What are you talking about?"

"She called the hotel you were supposed to be at, found out you weren't there."

Gordon took another drag from his smoke.

"Then she called the church you were supposed to be speaking at and found out the conference ended last night."

Samuel frowned acutely.

"How did you find all this out?"

"She called me, asked if I saw you."

Samuel grunted somewhat. Sylvia knew he and Gordon were close. He wasn't surprised she chose to call him.

"She told me she had a hunch where you were, and she was going to confirm her suspicions."

Gordon took another drag before flicking the butt into the street.

"So I headed to your house and luckily I got there just as she backed out."

Samuel again grunted his understanding.

"She was headed here, but I called and threw her off for the moment."

"What exactly did you say?"

"I told her you just called. We were meeting across the bridge. I followed until I was sure she was headed there, then I came over here to get you."

Samuel loosed a weighty breath.

"She is always in my damned way."

"Well once she figures out you're not over there, I'm pretty sure she is headed this way."

Gordon knew about Samuel's involvement with Tatiana and that his wife was extremely insecure still about the young woman.

"Good looking out man, although the timing wasn't the best."

Samuel chuckled. Gordon smiled.

"Guess you'll have to make up for it next time."

Getting in his own car, Gordon pulled away from the curb, just as Samuel started his vehicle and did the same. Crisis, for the moment, averted.

*****

Moments later the fire red Mercedes C-300 turned the corner and slowed down in front of Londen Plaza. Sylvia took her time looking for the black Mercedes, not seeing it. *You look like a fool out here.* Sylvia sighed thinking she was wrong about Samuel and drove away headed toward home. She couldn't help the fear. She knew how he felt about Tatiana. She could see it every time he looked at the young woman. *I know they were together.* Samuel denied it again and again during the time of their counseling sessions. Sylvia loved her husband with her whole heart and she did everything she could to be a good wife. She wanted kids, but Samuel was adamant about them not having any right now. *We have been married for almost 10 years, so when?*

The tears returned and ran down her cheek.

Part of her wanted to sit down and talk to Tatiana; ask her about Samuel and if anything ever went on between them. The other part of her was afraid of the answer. It would destroy her to find out Samuel cheated on her with anyone. Sighing deeply Sylvia pushed it out of her mind for now, not totally dismissing it, but not ready to act on it either. Still the memories from the past would not leave her. She thought about Virginia Reynolds and how she treated Tatiana all those years ago. *It is like she hates her own child.* Sylvia shook her head, feeling sorry for Tatiana once again. Virginia was the reason Samuel began counseling Tatiana. Sylvia never believed the young woman was as troubled and unruly as her mother made her out to be. *All teenagers go through their stages.* She rounded the corner to her home. Seeing Samuel's car once the garage lifted, Sylvia smiled. Pushing any further contemplation of what if out of her mind she got out and went inside to greet the man she loved.

*****

Jaden felt numb. He could not believe everything that transpired tonight. It was completely surreal. *Wiz is gone.* His heart heavy, the pain wore on his psyche. Jaden also had to process that one of his own was responsible for taking his mentors life. *He didn't pull the trigger.* Jaden tried his best to reason, but he knew he was reaching. Sharif was just as guilty as his partner in crime tonight. *What are you gonna do?* He owed it to Wiz to make sure his murderers came to justice, but Sharif was a good kid. Jaden knew in his heart he was just confused, mixed up and looking for something to fill the void obviously inside him. His cell rang. Jaden answered blindly. It was another of their brothers asking about tonight and giving direction for the group. He told Jaden they would hold a memorial for Wiz and he would get back to him with the details. Vaguely hearing the man as he spoke, Jaden managed to tell him that was fine and disconnect.

Rising finally from the couch, Jaden turned on the CD player and let the jazz float through the apartment. He headed to the shower trying to get his head together. Standing under the steaming hot spray, Jaden finally allowed the emotion he held all night to flow freely. He shed tears for his friend, his mentor, his brother, and the void his absence created. Jaden would be eternally grateful to Wiz for all the guidance he provided over the years. For helping him through his own dark time. Taking a new breath, Jaden made his decision about Sharif. Exiting the shower, he dried himself and dressed for bed. Heading into the kitchen, he made himself a drink and picked up his cell. He knew it was late. He hoped her phone was on vibrate as he dialed Tatiana's number. He wanted to leave her a message, explaining tonight, and the desire to have a few days alone. The call went straight to voicemail as Jaden smiled a tad hearing her voice.

"Hi baby."

He went on to tell her about Wiz's passing and that he would need a few days to get himself together.

"I'm fine baby, so don't worry and I will call you soon."

"Love you," he said softly before disconnecting.

He was through letting time go by without the people in his life knowing how he felt about them. He did love

Tatiana, very much. It was time she knew that. Draining his glass and making himself another he picked up the officer's card from his countertop. Jaden looked at it long and hard as he finished his second drink. Putting it down, he blew out a tired breath and dropped his glass into the sink. *Tackle all this crap tomorrow.* Walking into his bedroom, climbing into the king-sized bed, and pulling the covers over his head, Jaden prayed sleep found him quickly.

CHAPTER 9

SUNSHINE & RAIN

Naimah was nervous as hell. *Calm down girl, dang!* You would think it was her first date ever the way she anxiously waited for Ruben to pick her up. Naimah chuckled silently of her actions. She really liked him. She hoped they would get along and hook up. The soft knock came moments later. Opening the door, Naimah smiled brightly seeing Ruben standing on the other side.

"Hey."

"Come in."

Her parents insisted on meeting him before they went out, though Auntie Bettie already filled them in on what a good young man he was. Ruben held his own as Naimah made the introductions.

"Naimah has a 12:00 curfew."

Ruben smiled graciously at her mother's statement.

"I'll have Naimah home on time."

With nothing further, she and Ruben left headed to the theater.

"I'm sorry about that."

Naimah apologized, fully embarrassed, as Ruben smiled.

"It is good to have parents that care."

Taking her hand, he held it as they rode.

Naimah was giddy with excitement as they continued to talk and get to know each other. Ruben was an old soul she found out quickly. He told her about his parents having him late in life.

"My mom was forty-nine when I was born."

He went on to tell her about both their passing and his older sister raising him.

"I'm sorry about your parents, Ruben."

He smiled.

"Thanks."

They arrived and parked. Ruben came around opening her door and helping her from the truck. When they rounded the corner headed to the box office, Naimah saw Denzel and his friends. He looked up in tandem, spotting her with Ruben.

Denzel fought hard to control his desire to go slap Naimah. *Why the hell is she out with that damned loser?* Deciding he wanted to press the issue, Denzel casually walked over to the couple as they finished their ticket purchase.

"Wassup Naimah?"

Denzel pointedly gave her a look.

Ruben continued to hold Naimah's hand, hearing her sigh deeply.

"Hey Denzel."

"You didn't tell me you had a date."

Naimah sucked her teeth, taking a cavernous breath to stay her annoyance.

"Denzel…"

Ruben fought not to smile, having a pretty good idea what was about to come out of her mouth.

"For the last time, you and I don't get down like that."

Denzel's eyes narrowed in anger.

He mumbled crossly before turning and walking away. Ruben broke his silence as they went inside the theater toward the concession stand.

"He must really be feeling you."

"He's really working my nerves."

Ruben chuckled.

"Well we won't think about it anymore. Let's enjoy the movie."

Naimah smiled at him agreeing with his sentiment.

Denzel of course played off the confrontation for his friends, but inside he was seething. *Evidently this girl doesn't really understand who I am.* He watched them laughing and holding hands while they entered their theatre. Calming himself, Denzel began to plot. Whatever Denzel wanted, Denzel got. Naimah sure as hell was not going to be the exception to that rule. He smiled a wicked smiled and entered the theatre with his own friends. Tomorrow was a new day. Things were going to change drastically where he and his future girl were concerned. Finding himself totally at ease with his new plans, Denzel turned his attention to the screen and began laughing with his friends.

******

Tatiana remained at home all day. She called in sick, not being able to bring herself to leave the apartment. Samuel's visit scared the hell out of her. She got Jaden's voicemail this morning when she finally checked her phone. *I hope he is really alright.* Forcing herself, she sipped the tea she made. Her appetite was gone. She was listless. Tatiana knew she had to do something about the situation and it needed to be done now. Otherwise Samuel would destroy her life. She would find herself his prisoner yet another time. She popped the soup into the microwave and warmed it slightly, forcing herself to drink it down. After sitting for a few moments ensuring the soup wouldn't make a u-turn, Tatiana rose and headed to the shower.

She returned to her bedroom moments later and picked up the phone.

"Hello," the soft ladylike voice answered.

"Hey Auntie Jo," Tatiana spoke cheerfully.

"Hey baby."

Jorinda Abbey was Virginia's older sister and Tatiana's favorite aunt.

"How are you doing?"

"As well as can be expected."

Her aunt moved into the assisted living facility at exactly the same time Tatiana moved out of her apartment and on her own. She lived with her aunt since she was sixteen. Once things got too bad at home and Samuel became even more threatening.

"How are you doing baby?"

Jo heard the strain in the young woman's voice.

"I'm okay, Auntie."

She heard the audible sigh before the woman spoke again.

"Tatiana, what's wrong? I know you, so don't try and con me."

Tatiana chuckled.

"Just some stuff I need to deal with Auntie."

"Well I'm here if you need to talk."

Tatiana swallowed hard the knot in her throat. That was exactly what she needed; someone to talk too. To unburden herself of all the hurt and confusion from years past. Instead, she told her Auntie she would keep that in mind.

"I will be by to see you tomorrow if that's good?"

"Oh, I will definitely be looking forward to it," Jo assured. "I love you Tatiana."

Exhaling loudly and putting her cell down, Tatiana's mind took flight to a time and place she didn't want to go. *"Hello Tatiana," Samuel greeted as she walked into his office wondering why she was here. "Hello," she returned politely. "Tatiana, your parents think that you would benefit from some counseling," he explained calmly. "They are worried about some of the decisions and paths you seem to be taking." He never took his eyes off her. Tatiana sighed deeply and set her mind to simply get through the counseling and live her life. Unfortunately, it wouldn't be that easy.*

Things were good for the first couple of months, and then they changed. "Why are we having our session here," Tatiana asked as they entered his home and went into his study. "Because it will give us more privacy and you can feel completely at ease," Samuel told her amiably, smiling and asking if she wanted something to drink. Tatiana accepted his offer and took the coke he brought back. "Tell me about the drugs, Tatiana," he asked, watching her closely. "They weren't mine." "OK," Samuel replied. "What about the condoms?" Again, his gaze never wavered. "They weren't mine either." She grew slightly uneasy under his stare. "Are you still a virgin Tatiana?" She blushed deeply. "Yes," she finally answered in almost a whisper. She saw him smile somewhat and sip his iced tea. "Let's talk about your relationship with your mother," he threw out seeing the hurt immediately come to her face. "She hates me," Tatiana said softly as the first tear fell.

Samuel rose and came over to the chaise lounge where she sat, putting his arms around her and held her as she cried. "She doesn't hate you Tatiana," he told her sympathetically. "Your parents only want what's best for you." Tatiana clung to him needing to be held. Her father had not hugged her in months. Most times he ignored her very presence. Samuel stroked her gently as he grabbed a tissue and dried her tears. "It's ok," he told her softly. "I'm here," he added, kissing her cheek. Tatiana, continued to lie in his arms, her emotions in turmoil, when he kissed her again carefully on the lips. "I should call my mama now," Tatiana told him, trying to pull away, completely uncomfortable. "Shh, it's okay," Samuel told her comfortingly. "I know you're scared, and probably a little embarrassed," he went on as he continued to caress her. He turned her face to his once more, kissing her again, ardently as Tatiana kissed him back. "This is wrong," she told him pushing him away, guilty, consumed, embarrassed, and aroused all at once. "No baby, it's not wrong," Samuel told her kissing her once more.

Tatiana allowed him to undress her as he kissed her all over. "But, wait," she tried again as Samuel kissed her lips another time telling her how much he loved her and that they were doing the right thing. "Tatiana, you and I belong together," he told her, his hands finding her center and arousing her even more. Her mind was screaming at her to stop, but the things Samuel was doing to her body she couldn't deny the pleasure. "Do you believe I love you," Samuel asked managing to undress himself. "Tatiana, you are so special," he told her soothingly as he smoothly parted her legs and placed himself between them. Tatiana's head was spinning. What the hell was she doing? This was her Pastor. He was a married man, and he was twelve years older than her. She didn't get a chance to react to any of her thoughts as she felt the pain of Samuel entering her. "No, stop," Tatiana tried. Samuel kissed her impassioned in response as he continued to thrust into her, holding her tightly. Tatiana tried hard to control the tears as he continued inside her, murmuring how much he loved her in her ear. "Mmm," he moaned deeply as Tatiana felt his semen and he stopped moving.

Samuel looked into her eyes as he lay atop her, kissing her lips. "Tatiana, baby, we are one now," he told her as the tear trickled down her face. "Don't cry baby," he told her, finally removing himself from her. "We didn't do anything wrong today," he went on as he held her. "This was a natural expression of a man and woman loving each other," Samuel told her as Tatiana's tears finally stopped. "And you are all woman Tatiana, don't let anyone tell you differently. "She smiled to a degree liking the sound of that. "What about your wife, and my parents?" "This is our personal business Tatiana," Samuel told her with another kiss. "We will tell them in due time, OK?" She nodded yes. Samuel smiled, having sex with her once more before finally allowing her to dress and call Virginia to pick her up.

*****

They were sitting in his truck talking and enjoying the evening, sipping on the soft drinks they picked up at the convenience store.

"Did you enjoy the movie?"

"Yes, I really did," Naimah smiled. "How many brothers and sisters do you have?"

"Eight. Five sisters and three brothers."
Naimah thought to herself how big a family that was.
"You're the baby?"
Ruben smiled.
"I am the youngest."
Naimah chuckled.
"What about you?"
"I have two younger brothers."
"Can I ask you something?"

Naimah took in his demeanor curious what was so pressing, as she told him to go ahead and ask.
"What are your plans for your future?"
Naimah was thoughtful. She only had a few things mapped out, not really expecting her life to be that complicated given the situation she originally found herself in with Sharif. He made it known he expected her to give him a couple of babies and them to live together and continue in the movement together. Now, being here in Alabama, Naimah spent little, if any, time at all worrying about her future for now.
"After I finish high school, I would like to go to college."
Ruben continued to watch her.
"Probably start off with the community college here for a couple of years. I hear they have an excellent LPN program."
Ruben smiled the slightest bit. She seemed very grounded and he liked that.
"What about you?"
"I'm into construction. I like it, and I doubt I go back to school anytime soon."
Naimah nodded her understanding.

"Would that be a problem if we were together?"

Ruben watched her reaction closely.

Naimah smiled before regarding him again.

"If that's what you like to do and it pays the bills, what difference does it make?"

She was never one to be caught up in material things and flashy men. Ruben smiled fully and hugged her. Naimah was going to be all right, he told himself.

"I want to tell you some stuff, before you hear it from the street."

Naimah paid rapt attention.

"I've dated a few of the girls around here and a lot of them don't have really good stuff to say about me."

Naimah frowned.

"Why not?"

Loosing a breath, he opened his mouth to explain.

"Naimah, I'm a real down to earth guy. I like simple stuff like the movies, bowling, maybe a show or two."

She nodded, and he continued his explanation.

"Sometimes just hanging out at the house chilling and playing cards."

Naimah remained mute.

"Well, I have this reputation of being cheap with all these girls."

Naimah chuckled slightly.

"They tell everyone I am tight, I am boring, a country hick, stuff like that."

Naimah could tell the words spoken hurt him.

"Ruben, I used to live in the big city. All the crap these girls think is so great here is really just a whole lot of nonsense."

"I'm cool with the stuff you like to do."

Ruben smiled again.

"Stop worrying about all that gossip. I don't listen to that drama any way; I make up my own mind about a person."

Ruben continued to watch her, smiling.

"What?"

"I'm going to like being with you."

Ruben kissed her.

Naimah smiled back repeating the same sentiment as they kissed again, expressively. Pulling away, Ruben glanced at his watch.

"We should head back to your house. I don't want to give your parents any reason not to let me see you again."

Naimah looked at the instrument panel and saw the time was 11:30. They made it back to her house by 11:48 and Ruben walked her to the door.

"I will call you tomorrow."

"Okay."

"Goodnight."

Ruben kissed her lips once more before she let herself inside and closed the door.

He smiled all the way back to his truck still whistling happily as he drove.

CHAPTER 10

STRANGE BEDFELLOWS

Tatiana wanted the thoughts to stop but they just kept on playing as she continued to cry and endure. *The affair continued well into her sixteenth birthday when Samuel bought her a beautiful gold bracelet and took her to a motel where they celebrated together. He gave her wine and of course had sex with her. She missed her period a month later. Samuel never used birth control, telling her condoms were for people who didn't love each other like they did. Tatiana was terrified, but she summoned every ounce of strength to tell him during their next counseling session. "Hi baby," Samuel greeted her in his study. They continued meeting at his home now instead of the church. Of course no one questioned it, given his sterling reputation and integrity. Tatiana remembered thinking how well he had them fooled. "What's wrong," Samuel asked picking up on her demeanor. "I missed my period," Tatiana told him fearfully. He sighed before coming to her, taking her into his arms. "Guess that is it then," he told her calmly, stroking her face. "What do you mean," Tatiana asked, totally puzzled. Samuel smiled and kissed her lovingly. "I'm going to divorce Sylvia and marry you, so our child will have both his parents," he told her kissing her again at the end of the sentence. "We can't do that Samuel," Tatiana told him, alarmed. "My parents will flip!" She was sure her father would do something crazy. "You're my wife Tatiana. This baby proves how much I love you, and it's meant to be." He began to caress her body. They heard the* door close and Samuel hurriedly removed his hand from Tatiana's breast.

Sylvia knocked on his study door less than five minutes later. Samuel invited her in as she spoke to Tatiana and apologized for interrupting, leaving them once again alone. "Please, let's just get an abortion," Tatiana pleaded after Sylvia left. The guilt was killing her, and she knew she couldn't go through with marrying Samuel or being with him anymore. "No," he told her harshly. "You are not killing our child." Tatiana began to cry again. Samuel softened. "Baby, I know you're scared, but I promise, I am going to take care of you." Tatiana simply nodded and looked at her hands.

Samuel told Sylvia he was taking Tatiana home. He actually wanted the time alone to show her a few things, so she would understand fully who he was. That he meant what he said about them being together and him taking care of her. They arrived on the seedy side of town moments later, Tatiana questioning why they were there. "Relax baby," Samuel told her as she saw the man approach the car. "Gordon, this is Tatiana." Gordon greeted her and Tatiana politely returned the greeting. "This her," Gordon asked as Samuel smiled and stroked her face gently. "Yeah, this is my heart," he replied lovingly. "She's carrying my child," he told Gordon who gave him a look. "Damn," he said softly as Tatiana looked down at her hands again, embarrassed.

"Where is Lucky," Samuel asked. He was a street dealer and he owed them for the dope he got last week. "He's in the alley, fu-, um messed up," Gordon corrected himself remembering Tatiana was in the car. "Mmph okay," Samuel said exiting the vehicle and walking with Gordon down the dimly lit alley. Tatiana, curious, watched the two men as they *found the man she assumed was Lucky and began talking to him. Suddenly she saw Samuel begin kicking him and beating him as the man cringed helpless and defenseless. Tatiana's hands flew to her mouth to keep from screaming as she watched Samuel take the gun from his pocket and shoot the man point blank in his arm and leg. Calmly walking away, Samuel returned to the car where Tatiana sat horrified. "Like I told you baby," he spoke softly regarding her once again. "I will take care of you," he went on never taking his eyes from her. "But you can never leave me." He kissed the trembling girl before starting the car and once more continuing on their journey making small talk like the violence never happened.*

*****

Samuel thrust into her once more before finishing and collapsing, his body still shuddering from his orgasm. Sylvia smiled internally as her husband held her. They hadn't made love in a few weeks. Tonight he was spectacular. She frowned marginally as Samuel removed himself from her, making sure the condom he wore remained secure. Sighing quietly Sylvia tried not to concentrate on that. They finally made love and for her that was the beginning of them trying again. Things were very strained over the weeks, culminating last night when she accused him of cheating on her. She never intended to argue with him at all, just happy that he was home when she arrived, but Samuel's nonchalant attitude and vague answers to her questions sent her off the deep end. *Who are you sleeping with Samuel, Sylvia screamed at him. Samuel simply gave her a look and walked into their bedroom. She of course followed still screaming at him, calling him a filthy liar and a hypocrite. Samuel finally tired of the harping and pushed her violently onto the bed, yelling at her to shut up and leave him alone. Sylvia wasn't stupid, as angry as she was, she knew how far to push him. So she left him alone and went to sleep.*

Today they both walked around on eggshells most of the day. He came into their room moments earlier, apologizing and kissing her softly. Sylvia couldn't stay angry with him. She loved Samuel with every fiber of her being. When he began to touch her, she immediately responded, her body aching to be held and loved by him. Samuel began undressing her as she did the same for him, going down on him and pleasuring him almost to finish. Sylvia loved the way Samuel touched her, even though he would never pleasure her orally, he did have a way with his hands. After arousing her to his satisfaction, he put the condom on. *"Honey, why can't we make love without the condom this time," Sylvia tried, as Samuel sighed deeply. "He hasn't released me yet," he told her gently as he kissed her again and entered her.* As disappointed as she was by his statement, Sylvia couldn't deny the pleasure she felt with Samuel inside her.

"I have to go out for a while."

She still lay in bed, nude.

Sylvia was immediately on guard, but promised not to over react, it caused enough problems last night.

"OK honey."

Samuel smiled and came over to the bed, leaning down and kissing her.

"I will be at the church for a little while, if you want to call me."

Sylvia smiled.

"I trust you."

Guilt smacked her for the earlier thoughts.

Samuel smiled at her again as he grabbed his briefcase and headed out the door. Sylvia heard the garage lift moments later as she burrowed under the covers and closed her eyes to nap for a little while.

******

Tatiana finally managed to cry herself to sleep. Samuel found her curled in a fetal position in bed as he checked on her. He used the burglary tools again, but picked up her keys from the kitchen counter, removing the house key, knowing she had a spare to replace it. Samuel undressed and gingerly climbed into bed with Tatiana, putting his arms around her as she slept. She stirred to a degree but didn't awaken. Though she was finally asleep, Tatiana's mind raced. Now the memories haunted her even in her dreams.

"Who is the father," Virginia screamed. Tatiana said nothing and endured. Her mother confronted her about being pregnant, noticing the slight weight gain and occasional sickness she was experiencing. Virginia made her take a home pregnancy test, livid at the result. Tatiana didn't care about her mother screaming. It was the deep pained hurt and disappointment she saw in Garlan's eyes that crushed her. "Say something you little tramp," Virginia screamed. "Stop it Virginia," Garlan told her angrily. He knew she was upset, so was he, but he didn't like Virginia calling Tatiana names. Virginia grabbed Tatiana by the shoulders and began shaking her. "Who is this boy you let knock you up," she yelled once more. Tatiana saw the venom in her eyes.

Everything happened so quickly she didn't have time to react. Virginia's eyes narrowed, and the hate Tatiana saw in them chilled her to the core, as her mother deliberately pushed her backwards down the staircase. Tatiana screamed aloud as her father called out her name, trying to get to her. All she remembered was darkness. When she opened her eyes, Garlan was worriedly looking into her face. "Chip, honey, can you hear me?" His eyes searched hers for recognition. "Daddy…" Garlan sighed with deep relief. "Where are we," Tatiana asked weakly. Her entire body hurt, her head pounded, and she was cramping something fierce. "You're in the hospital baby." Memory returned, and Tatiana scanned the room for her mother, relieved she was not there. "She pushed me daddy." Garlan sighed slightly before answering her. "It was an accident honey," he told her sympathetically. "She was angry, you two were tussling back and forth." Tatiana shook her head vigorously. "You didn't see her face daddy. She wanted to kill me," Tatiana tried to explain. "Don't be dramatic Tatiana," Virginia's shrill voice rang out as she entered the room and heard Tatiana's accusations. "It was an unfortunate accident." There was no hint of genuine emotion in her voice.

"Pastor Conklin is here," she announced as Tatiana froze. Garlan gave her a quizzical glance but said nothing. "He has agreed to come and talk to you," Virginia went on. "Maybe he can find out who you have been in the streets having sex with." Both Samuel and Sylvia entered her hospital room. "How are you precious Tatiana," Sylvia asked genuinely concerned, making Tatiana feel even lower for the deception. "I'm okay First Lady," she returned, feeling Samuel's eyes boring into her flesh. The doctor entered while they were there. Virginia informed him they had nothing to hide from their leaders. Sighing, the doctor addressed both Garlan and Virginia. "The fall caused Tatiana to miscarry I'm afraid." Tatiana began to cry. Samuel's eyes turned blood red. "We will do a D&C in a few minutes to remove the tissue

from the uterus." Virginia told him that was fine and followed him out to sign papers. Garlan and Sylvia left moment's later, giving Samuel time to console Tatiana on her loss and try to find out who fathered the child.

He immediately came to her bedside, kissing her lips and stroking her face. "I'm sorry," she told him quietly beginning to cry. "Honey, this is not your fault," Samuel told her lovingly. "Tell me what happened," he pressed as Tatiana recalled what she could. "She was trying to kill me," she told him quietly. "I believe you baby," Samuel told her. He kissed her cheek and shared the story he conjured. He later told Virginia and Garlan that Tatiana refused to name the child's father, and since the baby was no longer an issue, they should just leave it alone and allow her to heal. Garlan had no problem with the recommendation. Virginia wanted answers. Irritated, Samuel finally called her out. "What is more important Virginia, finding out who made her pregnant or her getting well?" Virginia caught the underlying threat of his tone and left well enough alone.

Tatiana had the D&C and was released the next day. She immediately asked to go live with her Aunt Jorinda. After a few more days of begging and cajoling, Garlan acquiesced. Virginia hardly flinched as she helped her pack and dropped her off at the woman's Brooklyn apartment. Tatiana recalled the tense words that were exchanged when they thought she was out of earshot. "She needs to continue counseling," Virginia told Jorinda who scoffed. "I think she has had way more than enough of that counseling mess," she spat angrily. "Leave the girl alone, she isn't bad Virginia, she's a teenager." Virginia sucked her teeth. "You would say that," she threw out as Jorinda told her to watch the ground she was treading. "Well whatever," Virginia threw back. "She's your problem now," she spat and left without a goodbye. Tatiana flourished at her Aunt's. She managed to distance herself from Samuel but not without several threats and surprise visits while she was still in school. As time passed and after a couple run ins with her Auntie Jo, Samuel backed off and left her alone. Tatiana lived with Auntie Jo until last year when she finally got her own place and a new job.

Tatiana stirred and felt the arms around her, startling her from her sleep.

"Relax baby, it is just me."

Samuel pulled her back down to him.

"What are you doing here?"

Her mind was on overload, she couldn't deal with him right now. This afternoon, the memories and dreams totally drained her.

"I came to see about you."

Samuel stroked her back, his hands sliding effortlessly over her butt.

"You were having a bad dream."

"Yes. Are you staying all night?"

Tatiana hoped to gauge how long he was planning to be around.

"No. I actually have to leave in a little while."

He kissed her.

"Do you know how much I have missed you?"

Tatiana didn't like the look, or the way he was touching her now. She was terrified Samuel would make her have sex with him. *You're not fifteen anymore, call the cops, report him for rape.* Samuel spoke as if reading her mind.

"Tatiana, you do remember our history, right?"

Choosing not to answer, Tatiana waited on him to speak again.

"No one would believe I forced you. Even your parents would testify for me."

His hand found her breast and squeezed.

"Tatiana, I love you. I won't hurt you, but I won't let you leave me again either."

Samuel kissed her deeply, undressing her. Tatiana was scared and defeated all at once. He was right. No one would believe he forced her. The lock wasn't forced. She knew without a doubt her mother would cheerfully and willingly testify against her. Garlan might have reservations, but he too would get on the stand and tell the truth as he knew it. The tears came before she could stop them. Samuel wiped them away.

"It's you and me baby."

He kissed her slowly parting her legs again.

Tatiana tried to fight back.

"Stop it!"

The words fell harshly from him. Holding both her arms above her head he looked into her eyes. He began kissing his way down her body, finally letting her arms go.

Samuel wanted to make love to her, but he knew she wasn't ready yet. He could still see the apprehension in her eyes. He continued to kiss her body, gently licking her stomach, making his way lower until he was settled between her legs tasting her. Tatiana didn't want this at all, completely repulsed, but didn't dare push him away. She also knew she better start showing a reaction or he would really hurt her. Closing her eyes and blocking out her surroundings, Tatiana shut down and let her body run on auto pilot. Samuel felt her begin to flow and knew she was enjoying him. He doubled his effort as Tatiana's body contracted and she exhaled aloud.

Samuel smiled and kissed his way back up her body, finding her lips and kissing her once more.

"Feel better now, baby?"

Tatiana opened her eyes and gave him the answer she knew he wanted to hear.

"I have to go now, but I promise, we will be together soon."

Samuel rose covering her with the comforter. He dressed and walked over to her once more.

"I'll see you soon, baby."

Kissing her forehead, he finally left her alone.

I can't do this anymore. Not sure how she could stop it she closed her eyes praying she didn't wake up.

CHAPTER 11

IT FEELS RIGHT

Naimah was thoroughly enjoying her birthday. Her Auntie Bettie threw the huge BBQ for her at their house. They had a enormous backyard and it was decorated with string lights and balloons. The grills were rolling full steam, while the huge caldron pot boiled blue crabs. Tabby invited all their friends from school. Some of Auntie Bettie's friends and co-workers stopped by. As well as her own parent's friends and co-workers. Ruben was there. Unfortunately, so was Denzel. Pastor and Mrs. Padgett were invited and by proxy, their son. Sighing evenly Naimah pushed the thought from her mind. Denzel spent the majority of the afternoon slyly trying to get close to her.

Naimah just wanted him to back off and leave her alone. She and Tabby soon discovered why Sheila, Tabby's best friend, didn't like her. Seemed the girl held a huge crush on Denzel, seeing Naimah as a threat.
"I told that stupid girl you don't even like Denzel."
Tabby explained the situation as she and Naimah enjoyed BBQ together.
"I hope she believes you. Trust me if I knew how to get him to talk to her, I definitely would."
"Move over girl."
DonJuan teased Tabby, elbowing her as he and Ruben joined them at the small picnic table.
Chuckling Tabby complied, stealing a hotdog from his plate.

"You know that's gonna cost you later!"

Tabby burst into laughter at his declaration.

DonJuan teased Naimah now.

"Big 17. You feel old?"

Naimah laughed.

"If I do, then you must feel ancient."

They all laughed.

"Your Auntie Bettie be throwing down."

Ruben complimented the cooking, polishing off the potato salad on his plate.

"Naimah cooks like that too."

Reuben regarded her after Tabby's assertion.

"Do you?"

"I do okay."

"So when are you gonna cook for me?"

"Whenever you want."

"Definitely will be soon."

Pastor Padgett greeted them as he came over to the table.

"Hi everyone."

Every person politely returned his greeting before Denzel joined him, standing and staring directly at Naimah. Pastor Padgett handed her an envelope with a card contained.

"Happy birthday, Naimah."

"Thank you so much, Pastor Padgett."

Naimah rose hugging him lightly.

"Why don't you and I take a little walk, hmm?"

Naimah frowned a bit in confusion but remained respectful telling him okay. Ruben, Tabby, and DonJuan, all respired noticeably after they left. Ruben grew agitated voicing his displeasure aloud.

"So now he got daddy doing his dirt."

Tabby spoke up.

"He's probably giving her the speech y'all, that's all."

Ruben simply grunted. He didn't put anything past Denzel. He knew how desperately he wanted to be with Naimah.

Pastor Padgett and Naimah walked through the back yard away from the party.

"So how are you liking Alabama?"

"It's been really good."

"Mm, that's nice."

His reply garnered a curious look from her. The tone very much distracted.

"Naimah…."

They stopped walking. He was looking directly at her now.

"Yes?"

"I like to talk to all my young people when they get close to graduation…"

Pastor Padgett took in the young woman. He understood his son's attraction. Naimah was a very pretty girl, respectful, and seemingly level-headed.

"I want you to be careful of your decisions at this juncture in your life. Some things you cannot take back, so think before you act."

Naimah smiled.

"I will definitely do that Pastor Padgett."

He went on to give her a little more life advice. When he finished talking, Denzel seemed to materialize on cue.

"I'll leave you two alone."

Pastor Padgett smiled at them both as he walked away.

Inhaling a fresh breath, Naimah gathered herself for whatever trick Denzel held up his sleeve this time.

"Why," he asked simply.

Naimah frowned curiously.

"What are you talking about? Why what?"

Denzel took a deep breath and measured its release before speaking again.

"Why are you trying to hurt me by dating Ruben?"

Naimah let go her breath and addressed him.

"Denzel, seriously, let it go. I don't like you like that."

Weary of explaining, she prayed he was really hearing her.

"I am attracted to Ruben. He and I are a couple."

Denzel struggled not to go off.

"Sheila really likes you. Maybe you should talk to her, get to know her. You never know, you two might hit it off."

Denzel stepped closer, the anger in his expression, migrating to his voice.

"I don't want Sheila."

Ruben walking up on them cancelled any escalation.

"Everything cool?"

He watched them from the table since Denzel walked up and his father walked away. Ruben was sick and tired of Denzel trying to get with Naimah when the girl told him in every way she knew how that she didn't want him.

"Yeah, everything is fine."

Naimah smiled, glad he appeared when he did. Denzel scared the hell out of her. He was Sharif reincarnate. That chapter was well sealed for Naimah. Taking Ruben's outstretched hand, they began walking back to the party as she felt Denzel's eyes boring into her back.

Sheila, spoke to Denzel having wandered over herself seeing him and Naimah talking.

"Hey, Wassup?"

Denzel turned and regarded the girl silently for a few moments as his mind raced. *Might as well get this bush too.* He would deal with Naimah later, he made up his mind as Sheila smiled again. They walked further away from the party finding a nice secluded spot to talk and get better acquainted. Denzel chuckled silently moments later as he kissed Sheila, his tongue down her throat, his hand between her legs.

******

Ruben was talking to Naimah as they arrived at his sister's house.

"Damn, maybe he will back off now."

He still lived with her, the arrangement working out well since she had no children and wasn't married. They were alone tonight. His sister was out of town attending her best friend's family reunion.

"I sure hope so."

They sat down on the couch and turned on the TV.

"Happy birthday again baby."

Ruben sweetly kissed her.

"Thanks," she giggled.

"I bought you something."

"You didn't have to do that, Ruben. You coming to my party was present enough."

Ruben smiled and rose leaving her alone transitorily as he retrieved the gift.

He returned moments later and handed her the oblong felt box.

"What is this?"

"Open it and see special!"

Ruben laughed, poking her in the ribs.

Naimah chuckled opening the lid to the box, revealing the sterling silver charm bracelet, complete with three charms.

"Thank you, Ruben. This is really nice."

Ruben helped her put it on explaining the other two charms, stopping momentarily as he arrived at the third. The interlocking hearts.

"This one is for us."

Naimah smiled, genuinely moved at his thoughtfulness.

"This means so much to me."

Ruben kissed her again, their lust beginning to overtake them. He pulled away moments later, trying to gather himself.

"You want something to drink?"

Ruben needed very much to cool off after that kiss. Naimah couldn't believe how aroused she was. Her nipples were hard. Her breathing was uneven. She wanted Ruben more than anything right now.

"No, I am okay."

Ruben swallowed hard and tried to turn his attention to the TV set. He wanted her so much, but he didn't want to rush her.

Naimah noticing the family photos on the table commented on them.

"Your sister is pretty,"

"Thanks. This is my mom and dad."

Ruben picked up one of the large photos.

Naimah smiled looking at the handsome couple. Ruben seemed to have taken his light complexion from his father.

"They're a good-looking pair."

Ruben thanked her again taking the picture and putting it down once more. Naimah moved closer to Ruben, resting her head on his chest as they watched the movie playing. Ruben rubbed her back as he held her thinking how good she felt in his arms. Naimah quickly stole his heart. It scared Ruben how deeply he crashed head first into this relationship. Thinking of Denzel and his pursuit pissed him off all over again. *He is such a pompous ass.* Ruben kissed Naimah's forehead absently. She kissed his chest in return, beginning to stroke it. She looked up into his eyes and Ruben kissed her fervidly, carefully laying her down on the couch.

Naimah felt his hands caressing her breasts, squeezing them, as she moaned quietly. *Please don't stop this time.* Ruben's hands slid under her shirt, unhooking her bra. Ruben removed the clothing, kissing her breasts softly and sucking the nipples. Naimah was on fire. She absolutely loved the things Ruben was doing to her. She reached up helping him out of his shirt, admiring and caressing the well-developed chest and sexy pectorals. Ruben kissed her neck, removing her jeans and grasping her butt as the kiss heightened. His erection was at full attention wanting desperately to be inside her.

"Naimah…"

Pulling away for a moment, he looked into her eyes. "Baby, we don't have to do this, if you're not really ready."

Naimah smiled at how sweet this man was, again wanting to give her virginity to him.

"I want this, Ruben."

He smiled, removing his own jeans as they continued to kiss.

Naimah reached down touching his erection as Ruben groaned, removing her panties and touching her intimately. Naimah whimpered as Ruben continued to touch her.

He began slowly kissing his way down her body, as Naimah writhed in anticipation. His tongue found its mark and Naimah moaned deeply. Ruben loved the feel of her body, the taste of her, as he continued to please her. Bringing her to orgasm, he felt her spasm as she cried out gripping his shoulders. He returned to her lips kissing her intensely as he touched her with his erection.

"Are you sure baby?"

"I want you, Ruben."

He kissed her delicately, removed the condom from the end table beside them and put it on. After caressing her to readiness once more, kissing her yet another time, Ruben entered her.

Naimah was waiting for the pain they told her she would experience, but there was none. Ruben was inside her and all she felt was unbridled pleasure as they began to move together.

"Naimah, Naimah…"

He couldn't believe how right this felt with her.

"Yes Ruben, that's so good."

She cried passionately reaching orgasm again, right as he too reached the pinnacle of release holding her tightly, breathing hard.

They held each other kissing intermittently for a few moments more before Ruben removed himself from her and disposed of the condom. Cleaning themselves up, and dressing, they headed to his truck. They began to talk as Ruben drove her home.

"I promise never to make you regret tonight."

Naimah smiled and kissed him.

"I don't regret it."

Ruben smiled again, kissed her passionately and told her goodnight. Naimah promised to call him tomorrow as she exited the truck and waved once more before disappearing inside. Ruben smiled inside, entirely content, and started the truck heading home.

Cʜᴀᴘᴛᴇʀ 12

DISCOVERIES

Jaden's world was getting more and more complicated. He spent the last three days trying to find Sharif without luck. *I need to get to him before the police do.* He didn't turn Sharif in, but there was another witness unknown to Jaden, who saw the incident, and heard Jaden call out Sharif's name. The police were pressuring him to corroborate the witness's story, but so far Jaden avoided the pressure and said nothing. He needed to talk to Tatiana. He was neglecting her. She texted him regularly letting him know she was fine, asking if he needed anything. *I need to spend some time with her, so she knows how much I care.* His cell rang. Recognizing his parent's number, Jaden answered warmly.

He was frowning now as he listened to his father tell him about his mother's hospitalization.

"I'll fly out today."

"Thanks son, I appreciate it truly."

"It's not a problem dad."

Jaden loved his parents. There was nothing he wouldn't do for them. Disconnecting he immediately called Tatiana.

"Hi."

The sweet voice made him feel even guiltier for the neglect.

"Hi baby, I just got a call from my dad. My mom is in the hospital with bronchial pneumonia."

She gasped at the disclosure.

"Jaden is she okay?"

He exhaled before answering.

"She is serious right now, so I'm flying there in a little while."

"Okay, sounds good."

"Baby, I know it's asking a lot, but maybe you could fly down tomorrow and spend the weekend?"

"Yeah, I could do that."

Jaden smiled fully and gave her all the information she needed.

"I'll reserve your room and stuff once I get there. I'll pay for it of course."

"Jaden, I can pay for my own room."

"Tatiana."

Hearing the tone, she stopped arguing.

"OK, I'll see you tomorrow."

"That's fine."

"Will you call me when you get there?"

"Yes baby, of course. I can't wait to see you tomorrow." The longing shone evident in his voice.

"Me either."

After the hell her life was these last days, she desperately needed to be held by him.

"Love you," he said calmly and disconnected.

Jaden was still smiling as he packed. He was worried about his mother without doubt, but he was also excitedly looking forward to seeing Tatiana, holding her, kissing her. *Making love to her?* Jaden thought long and hard about it. He wanted that since he met her, but Jaden didn't want to rush what was coming along so beautifully between them. Tatiana was special. He wanted her to know that. Deciding he would just play it by ear, Jaden completed his task. Heading out the door he decided to make one more swing through the neighborhood and familiar hangouts. The prayer he would get lucky and actually find Sharif this time.

*****

Finally, having promised herself time and again to do it, Sylvia was cleaning out the attic. Samuel already left headed to the church to begin his day. She would join him later for several meetings with various auxiliaries.

"All this crap should have been thrown out a long time ago."

She opened the first box and began to go through the contents. Finding lots of papers no longer useful, she promptly shredded those, moving on to the next box. It was marked personal. Sylvia assumed it was just more paperwork Samuel should have thrown out long ago. Instead, Sylvia found lots of photographs. There were some from the first church Samuel pastored, featuring various events and gatherings. There were others from Christian Cathedral, the church here, as well as several photos of the two of them. She found another small envelope inside marked 'x-personal' and assumed these were their wedding photos.

Still smiling when she opened them, Sylvia began to look thru the stills. The smile left her face. Tears came to her eyes in their stead. They were pictures of Tatiana. Lots and lots of pictures of the girl with hearts and the word love written in various positions within the shots. *Please do not let this be what I think it is.* The lone tear rolled down her cheek. She continued to go through the stack as the pictures became more personal. Sylvia began weeping openly holding the picture of Samuel and Tatiana. His arm around her, kissing her on the lips. *She was a child!* Sylvia's mind screamed in pain while she continued to cry. Hurriedly putting the pictures back and fleeing to her room, she flung herself across the bed. Now it all made sense. Now Sylvia understood why Tatiana always seemed so frightened when she or Samuel came around. *She was scared I would find out. Could her husband, the man she loved, have done something as horrible as the thing implied in those pictures?* The hurt and fear took over. *I definitely need to talk to Tatiana.*

Sylvia heard the door close and knew Samuel returned. *He cannot suspect I know anything yet.* She hurriedly rose and went into the bathroom. Washing her face. Putting Visine in her eyes. She emerged moments later encountering Samuel in the bedroom, changing his clothes.

"Hi honey."

Sylvia summoned every ounce of acting skill she possessed, greeting him in return, even kissing him softly.

"Cleaning out the attic I see."

Sylvia prayed he didn't notice the photo box. Now she understood why he was so insistent that she not clean out his personal papers. *You didn't want me to know what a monster you were.* Sylvia continued to linger in disbelief behind the small smile she displayed for his benefit.

"I'll be back later."

Sylvia nodded.

"I'll be gone soon myself."

As soon as the door closed, she sat down hard on the bed, head in her hands, at a total loss of her next move.

*****

Samuel arrived letting himself inside. Heading to the kitchen he heard the water running and knew Tatiana was in the shower. He grabbed the bottle of water and made his way into the bedroom to wait for her to come out. Samuel greeted her as Tatiana walked into the room and stopped in her tracks.

"Hi baby."

"Hey."

Tatiana really didn't want to deal with him today. She was excited about her weekend with Jaden and spending time with him. Samuel walked over to her, pulling her close and kissing her deeply. Tatiana didn't fight him, simply allowing him to have his way.

"You smell delicious."

He started kissing her neck.

"Thanks."

There must be a way out of this hell she was enduring, Tatiana told herself as Samuel undid her towel gently caressing her breast.

"I need you."

Pulling her toward the bed, he pushed her effortlessly onto it. He began removing his shirt. Tatiana finally found her voice.

"Samuel…"

Pulling herself into a sitting position, she prayed this would work. Feigning irritation, she picked up speech another time.

"I'm sick of this."

He stopped undressing and regarded her curiously. He never heard Tatiana speak to him this way.

"I am tired of being the sideline bitch, the whore on the street."

Samuel's mouth dropped.

Feeling the performance and never taking her eyes off him, Tatiana went on.

"You come in here feeding me all this crap about you love me, and baby this, baby that. Well you know what, I'm done."

She rose, putting on her robe. Samuel continued to remain mute.

"If you're gonna divorce old girl and get with me, then do it!"

Tatiana stood right in his face now.

"Otherwise get the hell out of my life and stop playing with me!"

Samuel was absolutely outdone.

"It's not like that at all baby."

He didn't want Tatiana angry with him. He loved her with his whole heart. She just scared the hell out of him.

He reached out for her as she pushed him away, sucking her teeth.

"I am going to divorce her."

Tatiana gave him another look and rolled her eyes.

"Yeah, when? You've already been inside me Samuel. You knocked me up, remember?"

"Baby, please, just listen."

"I don't wanna hear anymore lies Samuel."

"Baby, what do I need to do to prove to you I'm serious?"

He hastily pleaded his case, looking into her eyes.

Praying he wouldn't actually follow through with so much to lose, she voiced the ultimatum.

"Show me the filed papers."

"Okay baby. But you have to give me a little time, okay?"

He kissed her as Tatiana allowed it.

"Fine. But you can't touch me until it is done."

Samuel sighed seriously.

"Baby, don't punish me like that."

"How do you think I feel Samuel?"

So far, so good. Tatiana's mind was racing thinking that her new approach might be just what she needed to rid herself of Samuel forever.

"What do you mean baby?"

Tatiana breathed loudly for effect. A silent plea of forgiveness for the lies about to be told.

"I lay here at night, wanting you, needing you. Thinking about how you touched me, how you made love to me."

Samuel stared into her eyes, staying silent.

"Then I think about how you are doing the same thing to her, and just lying to me."

"I don't do that Tatiana. I don't even have sex with her."

Tatiana scoffed. *You are such a liar.*

"Yeah right! Well you aren't having sex with me either. Not as long as you're still legally married to her."

Samuel yet another time respired aloud.

"OK baby."

He was already completely aroused standing this close to her, how was he going to not make love to her?

Pulling her to him and holding her, Samuel stroked her back. Tatiana thanked God silently, surprising even herself with the thought. Samuel began kissing her neck. Tatiana again played along. She moaned as he lightly kissed her breast, another time pushing her onto the bed.

Samuel lay atop her kissing her as his hands continued caressing her. He smoothly unzipped his pants and freed his erection, kissing Tatiana fervently as he prepared to enter her.

"No, stop! See that's the crap I am talking about!"

She produced tears, knowing his weakness.

"You think I'm just the screw bitch!"

Tatiana sobbed deeply as Samuel gathered himself and came to her.

"No, baby, I'm sorry, I'm sorry. I just want you so much Tatiana."

Switching lanes, he tried anew.

"Let me please you baby."

Tatiana frowned acutely.

"No, not like that."

Tatiana acquiesced, knowing she had to give something to keep him from violating her. Samuel smiled kissing her as she lay back and allowed him to taste her. He pleasured himself as he enjoyed her, finishing just as she did.

"I love you Tatiana. I'm going to prove that to you."

He planted another kiss on her lips.

"And don't you ever think of, or call yourself, a bitch or a whore again, do you hear me?"

"Yes."

He kissed her once more and left her alone, heading out to meet Gordon. Tatiana exhaled in relief thankful she was only forced to have oral sex with him. *Okay, that's a start, now what?*

CHAPTER 13

THE VEIL IS LIFTED

Tatiana gathered herself, showered and dressed heading to see her Auntie Jo like she promised. Finally leaving the subway and walking to the assisted living facility, Tatiana gathered herself. Her aunt knew her too well to fake it. She knocked moments later on her Aunt's door as the woman opened it smiling, and invited her in.

"Hey Auntie."

Tatiana hugged her tightly as Jorinda hugged her back.

"Sit down, let me get us some tea."

Tatiana smiled and did as her aunt requested. She relaxed finally for the first time in days. Being with Auntie Jo always made her feel safe and secure. Tatiana was also looking excitedly forward to seeing Jaden tomorrow. *Mmm, I need that man's good vibes so much right now.* Jorinda re-entered the room recapturing her attention.

"How are you doing baby?"

"I am doing okay, Auntie."

Tatiana sipped her tea.

Jo sighed heavily before addressing her niece again.

"Tatiana, now, you know I know you right?"

Tatiana remained mute.

"There's something very wrong with you right now, so why are you trying to hide it from me?"

Tatiana took a deep breath and put a smile on her face hoping to convince her aunt everything was fine.

"I'm okay, Auntie, for real."

Jorinda sat her cup down and crossed her arms in front of her.

"Tatiana Elizabeth. You're going to sit in my house and lie to my face now?"

Tatiana's eyes filled, and she looked away. She couldn't lie to Auntie Jo, but she was scared to death to tell her the truth.

"Baby, what is going on?"

Reaching over, Jorinda took Tatiana's hands into her own.

"Are you in trouble?"

Tatiana began to cry.

"Yes, but not the kind you're talking about."

Jorinda exhaled heavily once again.

"Baby, tell me what is wrong, I can't help you if I don't know."

Tatiana cried harder.

"I need to go, Auntie."

Jorinda wouldn't let go of her hand.

"Tatiana, talk to your Auntie. I love you, tell me."

Hearing her aunt say she loved her, Tatiana broke. She spent the next hour and forty-five minutes telling Jorinda everything about her, Samuel Conklin, and the unspeakable things that transpired between them seven years ago.

Jorinda was absolutely furious after listening to her niece. She held Tatiana rocking her gently as the young woman continued to sniffle. *I knew that nasty sonofabitch was doing something to this child.* Jorinda fumed confirming her long ago suspicions. Hearing of Virginia's role in all Tatiana's torment made her continue to see red. *She may be my sister, but she is still one evil bitch.* Tatiana finally quieted.

"Please don't hate me Auntie."

Jorinda smiled lovingly at her niece and caressed her face.

"I love you Tatiana. "

That settled, she spoke another time. Tatiana paid rapt attention.

"You listen to me baby. You were abused, manipulated, and lied too."

Jorinda prayed she was getting through.

"What that nasty, lying ass man did to you was not your fault."

"But I didn't fight him auntie, I just let it happen."

"Tatiana, you were fifteen years old. You stop letting that dog off the hook. What he did was dead ass wrong and HE knew it."

Tatiana sadly nodded her understanding.

"Mama hates me for all of it. Even the part she doesn't really know, I think she suspects, and she hates me."

Jorinda sighed evenly. Now was the time to set some things in order. Her mind told her it was the right thing to do as she watched her niece continue to struggle.

"Virginia is not your mother, Tatiana."

Tatiana's head snapped up. She eyed her aunt with disbelief.

"What are you talking about Auntie Jo? I was adopted?"

Jorinda loosed another breath, hating to hurt Tatiana any more than she already was. Her niece needed to know the truth. Then she could try to heal her hurt and get her life together.

"Not in the traditional sense, no."

"I don't understand."

What the hell else can go wrong today? Jorinda began speaking, breaking her thought.

"Your mama's name is Rachel. Rachel Elizabeth Abbey, she was our youngest sister."

Tatiana continued to remain mute waiting for more.

Taking a new breath Jorinda began to recount the story of Tatiana's conception and subsequent birth.

"Rae loved you. She and Garlan were excitedly looking forward to being a family and raising you together."

Tatiana smiled slightly.

"Virginia was jealous. She was always jealous of Rae. She wanted Garlan, but he only had eyes for Rae."

Tatiana noted the anger, the clenched jaw of her aunt when she spoke of Virginia.

"You were only a month old when she was killed."

Jorinda paused momentarily, as the tears came to her eyes.

"Senseless murder, all for the twenty dollars in her purse."

The tear escaped and rolled down her cheek.

"Of course, Virginia saw it as an opportunity to have Garlan finally, using you in the process."

Tatiana nodded her understanding.

"She treats you the way she does because every time she looks at you she sees Rae."

Tatiana thought how much that made sense.

"Garlan was always weak when it came to Virginia. I guess he felt like he owed her because she helped him with you."

Jorinda shrugged at the end of the sentence.

"We've been trying to work things out. Me and daddy, I mean."

Jorinda nodded thoughtfully.

"Do you have any pictures of Rachel, I mean, mama?"

Jo smiled and rose headed to her bedroom. She returned moments later with the photo albums and they spent the greater portion of the afternoon looking at them reminiscing.

"Now, we gotta figure out what to do about your problem."

Jorinda returned her attention back to Samuel and his obsessions.

"He's dangerous Auntie."

"Hmph, I am sure. But I have an idea."

Tatiana listened carefully as she began to elaborate.

"Do you think it would work?"

Jorinda, mind already working ahead, answered her.

"Yes,"

"Okay, I'll start when I come back."

"Where are you going?"

Tatiana told her about Jaden and his mother's illness.

"He sounds like a really nice man."

Tatiana smiled fully.

"He really is."

Jorinda loved seeing the happiness etched in her niece's face as she talked about Jaden. *She deserves this and so much more.* Her mind cataloged something she needed to do when Tatiana left.

"I'm heading out now Auntie. Thank you so much for listening, for telling the truth, for helping me."

Jorinda embraced her, holding her tightly.

"I'm sorry for all this happening to you Tatiana, but we're gonna make it right."

Tatiana smiled and nodded her understanding, finally leaving. Jorinda picked up the phone. Garlan answered on the third ring.

"Come see me right now."

Disconnecting she headed back to the kitchen to refresh her tea and wait on him to appear.

*****

Nakida sighed lightly looking over and seeing Jaden's empty cube once more. She heard that in addition to his friend being killed, there was now a family emergency. He took a one month leave of absence. *I wish I could be there for him right now.* Nakida remained hopelessly infatuated with Jaden. She just could not seem to shake the feelings or accept that he didn't return them.

Rahshaun placed the small sunshine bouquet on her desk as he passed by.

"Wassup Nakida."

Wary she gave him a look.

"What are these for?"

Rahshaun burst into laughter before answering.

"Damn girl, has it been that long since a brutha was just nice to your ass, that you forgot?"

Chuckling he walked away.

Nakida remained suspicious.

Something just ain't quite right with him. Her gaze followed the direction Rahshaun went. Nakida couldn't put her finger on it, but she felt it. It was a dark sinister feeling that Rahshaun was evil. She sighed deeply knowing it would sound silly if she told anyone. That was the best way she could think to describe it however. Nakida witnessed his in and out odd behavior firsthand on several occasions. Rahshaun was a dog true enough, but it was like he was forever trying to prove a point with the quantity of women he slept with. She also suspected violence was a common side dish served when dating or sleeping with the man. Nakida could never get Tisha to admit it, but after their lunch date and subsequent club date, the girl avoided Rahshaun like the plague. You could see the fear on her face when they were forced to be in close proximity. Exhaling once more pushing further contemplation aside, Nakida returned her attention to her own desk and began her day. She never noticed Rahshaun's quiet observation as she did.

*****

Garlan arrived an hour after Jorinda's call. He took the seat offered as she invited him in and handed him the cup of coffee he requested.

"What is so important, Jo?"

Sipping the steaming hot liquid, he watched her closely.

"Your daughter."

"Is there something wrong with Tatiana?"

The uneasy feeling splashed headlong in his gut.

"Where is your inhaler?"

Garlan was a chronic asthmatic and Jorinda knew what she was about to tell him would set him off. His last few attacks were what kept landing him in the hospital. She needed him in one piece and healthy as possible to help her get Tatiana out of the mess she was trapped in.

"I have it in my pocket."

The question only served to deepen his trepidation.

"Hmph, take it out and keep it in your hand."

Now he knew it was bad. Garlan did as she asked.

Jorinda took a deep breath and began to speak. "Did you know that Samuel Conklin took Tatiana's virginity when she was fifteen years old?"

Garlan's mouth dropped. His eyes turned fire red. Anger boiled inside him.

"What the hell are you talking about Jorinda?"

Jorinda sighed deeply and repeated what she said.

"We have been through all this nonsense. Tatiana saw Pastor Conklin for counseling. She developed a schoolgirl crush on him and started making up these accusations."

Jorinda sat up on the edge of her seat and looked him in the eye.

"Do you really believe that bullshit or does that just make it easier to know you failed that child and allowed Virginia to treat her like shit?"

Her anger neared the boiling point.

Jorinda was sick and tired of Garlan acting like a worn-out doormat, never using his backbone. Never standing up for either himself or his daughter.

"Did Tatiana tell you this, Jo? She lies, Jo, you know that."

Jorinda sucked her teeth in disgust.

"Tatiana has never lied to me Garlan. She has no reason to."

Gearing up anew, Jorinda didn't let up.

"I have met the good reverend Conklin. He is quite the piece of work."

Garlan retained his silence, sipping his coffee anew.

"But I'm sure none of your church members get it, because he has all of you so mesmerized."

Garlan sighed deeply, rubbing his temples methodically. He didn't want to rehash all this ancient history and deal with it again.

Jorinda wasn't finished with him just yet.

"I have seen how he looks at that child. Bet he didn't tell you all the times he showed up at Tatiana's school, without warning."

Garlan endured the tongue lashing.

"Or the times he showed up here, after 9:00 at night, talking about taking her out for ice cream to talk."

The memories began to betray him.

Garlan began recalling things he thought he saw when Tatiana and Pastor Conklin were together. Jorinda saw his wheels turning.

"Did she ever tell you who got her pregnant?"

Garlan again looked into her eyes, not wanting to hear what she was going to say next.

"He fathered that child, Garlan, Samuel Conklin."

Garlan began to wheeze, quickly unlocking his inhaler and taking the needed dosage. Jorinda gave him time to gather himself before speaking again.

"Tatiana has been through hell, and she is really messed up behind what this monster did to her."

Jorinda wasn't letting Garlan off the hook. She let him have another barrel when she continued speaking.

"Added to the crap you have allowed Virginia to do to her all these years, this child thinks she deserved all the things this man did to her. That her own mother hated her."

The tear escaped Garlan's eye. The actuality was hard and painful.

"She knows the truth now though."

"About Rachel?"

Jorinda nodded yes.

"How did she take it?"

His mind recalled the woman he loved with all his heart. "Relieved, happy, sad, all at the same time. I showed her pictures, told her about her mama, and helped her understand a little better."

Garlan nodded.

"I'm gonna kill him."

His mind went back to Samuel Conklin.

"No."

Garlan again regarded her.

"I have something way better in mind. Death would be too easy."

Nodding marginally, he remained mute as Jorinda explained the plan she devised, Tatiana's role, and his own part to be played.

"Let me know when you're ready."

Jorinda nodded her understanding. Garland rose from the chair heading out.

"I have a lot to get in order. Did Tatiana head home?"

"I think so. I know she's leaving town in the morning."

Garlan grunted his understanding and opened the door. "Thanks Jo."

Jorinda looked into his face seeing the hurt, the anger, and the determination. Garlan wasn't going to fail Tatiana again and she knew it.

"Talk to you soon, Garlan."

He nodded, closing the door.

Rahshaun boarded the elevator with Nakida, headed out for the day.

"Girl I know you're gonna be at Expressions tonight!"

Nakida chuckled.

"I thought about it."

Expressions was the hot new club recently opened uptown. They were having a blowout grand opening party with several celebrities promised in attendance. Rahshaun gave her a look as he smiled.

"Come on now, Nakida, you know you're going!"

She smiled somewhat, another time.

"You and Tiffany should go with me and my boy."

Nakida didn't know why but the request immediately made her uneasy. She just couldn't shake that feeling of darkness surrounding Rahshaun.

"Don't make a brutha beg."

Sighing, Nakida reluctantly agreed, calling Tiffany as she left the elevator.

"Hey chick."

Continuing the conversation, she made her request known.

"Yeah, that's cool girl. Ask him or his boy about getting us in VIP?"

"OK."

Disconnecting Nakida relayed Tiffany's request.

"She's down, but she wants to know about VIP?"

Rahshaun smiled and told her it was no problem.

I know Kenny gonna get that pussy, paying $50 to get in VIP. Rahshaun's dark thoughts deepend behind the smile as he and Nakida exited the building. The conversation resumed once they boarded the subway.

"So what time am I scooping you up?"
"Umm, what, say 10:00 or 10:30 I guess."
Rahshaun smiled and got her address. He threw out last minute instructions as she prepared to get off the train.
"See ya later girl. Make sure you're dressed to turn heads."
"I don't turn heads, I break necks!"
Rahshaun burst into laughter. Nakida, smiling, turned and walked away, never seeing the smile immediately vanish, replaced by the dark, brooding, scowl.

CHAPTER 14

HATERS WILL HATE

Naimah smiled thinking about Ruben and how good their relationship was going. They were going to celebrate their two-month anniversary this weekend. Denzel finally backed off and left her alone. Naimah was eternally grateful. He and Sheila were talking seriously. She could tell the girl was giddy with joy over the development. Naimah continued thinking to herself how silly some of the girls were here. Having overheard a couple of them talking about her, Ruben, and how stupid she was for dating him, she smirked. *"Girl, he is so tight, he doesn't want to spend any money on a chick or nothing."* Naimah found out Maria, the girl speaking, went out with Ruben on a couple of occasions. She was angry when he wouldn't buy her a designer purse she requested. *Silly brauds.* Ruben spoiled her scandalously since they made love on her birthday. He gave her money on almost a daily basis. He bought her jewelry and clothes without her asking.

Naimah loved him. There was no doubt in her mind that Ruben was who she wanted to spend the rest of her life with. She knew everyone would say she was too young to know that, only being seventeen, but she knew it. Naimah always asked God to send her one man and he be the right man. She knew in her heart that was the real reason she kept putting Sharif off. He wasn't for her. He was a bully and he would have hurt her again and again if she never escaped him. *I wonder what in the world is going on with him now?* Her cousins in New York told her the last they heard he had a couple of babies on the way and dropped out of the movement. *That boy is really troubled,* Reeling her mind in, she heard the bell ring. She rose to leave. Ruben was supposed to be waiting for her. They were going to eat, to a movie. He said he had a surprise for her. *Wonder what he's up to now?* Naimah smiled as she spotted the truck and hurried to get inside.

Ruben greeted her once she entered and buckled her seatbelt.

"Hey baby."

"Hey."

He leaned over and kissed her.

"You ready for tonight?"

"Yeah, and I am dying to know what the surprise is."

Ruben chuckled, started the truck, and said nothing.

*****

Denzel half listened as Sheila rambled on. His eyes were glued to Naimah getting into the truck with Ruben. *Saturday night.* They were having mandatory auxiliary meetings. Everyone who served in any capacity at the church was required to be present. Returning his attention to Sheila, Denzel finally spoke, shutting her up momentarily.

"What's up with you and Ronnie Whitaker?"

Sheila frowned somewhat.

"Nothing."

"Hmph."

Denzel never took his eyes from her.

"What are you trying to say Denzel?"

"I heard things."

Truthfully, he needed to start this fight and make sure it went down very publicly.

"I don't know who you've been talking too, or what you heard…"

"I heard you gave him some ass. That's what I heard."

Sheila slapped him. He slapped her back.

"No you didn't hit me!"

"You hit me, didn't you?!"

She eyed him hatefully. Denzel returned the look.

"Don't be mad at me because you're a whore and got caught in your lies."

Hearing the raised voices everyone began to take note.

"I'm not a whore!"

"Oh yeah? Then why did I get the panties the first day we talked, at Naimah's party?"

Sheila's fury grew.

"Well since we're telling shit, let me tell all these girls that think you're so great, that your dick is little and you don't even know how to eat a chick out!"

Denzel was furious.

"I guess my dick would be small to you, considering everybody that has run all up through you, you bitch!"

The counselor came out seeing the commotion.

"What is going on over here?"

Everyone began to quickly move away.

"Sheila, Denzel you two know better. Go home, school is over."

She stood watching until they both gathered their things and began walking away.

"This shit ain't over whore."

Denzel fixed her with an evil look as he got to his car.

"I'm not scared of you Denzel. You need to take your non fucking ass back to the church."

Sheila's defiance was brazened and without restraint.

"While you're praying, ask God to give you a bigger dick and some skills, bastard!"

Her friends giggled, all of them jumping into Sheila's car leaving him standing there boiling.

Oh I am going to make that bitch real sorry. Denzel darkly began making internal plans. He finally cranked his own vehicle spinning out of the parking lot.

*****

The evening was going by too fast as far as Ruben was concerned. He loved having Naimah in his arms. He held her while they watched the DVD they picked up. She told him she would rather spend the evening in with him, instead of at the theatre. It was things just like that; assuring Ruben he made the right choice in hooking up with Naimah. The thing that scared the hell out of him though was how deeply in love with this girl he was. Ruben was normally slow and meticulous about his relationships. A lot of the girls he thought were good for him, turned out not to be. Naimah was so different. She carried a maturity and wisdom far beyond her years. His sister told him she was his compliment. Two old souls who were here before. *She's good for you Ruben, don't push her away.* His sister's words rang in his mind again as Naimah shifted positions.

Ruben had been hurt before, a couple of times. He was extremely leery of putting his heart out there again, unguarded. Still he couldn't deny what he felt, or what he saw when Naimah looked into his eyes. *She loves me too.* Naimah spoke finally.

"You okay?"

Turning over she faced him waiting for an answer.

Ruben smiled looking into her beautiful face as he continued to hold her.

"I'm fine, baby."

He kissed her for emphasis.

"You've been really quiet tonight."

Ruben chuckled.

"Deep thought."

"Good thoughts, I hope."

"Yes, baby."

Ruben kissed her again, a little more insistent this time.

"What's the surprise, Ruben? You have kept me waiting all night."

Ruben laughed thinking the pout from her was cute.

"I have to tell you some things first."

"OK."

Naimah waited on him to speak.

Ruben took a deep breath, blowing it out slowly. "Naimah, I um…"

He hesitated. She didn't interrupt.

"I have met some girls I thought were, you know, really cool and that we hit it off."

Naimah watched him, seeing the emotion and feeling the struggle he was having telling her these things.

"Turned out they weren't."

Naimah picked up the tone.

"I'm sorry they hurt you, Ruben."

"I guess what I'm trying to say, Naimah, is that I love you, and I want you to always be a part of my life."
He produced the quarter carat diamond ring he bought for her. Naimah smiled fully, hugging Ruben tightly.
"I love you too, Ruben."
He slipped the ring on her finger.
"It is a promise ring. It just means you promise to be with me, exclusively."
Naimah smiled again.
"I promise, Ruben."
They began to kiss fervently their passion taking over.

Naimah couldn't describe how happy she was as Ruben continued to kiss and arouse her. She loved him without question. Now she knew for certain he felt the same way.
Ruben tasted her. The sensations wracked her body bringing a loud moan from her lips.
Naimah sighed softly, calling his name as she came hard, her body trembling in ecstasy. Ruben kissed his way up her body, finding her lips as they began to kiss passionately once more.
Ruben groaned quietly as he slid inside Naimah and began making love to her. Their bodies rocked together in rhythmic motion as the heat rose between them. Naimah cried out gripping his butt and pulling him deeper inside as she came hard once more.
"Girl, shit!"
Ruben came holding her tightly, caution thrown to the wind, until he returned to reality remembering he wasn't wearing a condom.
"I'm sorry, Naimah baby."

"It's okay Ruben."

Naimah felt slightly uneasy but tried to make the best of it.

"It was an accident. I think it will be okay."

Ruben loosed a silent breath glad she wasn't angry with him.

"I hope so."

They dressed and finished watching the movie, putting it out of their mind. Hoping for the best.

*****

Still smiling, Denzel pulled into Anthony's driveway.

"Yo, I'm here."

Anthony called earlier telling him Sheila and her girls were there, smoking weed, drinking and shooting the breeze. Anthony was one of Denzel's close friends. That seemingly didn't matter to Shonda, Sheila's friend who had a serious crush on him.

"I waited until that trick Sheila was good and buzzed before I called you."

Denzel arrived at the basement door, Anthony beside him as they talked. Anthony knew about the earlier stunt she pulled and Denzel's desire to get even. This was Anthony's private sanctuary. His parents seldom ventured down to check on the activities going on within its walls.

"Where is the tramp?"

Anthony pointed her out.

"Over there."

Sheila was faded, and he knew it. Denzel saw her, eyes half closed, downing yet another beer. Anthony told him she already finished at least three, added to several shots of Patrôn.

"I need her in the room alone."

Anthony nodded his understanding. There was a separate small space in the basement blocked with its own door. He needed a little privacy for what he had in mind. Anthony immediately whispered the plan in another friend's ear. They both smiled and went to Sheila convincing her to come with them. Anthony's other best friend kept Shonda and the rest of the girls busy playing dominoes. Sheila was higher than she could ever recall. She acknowledged the impairment to herself as the young men sat her on the small twin sized bed.

"Here girl, hit this shit."

Anthony egged her on, giving her another shot of tequila. Sheila giggled and downed the shot quickly feeling the rush immediately. Anthony stepped back. Darquavius, the other friend who help bring Sheila in the small room, stepped to her and began touching her breasts.

"Stop Quay."

"Don't be like that Sheila."

Squeezing her breast again, he continued to lay the trap as Denzel waited and watched.

Sheila felt herself heating up. Having received no satisfaction from her encounters with Denzel she was horny as hell. He really was a lousy lay in her mind. She allowed Darquavius to remove her top and bra.

"Baby you are so fine."

Quay suppressed his laughter as he continued to massage her bare breasts.

Anthony returned and handed Denzel the camera.

"Make sure you don't get Quay's face."

Denzel nodded and turned the mechanism on. Darquavius managed to talk Sheila into undressing. She was lying naked now on the bed as he stood beside it. His hardness residenced in her mouth sucking him greedily. Denzel smiled documenting every moment of it.

"You gonna let me hit it girl?"

Sheila moaned and writhed from him fingering her.

"Yeah, mmhmm."

Darquavius grinned ear to ear and put on the condom. He climbed into bed and entered her. Sheila moaned her satisfaction. Darquavius thrust into her again and again. He came soon afterward and rose from her.

"Damn, Sheila."

She continued to lie on the bed, legs wide open, almost passed out.

"I enjoyed beating the hell outta that pussy baby."

He chuckled. Darquavius stepped to Denzel as they exchanged glances and chuckled again.

Denzel walked over to the bed, lowered his pants. He put on the condom turning Sheila over and pulling her to her knees. She remained lucid enough to comply, thinking Darquavius was about to sex her again. Making sure he had the right angle, Darquavius stood with the camera positioned, sure not to show Denzel's face. His friend rammed himself into Sheila anally. She cried out. Denzel hurriedly covered her mouth continuing his assault. Too drunk and high to fight, Sheila gave in, allowing herself to be violated.

Denzel held her tightly thrusting repeatedly until his anger finally came full circle.

"That was some true porno shit right there!"

Darquavius chuckled after the declaration, putting the camera on pause.

Sheila flopped onto the bed after Denzel released her. He rose putting his clothes on.

"Wake her up so she leaves with Shonda."

Anthony nodded agreement. Taking the camera and the footage, Denzel stealthily made his way out of the basement, undetected.

******

Naimah and Tabby were talking on the phone. She explained tonight and the accident while making love.

"You need to get on the pill."

Naimah sighed.

"How am I gonna do that without telling Mama?"

Tabby giggled.

"Girl, here you can go to the clinic at sixteen and get them without your parent's permission."

"Wow, really?"

"Yep, you wanna go tomorrow?"

"Yeah, because I don't want to get pregnant right now."

"We can get them to give you a morning after pill too."

Naimah sighed with relief after Tabby's declaration.

"Thanks girl."

"So you and Ruben are engaged now or what?"

Naimah chuckled and repeated what Ruben told her, about it being a promise ring.

"Mmmhmm. That boy is sprung."

Tabby laughed as Naimah joined her.

"I am too, but I'll never admit it."

Both girls laughed another time.

"He said he was serious with a couple girls, but they hurt him."

Tabby confirmed Ruben's statement.

"We actually thought he was gonna marry Laurell."

Tabby spoke aloud of Ruben's old girlfriend, peaking Naimah's interest.

"What happened?"

"She cheated on him, with one of the dudes he worked with."

"Dang!"

"Yeah, it was messed up, because Ruben, he doesn't treat a chick wrong."

Tabby took a sip of her drink as she continued to talk. "He's good people, but he is not flashy, or got that bad boy thing going. So I guess he was too square for old girl."

Naimah sucked her teeth in disgust.

"Where is she now?"

Tabby chuckled again.

"She's still here, trying to holla at Ruben every time she sees him."

Naimah's jealousy instantly kindled.

"That trick better stay away from my man."

Tabby burst into laughter.

"Girl you ain't got jack to worry about. Ruben was done with that ass when he walked into her room and found old dude up between her legs."

Naimah calmed slightly.

Her line beeped and she saw Ruben's name on the I.D.

"Lemme go girl, that is Ruben."

"OK cool, but let's meet up in the morning, 8:00, to go to the clinic."

Naimah confirmed the time and clicked over.

"Hey."

"Hey baby, I just wanted to apologize again for tonight Naimah."

Ruben prayed she wasn't angry.

"I would never try and hurt you like that, you know."

"Ruben, I told you, it's okay. I know it was an accident." She smiled as she talked to him.

"I'm going to the clinic in the morning, get the morning after pill, and try to get on some birth control, so we don't have to worry about this again."

Ruben smiled now. His decision again confirmed. Naimah was absolutely the best choice in a woman he made in a very long time.

"OK baby. Do you want me to go with you?"

"Thanks for offering, but Tabby is going with me."

"I'll let you go to sleep now. Sweet dreams baby."

Naimah returned the sentiment and disconnected. Ruben's cell rang immediately afterward. He looked at the I.D., thinking Naimah called right back. He scowled deeply seeing Laurell's name. *Damn. girl, catch a clue.* Ignoring the call, he sent it straight to voicemail.

*****

Denzel enjoyed his Pepsi smiling as he watched the images on his screen. He uploaded the footage as soon as he got home. Using the bogus email, he set up to do his dirt, he set up a mailing list and sent the link to everyone on it. By Monday morning when they returned to school, Sheila would be the talk of the town. He chuckled of his revenge and logged out. He clicked on another file in his arsenal and sat admiring the photos of Naimah contained. He heralded quite the collection. There were photos of her at church, at school, various social events. There were a couple that made him frown. He only kept them to keep his anger fueled against Ruben. He hated the stills of them kissing, or him touching her. Denzel paid dearly for those shots.

Hearing footsteps Denzel immediately closed the files and opened his main browser, playing a video game as his father knocked lightly on his door.
"Come in."
"Hey son, how is it going," Daniel Padgett greeted him.
"Pretty good dad. Can't complain."
He chuckled at his comment, his father joined him.
"I just wanted to stop in and see how you are doing before I went to bed. Make sure you have all your notes and everything in order for the meetings tomorrow."
Denzel assured him he was ready.
"May I have a copy of your itinerary?"
Denzel told him of his desire to meet with his auxiliary heads and member's one on one before setting up the actual meetings. Denzel handed him the list as his father looked it over.
"Looks good, son. I see Naimah is still working with you on the anniversary project."
"Yes, we're moving full steam ahead."
"She couldn't come earlier?"
Daniel, seeing the girl was last on the list, queried without malice.
"No, she said that was the best time for her."

Denzel lied without hesitation. Truthfully Naimah asked to come as early as possible.

"Hmph, okay, that's fine. See you tomorrow son, good night."

"Good night dad."

As soon as his father closed the door, Denzel opened the file again. Looking at the photographs, tracing Naimah's face with his finger he sighed softly. *The one that should have been mine.* Denzel closed the file, turned off the computer, and went to bed. Tomorrow was a new day.

CHAPTER 15

REVEALED

*H*ow *the hell did we end up here?* Nakida watched Rahshaun warily. The evening started off great. He picked her up at 10:15 and they headed to Expressions, meeting Tiffany and his friend Kenny. They went into the club and of course VIP like Rahshaun promised. *"What do you want to drink,"* Rahshaun asked. *"White Russian,"* Nakida replied. Rahshaun was the perfect gentleman all evening as they laughed, talked, danced and drank. When he suggested taking the party to his house once they exited the club, both Nakida and Tiffany were cool with the idea. Arriving at his place, things were still calm as they came in, got comfortable, and started playing cards. *"I'm beginning to think we've been set up Kenny,"* Rahshaun *laughed with his friend. Nakida and Tiffany beat them a third straight set of spades. "We just got that shark action going on, don't hate,"* Tiffany *teased. Kenny chuckled and brought her the drink she asked for.*

Nakida also enjoyed her drink as Rahshaun pulled out a DVD and asked if they wanted to watch. Shrugging Nakida told him it was cool. She saw Tiffany and Kenny out of the corner of her eye indulging in kissing and heavy petting. *I hope Rahshaun doesn't think we're going to do that shit too.* Nakida continued to be plagued by that bad feeling about Rahshaun. So far tonight, he didn't do anything out of the ordinary to warrant her continued emotional state of darkness.

"Why don't we go watch this in my room," Rahshaun told her. Nakida gave him a look. He chuckled before nodding toward Kenny and Tiffany. *"Give them a little privacy."* Nakida noticed the couple getting hot and heavy with their play. *"OK, I guess."* She remained on guard as Rahshaun grabbed the DVD and showed her to his room. She missed the looks he and Kenny exchanged.

The foot bench sitting at the end of his bed was plush and very inviting. Nakida sat down making herself comfortable as he started the DVD. *"Your back is gonna hurt sitting on that thing after a while,* Rahshaun told her jovially. *"I don't bite girl, come sit up here by me."* Nakida finally rose and joined him on the huge king-sized bed, taking in the room and the furnishings. Rahshaun had good taste she admitted, loving the black, crème, and gold coloring in the room. Everything seemed to blend and match perfectly. Rahshaun burst into laughter at a scene in the movie, interrupting her thoughts. Nakida began to relax and enjoy the movie when the sharp scream pierced the atmosphere. *"What the hell,"* Nakida mumbled trying to rise from the bed. *Rahshaun grabbed her and held her tightly. "Nah, how about you just stay here and let them handle their business." The hiss of his voice in her ear brought goosebumps on her skin.* Nakida heard Tiffany scream shortly once more as the sound of something crashing and breaking added to the foray. *"Let go of me," Nakida yelled trying to free herself and get to her friend. "Re-fucking-lax," Rahshaun told her acidly.* "See nice and quiet now."

Rahshaun's voice again snapped Nakida's thoughts bringing her back to the present.

Terrified her mind raced wondering what happened to her friend. Tiffany remained deathly quiet since her screams moments earlier.

"Please Rahshaun. Just let us go, we won't tell anyone."

Holding her tightly, Rahshaun kissed her neck tenderly.

"Tell them what? You and your girl came here willingly…"

Biting her earlobe, he continued to spin the tale.

"We all got to drinking, kissing, shit just happened."

Nakida finally understood what she felt about him. Rahshaun was a date rapist and his game stayed on point. Everything he said was true. Proving force would definitely be hard, if not impossible.

The knock on the door made her jump.

"Yeah man."

"I'm taking old girl home."

"Where is Tiffany, what did you do?!!"

"Calm down, Nakida," he told her in her ear. "Bring her in here so Nakida can stop tripping."

The door opened, and Kenny pushed Tiffany into the room. Nakida rose and went to her friend who was barely conscious.

"Nakida, I gotta go home."

"Yeah, come on."

She tried to walk by Kenny with her friend.

"I got her."

Breaking her hold on Tiffany, he pushed Nakida back into the room with Rahshaun.

"You got some unfinished business."

His expression smugly arrogant as Rahshaun walked up behind Nakida and grabbed her again.

Nakida screamed trying to fight as Rahshaun threw her onto the bed. He put his hands around her throat.

"Hush!"

Nakida stopped fighting and he let go of her throat. Kenny chuckled, telling Rahshaun he was out, and he would see him later. Grunting his acknowledgement, Rahshaun continued to regard Nakida as his anger grew.

"You thought it was cute the way you kept rejecting me huh?!"

Ripping her shirt open and exposing her bra, he immediately tore it from her body revealing her breasts.

"Nice."

Nakida knew without a doubt Rahshaun was dangerous and unbalanced. She just prayed he didn't kill her when he raped her. She already settled in her mind that he was going to violate her, Nakida just wanted to live to get through it.

"I'm going to fuck you until my heart's content tonight, did you know that?"

Reaching under her skirt the thong yielded to the rough tug.

Nakida remained silent just wanting it over.

"You are so fine, Nakida, shit."

Rahshaun unzipped his pants and removed them as well as his underwear.

He whipped his shirt over his head and returned to her, naked. He took her skirt off as well as the torn shirt, regarding her all the while.

"You scared?"

"Please Rahshaun, don't hurt me."

Rahshaun smiled and kissed her hard.

"I can't promise you that."
Rubbing his erection against her, he taunted her anew.
"You will always remember this night Nakida."
"Please…"
Rahshaun parted her legs. Nakida screamed shortly.
The front door splintered moments later. She heard voices yelling as someone pulled Rahshaun off her.
"Cover her!"
One of the officers yelled directives as they cuffed Rahshaun and began reading him his rights.
"What's going on?"
Nakida managed to gather herself as the shock began to wear off slightly.
The lead officer explained that they were called by a neighbor who heard screaming and fighting earlier. He called again when officers failed to show up.
"We heard you scream as we were about to knock."
Nakida nodded absently.
"You're going to have to go to the hospital, let them examine you."
"Yeah, okay, he had a friend…"
The officer nodded.
"Yes, we detained them downstairs. They were leaving as we arrived. We stopped them because the young lady was acting strangely."
Nakida exhaled loudly, relieved that the police showed up when they did and that both Kenny and Rahshaun were in custody.
"She wanted it!"
Rahshaun yelled the typical drivel as they let him put on his pants and walked him toward the door.

"She's a fucking tease, a lying bitch!"
The cop shook his head and helped Nakida to the elevator, headed downstairs where the ambulance waited.

*****

Tatiana heard the knock and froze. *Samuel has your key.* The recollection brought some measure of relief that he wasn't stopping by again.
"Daddy?"
"Can I come in?"
Tatiana nodded and moved out of the way.
"What brings you by, daddy?"
"I just left your Auntie Jorinda."
Garlan never took his eyes off her.
Tatiana felt the tears come as she swallowed hard.
"Oh."
Garlan sighed intensely seeing the hurt and struggle.
"Chip, I'm sorry honey."
Going to her, he took her into his arms.
Tatiana hugged her father back, holding on tightly as her tears flowed.
"I'm sorry I failed you baby, and let you down. I won't let him hurt you ever again though Chip, I promise."
Garlan felt her body shake as she continued to hug him and cry.
Garlan held her until she stopped crying, then let her go.
"Baby, I'm sorry I didn't believe you all those years ago."
Tatiana smiled marginally.
"I'm just glad you believe me now, daddy."
"Jo shared her plans with me."

Tatiana nodded absently.

"Honey, are you sure you can do this?"

"Yeah, I mean, I have to."

Garlan grunted noncommittal.

"Daddy…"

Garlan regarded her waiting for her to complete the sentence.

"Tell me about my real mama."

He gathered himself and told Tatiana all about Rachael, how much she loved her, and how much he himself missed her even now.

"I see her every time I look at you."

Garlan gazed at her, the love in his voice coming through.

Tatiana smiled. She saw pictures of her mother admitting they favored greatly.

"Chip?"

"Yes daddy?"

"Did Virginia know?"

The pain reflected in his eyes once the words left his lips.

"I never told her."

Tatiana skirted the answer for his sake. She believed with her whole heart that her mother, well her aunt, knew all about the things Samuel was doing to her. She planned to prove it too. Garlan grunted again but said nothing.

"Jo tells me you have a boyfriend."

Tatiana blushed and told her father about Jaden.

"He sounds like a fine young man. You're going to have to tell him the truth though, Chip."

Tatiana's eyes teared again.

"You know that, right?"

Tatiana nodded shortly.

"I know."

Garlan didn't push any more. Rising he told Tatiana he would talk to her again soon.

"Have fun honey."

Hugging her tightly once more, he reassured her of his support, while stroking her face.

"I am going to play my part Chip. I'm here if you need me, call me."

Tatiana smiled brightly and kissed his cheek.

"Thank you, daddy."

Garlan smiled and left. Tatiana smiled leaning against the closed door. She felt just a little better now. Her confidence boosted that they could indeed pull this off.

*****

Sylvia was about to burst. She was trying as hard as she could to be normal. So far she seemed to be doing okay. Samuel didn't question her moods. She just could not wrap her mind around the thought of her husband having an affair with a fifteen-year old child. *You're racing to conclusions.* There was no proof that those photos were anything more than a young woman's infatuation with her pastor. *What about the picture of his kissing her, the photos of her in the lingerie?*

"She probably sent those to him."

As for the kiss, it was innocent enough. Samuel was very affectionate. He probably didn't want to hurt the young woman's feelings when she turned her lips to his, as he aimed for her cheek. Sylvia didn't want to think about it anymore. Her head was pounding. She couldn't breathe. *You better step up your game.* Even if he didn't have an affair with Tatiana, she dismissed her suspicions; there was always the, what if, factor.

Samuel entered the house moments later, mind still whirling from Tatiana's ultimatum. He couldn't be angry with her. He made her wait almost seven years and he was still married to Sylvia. *I just need time to get everything set up.* Samuel grabbed a glass of wine. He loved Tatiana so much. He would do anything to be with her. Samuel knew he needed to move up his plans and quick. Time was not on his side anymore. He already knew she was seeing someone else. What if she decided to move on and stopped loving him? Samuel grew angry at the thought. He didn't want any other man touching her, kissing her, making love to her. Tatiana belonged explicitly to him and that was that. He continued to brood in his thoughts, not hearing Sylvia as she entered the kitchen.

"Hi honey."

Samuel turned to her and stopped, taking her in.

What is this about? Suspicion bloomed fully as he sipped his wine. Sylvia was clad in a racy nightie, see through, with sexy heeled slippers. Normally she wore a very modest nightgown and her slides.

"Hi there. You look nice."

Sylvia smiled and thanked him.

"Are you hungry?"

As Samuel continued to eye her she hoped he got turned on.

"I grabbed something while I was out."

She is up to something.

Walking over to her and pulling her to him, he began weeding out her ulterior motives.

"Why are you all sexed up like this?"

"Just wanted to look nice for you, that's all."

Samuels hands slid down her butt, squeezing.

"I like it."

Sylvia smiled invisibly as his hands ventured under the nightie and began touching her.

"How about we head on into this bedroom?"

Samuel allowed Sylvia to undress him, closing his eyes and enjoying her mouth on him as she gave him head.

"Nice."

Sylvia worked him over greedily. She was on fire wanting Samuel as he pushed her away, telling her he wanted to make love now. He stripped the nightgown quickly and pushed her back onto the bed.

"You want this?"

Holding his erection in his hands, he held her eyes captive.

"Yes, right now."

Samuel smiled, reaching into the nightstand and taking out the condom.

"Please Samuel, just this once."

Just like I figured. He congratulated himself at having learned her true motives for the outfit. *Sylvia was trying to trap him.* Samuel tossed the condom aside. She smiled as he kissed her intensely and entered her.

"Mmm, yessss."

He held her tightly as she reached orgasm and he concentrated on his own finish. Just as he came Samuel pulled out. *Stupid bitch.* He heard Sylvia sigh softly, knowing she was disappointed. *He would screw her and enjoy getting his nut, but he would never impregnate her.*

Samuel kissed her and rose headed to the shower. Sylvia fought to keep the tears from escaping as the realization finally dawned. It wasn't that they couldn't have children together. Samuel didn't want children with her.

CHAPTER 16

LOVE & REGRETS

Saturday morning arrived bright and sunny. Tatiana stepped off the plane and walked inside the Miami International Airport terminal. She spotted Jaden just as she collected her other bag from the carousel.

"Hi baby. How was your flight,"

He added a kiss to the cheerful greeting, taking her bags from her.

"Flight was good, and I'm fine."

Her last statement was true, now that she was here with him. The weather was just what everyone warned. Balmy, sunny, temperatures. *Typical retiree destination.* Jaden opened her car door for her and she got inside. He put her bags in the trunk, joining her moments later inside the vehicle.

"How is your mom?"

"She has improved a little."

"Well that's good news, right?"

She noted the worry still on his face.

"Yeah, every little bit helps."

Jaden smiled at her.

"We'll head over to the hotel and get you settled. Then we'll head to the hospital, so I can check on my pops, maybe relieve him for a little while."

"Of course, Jaden, that will be fine."

She loved the palm trees and the view of the ocean as they passed over one of the bridges headed downtown.

They arrived moments later at the Hilton-Bentley hotel.
"This is South Beach. I thought you would like to be close to the water."
"Wow, it's beautiful."
Tatiana inhaled deeply the sea salted air.
Jaden smiled and took her bags following her inside to the lobby.

After retrieving the room key, Jaden and Tatiana took the elevator to the twelfth floor and her room.
"Thank you so much for coming down here, baby."
Tatiana turned to him and hugged him tightly.
"I'm happy to come."
Looking around, she turned to him, eyebrow raised.
"Jaden, a simple room would have been fine."
He chuckled at her declaration. The room was exquisite; from the rose colored, quilted, gold framed headboard on the king-sized bed, to the glass enclosed sitting area with the patio she could walk out onto and see the ocean, feel the breeze and smell the air.
"I wanted you to be comfortable."
This man is wonderful. Tatiana pinched herself internally behind the smile on her face. Jaden kissed her again, telling her how very much he missed her.
"Are you sure you're okay?"
"I'm better now with you here baby."
Tatiana smiled, taking his hand. Glancing at the time she put her thoughts into words.
"We need to head to the hospital. We can have dinner on the balcony."
"Sounds like a wonderful idea," Jaden smiled.

******

Naimah and Tabby were laughing amongst themselves after leaving the clinic and heading back home.

"They gave you the morning after one?"

"Yes, and three packs of birth control pills. I can start taking them right after my period."

They stopped at the local Family dollar and headed inside to pick up a couple of items.

"Wanna see his ex?"

Tabby spotted the girl on the next isle.

Naimah frowned quizzically.

"Laurell," Tabby said plainly.

"Oh, yeah, I wanna see Miss Thang."

Tabby chuckled. Grabbing a can of air freshener, the two girls walked around the corner to the next isle. Laurell was perusing the various offerings of bath soap the store carried.

"Hey Laurell. Wassup?"

The young woman turned around.

"Oh hi, Tabby."

Naimah noticed that her smile never reached her eyes.

"This is Naimah," she replied introducing the two girls.

"Hi Naimah."

"Just wanted to say hi."

Just before they left earshot, Tabby spoke again.

"Didn't Ruben say he needs some tire shine or something?"

Laurell gave them her attention again hearing the man's name. *I wonder if she would tell me what's going on with him now?* Turning once more to walk back down the same aisle, since the auto products were on the opposite side where Laurell stood, Tabby and Naimah walked by her.

"Um, Tabby…"

"Yeah, what's up?"

Naimah pretended to look for the tire shine product while Tabby spoke to Laurell.

"How is Ruben these days?"

Naimah took the girl in. She was cute, short haircut spiked at the top. Naimah could tell the girl was still smarting from Ruben breaking up with her. *Too bad.* Naimah shrugged. *You shouldn't have cheated on him.*

"He's fine Laurell. But Naimah could probably answer that question better than I could."

Laurell's eyes found Naimah's.

"She and Ruben are kicking it now."

Laurell's eyes narrowed. She turned walking away without another word. Tabby burst into laughter, but Naimah felt bad. She knew Laurell was hurt and embarrassed. That wasn't her intention.

"Come on."

Tabby's words broke her pondering as they headed to the counter and paid for their items.

Naimah saw Laurell once more as they exited the store. She was getting into her car. She looked directly into Naimah's eyes another time and said nothing. Naimah sighed regretfully as she looked at the girl, swearing she could see tears in her eyes.

******

Ruben checked his phone, feeling the vibration. He read the text from Laurell and frowned deeply. 'I met ur girl,' the message read. 'ur not over me Ruben, I no ur not,' it continued as he sighed again. 'I made a mistake and I am sorry, plz stop punishing me' the girl typed. 'let's make up baby and be happy again, I still luv u so much.' He swiftly deleted it. *How in the world did she meet Naimah?* DonJuan walked up and they started to shoot the breeze. He forgot all about Laurell's text, or her meeting Naimah. They headed inside the Waffle house and ordered a late breakfast.

"You and Naimah hitting it off I see."

DonJuan cranked up teasing him while they waited. Ruben smiled.

"Yeah, we're straight."

"Her and Tabby went to the clinic."

Ruben nodded his knowledge.

"Got caught up last night."

His friend grunted at the admission.

"Yeah me and Tabby had a couple close calls too."

The waitress set the food in front of them. His cell rang while they were eating. Ruben smiled seeing Naimah's name on the I.D.

"Hey baby."

DonJuan continued to devour his meal.

"How did everything go?"

Naimah filled him in, telling him about her and Tabby running into Laurell at the family dollar store.

"It's cool."

Ruben never mentioned the text message. He was done with Laurell. Cheating on Naimah never crossed his mind.

"Where are you?"

Ruben chuckled.

"Waffle House, with DonJuan."

"Cool, we're close to that."

"Come on then, we're still here."

"Tabby and Naimah are on their way."

"Everything straight with her at the clinic?"

"She said everything was fine. She ran into Laurell."

DonJuan sucked his teeth annoyed.

"She still tryna get back with you?"

Ruben nodded yes.

"Don't know why chicks want to get a brain, after they messed up."

They both chuckled and continued their meals waiting on the girls to arrive.

******

Denzel laughed as he and Anthony talked. The video made the rounds. Everyone posted the link on their Facebook page, Myspace, Hi-Five and other social networks.

"Man, she called here screaming and crying, talking about I set her up and shit!"

Denzel continued to smile listening to Anthony finish the story.

"I told that tramp she didn't know who she was fooling with. She was the one drinking and smoking, losing her damned mind."

Denzel interjected.

"Bet she won't be miss fly at the mouth come Monday."

"Ha, you got that right! You gonna come hang tonight?"

Denzel sighed evenly before answering.

"Got a full day of church duty."

Anthony chuckled again. Darquavius piped up in the background.

"Tell that fool church is on Sunday!"

Denzel laughed with them.

"Only good thing is hanging with Naimah later tonight."

"You still tryna holla at baby," Anthony asked.

"She is my cup of tea."

"I get it, but she's still with Ruben, and I think they're hitting the skins too."

Denzel's facial expression darkened.

"How do you know that?"

"I overheard her and Tabby talking one day a while back, and from what I heard, it sure sounded like they were banging."

Denzel blew his breath out slowly, before addressing Anthony.

"Well even if they are, everyone is entitled to one mistake."

"True. Hit me back later, let me know if you made any progress."

Denzel assured him he would and disconnected. Rising he headed out to the church thoughts of Naimah still playing in his mind.

*****

Laurell watched Ruben and Naimah interacting, growing more and more furious. *That heffa is not gonna take my man from me!* Boldly rising she walked across the street to the Target parking lot where the two were. Ruben was holding Naimah, smiling and telling her something in her ear as Laurell got closer. She saw them kiss and lost it.

"What is this shit?!"

Ruben turned regarding her with surprise. Naimah remained quiet waiting to see what the girl's game was.

"Why are you here, Laurell?"

"What do you mean, why am I here…."

She began to yell as people regarded them curiously walking in and out of the store.

"You're my boyfriend, and you're here with a chick that ain't me!"

Laurell prayed her strategy would work and Naimah would think Ruben was cheating on her.

Naimah raised an eyebrow. She was about to speak when Ruben cut her off.

"Laurell, you and I broke up almost six months ago."

His his anger began to rise.

"You cheated on me, I caught you, we were done."

Laurell held her ground.

"Stop lying to this girl Ruben! You and I had sex less than three months ago, or did you forget that?"

Ruben caught his breath, stunned. He basically overlooked that drunken night three months ago. He ran into her at the convenience store and she brought him back to her apartment, seducing him. Her having her own place was one of the things that drew him to her. He thought the one-year age difference would make her more mature than the girls his own age. He was wrong. Her being nineteen didn't mean anything when it came to faithfulness. Naimah turned to him, the question in her face. Laurell smiled faintly believing she was beginning to make progress.

"It was before us Naimah."

Ruben sincerely prayed she heard him.

"You protected yourself?"

Ruben nodded he had. Naimah asked her next question.

"Do you wanna be back with her?"

Ruben replied without hesitation.

"No. I love you Naimah that's why I gave you a ring."

Laurell endured trying hard to block the tears hearing him say he loved the girl and gave her a ring. Naimah turned her attention to Laurell and regarded her a few moments more in silence. Sstepping to her she began speaking.

"I'm not trying to be your enemy. But me and Ruben, we are together."

Never taking her eyes from the girl Naimah continued laying the blueprint before her.

"You blew your chance, now I'm here, and I'm not going anywhere."

The first tear rolled down Laurell's cheek.

"Don't embarrass yourself out here anymore, seriously."

Ruben opened the truck door and Naimah walked away leaving Laurell standing alone. Ruben closed the door, heading to the driver's side, getting in. He started the truck, backed out and left Laurell standing in the parking lot, sobbing aloud. She slowly made her way to her own vehicle.

"I have never cheated on you Naimah."

She pushed her breath through marginally opened lips before answering him.

"I believe you. I just hope that's the end of it."

"Me too."

"You could have told me about that night you know. I wouldn't have been mad."

Ruben swallowed his embarrassment.

"I was ashamed of myself for that night. I just wanted to forget about it."

Naimah nodded her understanding.

"You want to go to the house with me?"

Ruben wanted very much to make love. He still felt an underlying irritation from Naimah. He didn't want to lose her.

"I can't. I have to go over to the church and have that meeting."

Reuben suppressed the chuckle hearing the dry tone. She definitely didn't seem eager to attend.

"I can pick you up afterward."

Ruben kissed her hand.

"What time do you think it will be done?"

"Come back around 8:00."

That was two hours from now. More than enough time in her mind to be spent with Denzel.

"I'll be here baby."

They kissed another time when he dropped her off in front of the church. She stroked his face and looked into his eyes.

"I'm not mad at you Ruben."

He smiled finally.

"I'll see you at 8:00."

Naimah waved before turning headed inside to the auxiliary meeting room.

*****

Jaden knocked lightly on the door. Tatiana answered looking ravishing.

"Hey," she greeted inviting him in.

Jaden took in the sapphire green sun dress. Form fitting, spaghetti strap, it afforded a generous view of her beautifully perfect cleavage.

"I brought some wine for dinner."

"Oh, that was nice."

Their food arrived moments later from the kitchen downstairs. They took it outside on the patio and sat down, relaxing together. Tatiana accompanied him earlier to the hospital meeting his father. Andrew Payne was Jaden's male model she could tell. His father was a complete gentleman. She could see plenty of his teaching in his son. They stayed at the hospital all afternoon while his father went home and got some much needed rest, took care of daily business for the household, and ran errands. He returned right around 7:30, insisting that Jaden leave and show Tatiana a good time tonight.

"I'm supposed to be showing you the city."

Looking into her eyes as they enjoyed their wine, he smiled at her another time.

"I'm enjoying the view just fine."

Jaden chuckled aloud, returning to his meal.

"Was there a service or something for your friend?"

"There was a memorial by the Percenters, then his parents held a private service and burial in Philadelphia."

"That is nice, that the group remembered him."

Jaden grunted his agreement.

"The police arrested Sharif."

Jaden sighed extremely digesting her words.

"I never wanted that."

Tatiana reached across the table, putting her hand atop his.

"You did your best, Jaden."

Tatiana knew how much Jaden cared for the kids in his group. She also knew somewhere inside he was taking this as a very personal failure.

"There's a boxing match on TV."
Jaden chortled before answering her back.
"What do you know about boxing?"
Tatiana, hand on her hip, gave him a teasing look as she rose to go back inside.
"What are you trying to say Jaden?"

They were inside the expansive bedroom suite, propped on the bed, as Jaden held her in his arms. He was trying to concentrate on the combatants in the ring. Tatiana's perfume, smooth skin, and soft warmth were distractions he wasn't sure he could overcome. Without thinking, Jaden kissed her neck. Tatiana sighed noiselessly, moving even closer to him. He kissed it again. She turned to him, looking into his eyes. Jaden picked up the remote and turned the set off. The soft roar of the ocean relaxed them as he pulled her to her feet and unzipped the sundress. Slowly and sensuously he removed it from her shoulders, kissing them lightly in the process. Tatiana closed her eyes enjoying every nuance of his touch as the dress passed her chest. The soft breeze coming thru the open balcony door made her nipples harden.

Jaden kissed them as she exhaled, completely at his mercy. He continued taking the dress down, her thong now exposed as he kissed her stomach. Tatiana thought she was going to pass out the way Jaden was touching and arousing her. The dress finally at her feet, Tatiana stepped out of it. Jaden made his way back to her lips, dripping soft butterfly kisses all over her body as he enjoyed the trip. Tatiana reached out and removed his shirt; undoing his pants and helping him undress. Now that they were both naked, she took the time to take him in. Jaden was stunning. His body toned and sculpted. His manhood at full attention, promising her a night of unbridled pleasure. Kissing her fervently, Jaden picked Tatiana up and placed her on the bed, climbing in with her. He licked her nipples, sucking them, as she moaned aloud. Reaching into the ice bucket on the nightstand, he removed several cubes, putting some in his mouth, the others in his hand. Tatiana gasped audibly as he touched her rubbing the ice on her swollen nipples, giving her sensations she never experienced before.

Letting the ice melt on her warm skin, Jaden repeated the gesture on her entire body. Gently opening her legs, Jaden went to work, using the ice in his mouth on her throbbing sex. Tatiana arched her back, rising off the mattress. *I knew this man was going to shake my foundation.* Jaden continued to arouse and tease her. She couldn't wait to feel him inside her. Tatiana exploded with the first orgasm. Jaden continued to taste her. Tatiana purred softly, lost in the symposium of pleasure derived from his tongue. Bringing her once again to the threshold, Jaden stopped, not allowing her to fall over just yet. He kissed her stomach, licking it as Tatiana's breathing increased. She urged him to take her. Jaden continued to take his time making his way back up her body. Kissing her neck and nibbling it gently. Tatiana was about to die she was sure from the anticipation. Jaden began kissing her lips, moving to her cheeks, the bridge of her nose, and both her eyelids. He kissed her ear, whispering into it as he did.

"Now the two, become one."

Tatiana felt him enter her and moaned stridently loving the feel of him. Jaden made love to her with slow,

disciplined, strokes. Tatiana drove her nails into his back and wrapped her legs around his waist. He lifted her to almost a sitting position, placing her against the headboard and pushed his length completely inside her. Tatiana's eyes rolled back into her head as she opened her mouth and let out the guttural scream of pleasure. Jaden brought her to yet another orgasm. Jaden continued the slow, opulent pace for the next forty-five minutes before pulling Tatiana tightly to his body and exploding with his own mind-blowing finish. Tatiana held him while they both tried to return their breathing to normal. Jaden began to kiss her lips delicately again, looking into her eyes as he spoke once more.
"Perfection."

CHAPTER 17

MASKED MONSTERS

Denzel enjoyed his time with Naimah. They were alone in the auxiliary room making plans for his father's pastoral anniversary next month. Denzel rose headed to the kitchen for a bottle of water.

"You want anything?"

"No, I'm good."

Nodding acknowledgement of her answer, Denzel exited the room, returning moments later.

Naimah was busy flipping through a book of robe samples for the gift they were presenting Pastor Padgett. She never saw Denzel lock the door or slyly slide and prop the chair behind it. Walking back to Naimah he sat down on the carpeted floor next to her. There were three small steps and she was leaning on them as she flipped through the book. Pointing at one of the robes featured, she garnered Denzel's attention and spoke.

"This is really nice."

Denzel looked over into the book.

"Yes, that's a nice choice. Can you hand me my pad from behind you, on the table?"

Denzel knew her reaching for the requested item would put Naimah in almost a laying position.

She did as he asked, and he made his move. Pouncing on her, he held her down on the floor.

"Get off me, Denzel!"

Instead Denzel kissed her, putting his weight on top of her making her immobile. Turning her head side to side, Naimah made him stop.

"Get off me!"

She yelled louder this time, hoping someone heard her.

"Nobody's here, Naimah. Everyone left at 7:00."

"Denzel stop, get off me!"

Her anger poured like lava as Sharif and his abuse flashed vividly in her mind's eye.

"I told you that I wasn't giving up."

He was breathing hard as his hands touched her.

Naimah grew even angrier that she was wearing a skirt. She put it on earlier. Her mom remained very much stuck in tradition and didn't allow her to wear jeans inside church like some of the other kids. Denzel easily grabbed her panties, pulling on them as Naimah heard the material rip.

"No, Denzel, stop, damn!"

Denzel chuckled and kissed her again. He finally succeeded in ripping the panties off.

"Mm, Naimah."

His voice became a hushed whisper as he began touching her intimately.

Naimah managed to free one arm. She hit him in the face as hard as she could. Denzel, furious that she struck him, struck her back, letting go the other arm. Naimah began to fight with all that was in her. She fought for all the abuse heaped on her by Sharif. She fought to save herself from all the torment Denzel served her in the short time she knew him. Denzel slapped her hard. He sat on her chest straddling her, beginning to beat her with his fists. Naimah's mouth was bleeding but she continued to fight.

"Stop it, you know you want this!"

Denzel pinned her arms down and freed his erection.

"Let's see you explain this shit to Ruben!"

Naimah began to scream for help, praying someone, anyone, would hear her.

"Shut up!"

Naimah continued to scream, tears flowing, when she heard the sound. Someone was trying to get in. She glanced at the door seeing the chair propped behind it, continuing to fight as best she could. Denzel was completely engrossed in his pleasure continuing to assault the brutalized girl. Finally, after what seemed like forever in her mind, the door burst open and she felt Denzel's weight come off her body.

"Oh my god," she heard a woman screaming.

"Stop Ruben, you're going to kill him, stop!"

DonJuan held Ruben back, his friend breathing hard.

Denzel was trying to catch his breath from the punches to his midsection by Ruben. His nose bled from another well placed left hook.

Daniel and his wife were just about to leave when they saw Denzel's car and Ruben's truck. The came over to make sure everything and everyone was all right and give Denzel instructions on locking the church when the meeting was done. Rebecca Padgett held Naimah, rocking her and crying. Naimah was unconscious. She passed out as Denzel was snatched from her body.

"Denzel, what the hell have you done?!"

Daniel remained incredulous with the sight before him.

"Call 911," Rebecca told her husband.

Ruben was beside himself seeing Naimah, bloodied, battered and now unconscious. He replayed the scene as they ran in. Denzel was on top of her thrusting into her as she screamed. It was about to drive him over the edge.

Pastor Padgett took Denzel to another room. DonJuan continued to try and calm Ruben. He was glad he came with him to pick Naimah up. *That damned boy is crazy as hell.* The ambulance arrived moments later as did Naimah's parents. Her father was livid. Both Ruben and DonJuan tried to keep him from killing not only Denzel, but Pastor Padgett as well.

"Everybody told you that boy was doing crazy shit, but you didn't want to hear it!"

Daniel was devastated with the act committed by his only son. The police arrived moments later as Naimah's father told them he wanted Denzel arrested. Daniel and Rebecca both wept openly as the officer's placed him in handcuffs and put him into a squad car. Naimah was loaded into the ambulance as Ruben raced to his truck. He knew they would take her to Cooper Green Mercy hospital. DonJuan jumped in the passenger seat as they followed the ambulance. Naimah's parents followed as well.

"Calm down man, she is going to be okay."

DonJuan sought to console Ruben seeing his death grip on the steering wheel.

"She better be."

He angrily replayed the scene again in his mind. Naimah was his baby and that animal was hurting her. Ruben finally arrived and parked. He hurried into emergency to join Naimah's parents.

The doctor emerged moments later regarding all the worried people in the waiting room..

"She is fine. The damage was superficial. The swelling will go down quickly."

Several heads nodded understanding hearing the words.

"We are processing a rape kit now."

Her father's eyes turned red. Her mother began to cry softly, before voicing her concern.

"Is she going to be okay?"

"Yes ma'am. She should recover in no time."

Everyone breathed a collective sigh of relief.

"Can we see her," her mother asked once more.

"After the police have what they need, then you can see her for a few moments."

Leaving them all alone in the waiting room, the doctor returned to his patients.

"They better keep that punk ass boy in jail."

Ruben and DonJuan both nodded their agreement to Naimah's father's statement. Her mother interceded.

"Let the law handle it y'all."

Her husband sucked his teeth and said nothing.

The nurse returned to the waiting room almost an hour later telling them the police were finished and they could see Naimah now.

Her father called out when the young man remained seated.

"Come on Ruben."

Smiling marginally, he rose and followed her parents to her room. DonJuan waited on Tabby to arrive.

*****

Daniel prayed for guidance, for forgiveness, for healing with Naimah and her parents. *My son is a monster.* He never in his wildest imagination would have believed his own flesh and blood could stoop so low. Rebecca joined him moments later explaining that Denzel was in his room. They immediately called their attorney who got them a quick bond. Until Naimah gave a statement it was simply a domestic incident. Daniel swallowed hard and said nothing. Rebecca left him alone and went to their bedroom. She needed very much to pray and get some answers, some peace, of her own.

Rising finally Daniel made his way down the hallway that led to Denzel's room. Passing the mirror he stopped and gazed into the glass for a long time, looking deeply into his own eyes. Tearing himself away he made his way to the boy's room, standing outside the closed door. He listened intently for any sound and heard none. Carefully opening the door, Daniel came inside and found the bed empty. *Where is he?* Denzel suddenly materialized from the hallway, glass of soda in hand.

He greeted his father quietly, unable to maintain eye contact.

"Hey dad."

Daniel regarded him silently a bit longer before returning the greeting.

"How many others have there been, Denzel?"

Daniel never took his eyes off his son.

"It's not like that, Dad."

"Stop with the lies. Now is the time for truth, and repentance."

Denzel sighed. *Here we go with this drama.* Denzel searched his mind for the answers he knew his father wanted to hear.

"It is all a big misunderstanding. When Naimah wakes up, she will tell you the same thing."

Daniel regarded the calm demeanor in which his son spoke and continued to lie to him.

"So, you think she wanted to have sex with you?"

Denzel sighed again.

"She just got scared, that'st all."

"You never answered my question? How many others have there been?"

"Dad, I've been having sex for a while now."

Denzel grew agitated with the badgering.

"Half these tricks want to play and tease, but they know they wanna fuck."

Daniel wasn't shocked by the language. He was too numb looking at the monster he gave life.

Denzel thought his father would yell when he used the curse word, but he didn't. He actually remained eerily silent. The slight clicking sound caught his attention as he finally looked up into the man's face. Denzel's eyes grew big.

"What, are you serious?"

"You are a monster."

Daniel continued, speaking serenely as the first tear rolled down his cheek.

"How many innocent girls' lives have you destroyed?"

Denzel remained speechless.

"How many more will you hurt in your reign? We raised you better than this, gave you everything, every opportunity."

"Where did we go wrong?"

Daniel finally refocused his gaze, regarding Denzel again.

"No more."

"Dad, wait, I--."

The deafening boom of the Beretta M9 permeated the house as the bullet penetrated his heart.

Rebecca entered the room moments later hearing the sounds, screaming hysterically now as she ran to her son. Denzel continued to stare at his father, eyes fixed, no life left.

"God forgive me."

Daniel finally spoke putting the gun down and with composure left the room.

Calling the police, he went outside to sit on his front porch, waiting for them to arrive.

*****

Ruben remained in the background as Naimah's mother and father talked trying to soothe her. He was trying hard to stay strong, but seeing her face bruised and swollen hurt more than words could express. He wanted so much to take away the pain. He wished he could turn back time and stop the attack from ever happening.

"We're leaving now baby."

Naimah's mother kissed her cheek delicately after the words. Her father mimicked the action, kissing her other cheek. His voice fractured the quiet.

"We'll be back in the morning to get you."

Naimah smiled a small portion.

"Okay."

"Good night Ruben," her parents spoke in tandem leaving them alone.

Ruben swallowed hard gathering his nerve and walked over to her bedside. Naimah turned her head away from him. Taking a deep breath, knowing she was embarrassed, Ruben stroked her cheek.

Naimah closed her eyes at his touch, tears trickled down her face.

"Baby, please look at me."

Naimah shook her head no and continued to cry.

"Please, Naimah. You have nothing to be ashamed of baby."

Ruben kissed her cheek. Naimah cried harder.

"I love you baby. I'm sorry I wasn't there when you needed me."

Naimah finally opened her eyes and regarded him. She noted the sincerity of his statements.

"I didn't lead him on, Ruben, I didn't!"

"Shh, baby, calm down. I know that."

Ruben touched her face again. Naimah began to relax once more.

"Denzel is a damned animal," Ruben angrily voiced.

"I never thought he would flip out on me like he did."

Ruben nodded.

"You're safe now baby. Denzel will never hurt you again."

Ruben had no idea how very right he was.

The door opened after the soft knock. Tabby entered, accompanied by Auntie Bettie and DonJuan.

"Hey baby, how are you feeling?"

"I am okay Auntie."

Tabby came over and hugged her, crying herself. Naimah waved at DonJuan as he smiled and stood beside Ruben.

"I only have to stay overnight."

Bettie nodded her understanding.

"Well you know I had to come and see about my baby." Naimah smiled fully. She loved her Aunt and Bettie let her know that love was reciprocated on a daily basis.

"We're going to leave you alone now. I just had to see for myself that you were all right."

She added another kiss to her niece's cheek before her, DonJuan, and Ruben, walked out of the door.

"I'll be right back," Ruben told her as Naimah nodded.

Tabby remained seated on the side of her bed.

"He's dead.

Naimah frowned, at a loss listening to her cousins' words.

"Denzel."

Naimah's eyes grew big.

Ruben walked in at that moment taking in the expression on her face, knowing Tabby told her about Denzel. DonJuan enlightened him as they all stood in the hallway.

"Can I talk to Naimah, Tabby?"

Tabby nodded.

"I'll see you tomorrow."

Ruben sat in the spot Tabby occupied moments earlier and took Naimah's hands into his own, the questions still etched in her face.

"His dad shot him."

Naimah's mouth dropped.

"Pastor Padgett?"

Was this some sick joke?

"Yeah."

"Pastor Padgett killed his own son?"

Naimah asked the question once more for her sanity.

Ruben again nodded in the affirmative. She was speechless. Naimah didn't know how to feel. On the one hand she was glad Denzel would never hurt her or another girl. On the other, she felt deep pity for Pastor Padgett living with the knowledge he killed his only child. Ruben took her into his arms and held her. They continued to sit in silence, both their minds spinning.

*****

Everyone was in a state of shock as news spread around the small community of the attack and subsequent murder. Daniel Padgett sat stoically in a holding cell waiting to be processed. He saw the people moving around, heard them speaking, but he wasn't here. His mind shut down and ceased to function rationally from the moment he walked into the auxiliary room at the church and saw Denzel brutally assaulting Naimah. He could still hear the girls pained screams, see the blood cascading from her mouth. He saw his son thrusting into her as if it were nothing. The horror replayed itself repeatedly on loop for Daniel. No matter how often he closed his eyes, he saw it and knew he was responsible for it.

Killing Denzel was the hardest thing he was ever pushed to do. Daniel reflected as he continued to sit in the cell. He prayed about it long and hard. He thought about Naimah's father and the things he said. Daniel knew Denzel was out of control. He drank, had sex, cursed, and did all manner of sinful things. Never, never in his wildest imagination could he imagine his son the sexual predator and sadist he became. Rebecca berated him well after the police handcuffed him and put him into the car. Daniel couldn't be angry with her. Denzel was her only child. She didn't see the evil in him. Even at the end she thought he could be saved, rehabilitated and changed. *You never gave him the chance to find out, did you?* Sighing without sound Daniel pushed the thoughts away. In his mind he did the right thing. The legal system would not have protected Naimah and other innocent unsuspecting girls like her. Today's justice gave the criminal more rights than the victim. Daniel bitterly held these statistics for facts, as the jailer came and told him they were finally ready for him.

CHAPTER 18

DANGEROUS DELUSIONS

Tatiana floated on cloud nine even sitting at work on a cloudy, rainy, Monday morning. The weekend with Jaden undeniably wonderful. She felt so complete, energized and ready to rid herself of Samuel once and for all. She loved Jaden. She knew without doubt he returned that love. Loosing a silent breath, Tatiana pulled out her cell and texted him. Samuel answered back almost immediately accepting her invitation to spend some time tonight. *Be careful with this man, you know he is volatile.* Tatiana acknowledged the thought then put it out of her mind. Her cell rang. She smiled seeing Jaden's name on the I.D.

"Hi." she greeted cheerfully.

"Hey baby."

She could imagine the smile on his face from his tone.

"How is your mom?"

"She's made a lot of improvement, responding well to the new treatment."

"I am really happy to hear that."

"I truly appreciate you coming down this weekend."

Tatiana smiled.

"It was fun, Jaden, I didn't mind at all."

She kept smiling, thinking of their lovemaking.

Jaden was the most wonderful and incredible man she met in a long time.

"So I won't have to twist your arm to get you to come back next weekend?"

Tatiana chuckled.

"No, you won't have to twist my arm."

"Great, I'll reserve your room again. Do you want to stay at the same place?"

"Yes, it was a great hotel, and it holds special memories."

Jaden laughed again.

"Okay, bring swimwear this time."

Tatiana smiled again looking at the dreary weather outside.

"You got it."

"I'll let you go baby. Call me later when you get off."

"I will but it might be kinda late."

Tatiana didn't want to risk talking to him and Samuel showing up.

"That's fine, have a great day. Love you."

Tatiana smiled and returned the sentiment, finally disconnecting, praying her work day hurried by.

*****

Samuel smiled contentedly as he drove to meet Gordon. *Get to see my baby tonight.* He excitedly recalled the early morning text and Tatiana wanting to spend time. He knew she would come around and admit her love for him sooner or later. *You know how Tatiana is.* His mind went another time to their last conversation. He had to make a move very soon. Sylvia was going to make it hard. He already knew that. Clingy and needy, she would fight the divorce tooth and nail. *Especially if she finds out about Tatiana.* He exhaled cavernously. He needed her out of the way. Samuel turned into the entrance and parked the Benz. Taking a deep breath and saying a silent prayer he got out.

He headed inside the glass enclosed skyscraper. Passing through the huge glass rotating doors, Samuel stood inside the ornate lobby and looked for the directory.

Finding it finally on the other side of the beautifully manicured manmade waterfall, he looked for the name and suite location of his destination. Grabbing the information, he turned his attention to the bank of elevators located in the main lobby and went to call a car. The wait was short. He boarded almost immediately. Pushing the button, he continued to think over his situation as the doors closed and the sleek carrier made its way upward. The elevator bell sounded rousing Samuel from his deep thought. He stepped out onto the fifteenth floor and looked once again for suite 1542. Arriving moments later he let himself inside the offices. The décor and plush amenities contained were impressive.

"May I help you sir?"

Samuel took in the woman. Light complexioned with shockingly jet-black hair. The red lipstick gave her a garish appearance. It took away from the natural beauty of her emerald green eyes and full contoured lips.

"I have an appointment."

After checking her computer, she smiled and led him to another expansive office. Showing him to a seat, she offered refreshments. Samuel asked for coffee.

"Good morning Pastor Conklin."

Christopher Michaels entered the office, booming voice filling the room.

The receptionist followed immediately behind. Handing Samuel the coffee, she left them to their business. Samuel took Christopher in as the man gathered notes and obtained his own cup of coffee. He was tall like Samuel, but thin and frail looking. His eyes were like a hawk. Darting back and forth, they gave the appearance of a hunter constantly seeking prey.

"How can I help you today?"

Inhaling a deep breath and casually expelling it, Samuel finally spoke.

"I need to obtain a divorce as quickly and discreetly as possible."

"Tell me the situation."

Christopher allowed Samuel to tell him everything he needed to know. After he spoke, Samuel waited on the attorney's response.

Christopher Michaels came highly recommended to him by another of his fellow ministry contacts. The man secured him a divorce, quickly and quietly, without so much as a ripple effect in his church.

"Is she going to fight it?"

Samuel sighed again.

"Probably."

"Hmph. Is there another woman involved?"

Being fully honest and transparent, Samuel answered his query without malice.

"Yes, but she has no knowledge of that."

Christopher nodded thoughtfully but said nothing for a few moments more.

"I think I can help you. There are some things I will need."

Samuel, delighted the man could help, paid rapt attention. He would bring Christopher whatever he wanted if it would get his freedom and give him his Tatiana back. Samuel made mental notes. They shook hands after the meeting and Samuel told Christopher he would see him soon.

*****

Sylvia tried to calm her nerves when she saw Virginia arrive at the restaurant. She arranged the lunch date hoping to garner more information on Tatiana and whatever may have been going on between her and Samuel. *And what still may be going on.* Virginia reached the table and smiled, greeting Sylvia.

"I was really surprised to get your call."

Virginia didn't know what the woman wanted but she hoped there was no drama. Careful and meticulous about her private life, you could never be too careful. Sylvia smiled back and began to spin the yarn.

"I just thought it would be nice if we spent some time. We haven't hung out with each other for a very long time, and I missed it."

Virginia smiled hearing the woman's explanation, satisfied that her secrets were still intact. They perused the menus delivered by their server, each deciding on an appetizer, drink, and entrée.

"How is Garlan, still recovering I hope."

"Yes, he is doing fine. The doctor gave him a new type of inhaler, and that seems to be working for him."

Candidly, she was more than tired of playing nurse to Garlan and his asthma. *This wasn't what I bargained for all those years ago.* Sylvia's voice broke her thought once more.

"It was good to see Tatiana at the hospital."

Virginia took a quick breath trying to keep her façade in place. Tatiana was another source of angst for her. Every time she looked into the young woman's face she saw her sister, Rachael.

"I'm glad you got the chance to see her. She still won't attend church."

Sylvia nodded.

"So, the counseling didn't help at all?"

The question steered the conversation more in the direction she wanted.

"No, not really it seems."

"Samuel is really disappointed with himself about that."

Virginia regarded her again.

"He shouldn't be. Pastor Conklin did all he could for Tatiana. She was bound and determined to rebel, and she did."

Sylvia grunted her understanding.

"Did she ever tell you about the boy she was involved with then? The one who got her pregnant?"

Virginia frowned somewhat.

"No."

Sylvia let the conversation go.

The server returned with their food. They began to eat making conversation about church, social issues and generalities. Sylvia knew she would glean no information worth using from Virginia. If there was an affair, she obviously was clueless about it. *Why are you pursuing this? You said yourself it was a schoolgirl crush; let this go.* The nagging doubt gnawed at her insides. Recalling the times Samuel and Tatiana interacted at church or church functions. Sylvia remembered the light in his eyes as he looked at the young woman. *He has never looked at me like that, ever.* Sylvia became sad and melancholy at the thought. She shook the blues and began talking to Virginia again as they enjoyed desert.

"This was a wonderful idea, Sylvia. I really needed this."

"I enjoyed it myself. We will have to do it again, soon."

They paid their respective checks and rose to leave. Walking Virginia outside, Sylvia hugged her and bid her goodbye. Virginia watched her walk away as her mind whirled. *Now what exactly was today really about? Maybe I need to make sure everything is still all right.* Pulling out her cell, she made a call.

*****

Tatiana prepared for her visitor. She showered and changed upon her arrival home from work. She wore a soft pink tank top, paired with white khaki capris. She didn't want Samuel to get the idea they were doing anything outside of talking. She was nervous as hell and scared to death. If he even suspected she was up to anything, he would hurt her. Tatiana wasn't too sure he wouldn't kill her. Taking another cleansing breath, she remembered the encouragement from her Auntie Jo and her father. *You can do this.* She fortified her determination as she put the kettle on for tea. *You hafta get this man out of your life once and for all.* She tidied the apartment, put everything in place. Hearing the kettle singing its song of readiness she went back to the kitchen to retrieve her tea.

Tatiana heard the lock turn moments after settling into her favorite easy chair and flipping on the TV.

"Hi baby."

Samuel smiled at her, throwing his keys on her counter. "Hey."

He took off his suit jacket, threw it over the chair and came over to her, leaning down kissing her lips.

"How was your day?"

Headed back to her kitchen, he threw the question over his shoulder.

"It was okay. Another Monday, you know."

He returned with a bottle of water, pulling her out of the chair and sitting down.

"Come here."

Smiling he pulled her back into the chair, sitting on his lap.

"You smell good."

He kissed her neck as Tatiana smiled and thanked him for the compliment.

"How was your day?"

"Very productive," Samuel smiled.

"That's good."

Samuel couldn't believe how right it felt being here with her. He was absolutely at peace enjoying the solitude of them being together, just talking.

"I am glad you wanted to see me baby."

Samuel smiled as he looked into her eyes.

Tatiana smiled a bit and averted her eyes.

Still so shy. Samuel pulled her back into his arms another time. Laying against his chest, Tatiana began her probe.

"Samuel?"

"Hmm?"

"Do you and Gordon still do your thing at the spot?"

"Why did you ask me that?"

Tatiana shrugged.

"I thought we were talking."

"That's stuff you don't need to worry about."

Tatiana rose and looked him in the eye.

"Oh, okay, I get it."

The irritation laced heavily in her voice when she spoke anew.

"You know everything there is to know about me, but you can have secrets from me, is that how it is?!"

Samuel hurriedly tried to defuse the situation, pulling her back to him.

"Baby it's not like that."

Tatiana jumped from his lap, hand on her hip.

"So what is it like then? How am I supposed to be with you and you keep stuff from me? I will not be Sylvia!"

Samuel rose and stepped to her.

"Baby calm down."

Tatiana turned her head and refused to look at him.

"Yes baby. me and Gordon still do our thing."

She regarded him once more.

"Tell me about it."

Samuel sighed deeply, looking into her eyes trying to decide. *This girl is gonna be my undoing.* Samuel loved her. Telling her no was not in his vocabulary.

"OK."

"I just wanna share everything in your life."

Samuel leaned in kissing her deeply and Tatiana kissed him back.

"Come sit back down."

She smiled finally and followed him back to the loveseat. Tatiana relaxed in his arms as he began to tell her about his other life.

*****

Garlan was uneasy about the whole plan, but he knew Jorinda was right. This was the only way they could free Tatiana from Samuel. *My poor baby. This is entirely my fault.* Picking up the phone he called Jorinda. He needed to know what was going on. *If that bastard hurts my daughter again.* Seeing Samuel Conklin's blood, he tried to calm himself.

"Hello."

"Hey Jo. Have you heard from Tatiana?"

"Yes, she called a few moments ago. She's fine and she said everything went well."

Garlan grunted his acknowledgement.

"I just pray we can pull this off quickly."

Jorinda breathed lightly.

"Yes, me too. That man is wicked."

Garlan agreed with her sentiment when she switched gears on him.

"Have you decided what you're going to do?"

"Yes."

He calmly enlightened her.

"Hmph, well I totally understand."

"I feel so guilty about Tatiana."

Jorinda knew he loved his daughter, he was just weak. It was the one fault she mentioned to Rae when they dated.

"I am sure you two can work things out Garlan. Tatiana loves you."

"I sure hope we can Jo. I owe her so much. Every time I think of that animal hurting her, getting her pregnant, using her…"

His breathing became mildly labored.

"Garlan, use your inhaler."

She heard the hiss of the instrument moments later.

"Just stick to our plan Garlan. When this is said and done, Samuel Conklin will never, ever, bother Tatiana again."

Garlan another time agreed with her as his breathing calmed.

"I hear Virginia coming up, so let me go."

She acknowledged his statement, promising to keep him updated as they disconnected. *Please God, protect my daughter and let us get through this unscathed and in one piece.* He finished the heartfelt prayer just as the door opened and Virginia walked inside.

CHAPTER 19

SAINTLY SINNERS

Tatiana didn't know how much longer she could keep up the pretenses. Nearly three weeks were passed, and they still didn't have enough information, according to the one detective who would actually talk to them. He would tell her vaguely about what he and Gordon were into, but he would never give her specifics. He was also becoming more and more insistent about having sex. Tatiana blinked away the tears that wanted to come trying to concentrate instead on the good things in her life right now. She and Jaden were coming along nicely, getting closer and closer. She didn't go to see him this weekend. His mother was finally released. Tatiana thought it better if they all spent some time, just family, before she met her. Jaden reluctantly agreed. He told her he understood her reasoning. He loved her all the more for it. *You have got to sit him down and tell him the truth.*

Tatiana sighed all over again. She already didn't want to have the conversation with Jaden. The fact that Samuel was still very much a part of her life, made it even worse. *How can I get him to admit anything worth using to me?* Rising, she had an idea, but it was going to take all her strength to pull off. Tatiana headed toward her shower. She stepped under the spray, mind whirling as she continued to contemplate what she was about to do. *I have to, it is the only way to jumpstart things.* Finishing her bath and heading into her room to dress.

Tatiana regarded herself moments later, deciding she looked good enough to accomplish her mission and headed out the door. She took the subway, mind wandering as she rode. *Just don't let him leave me when I tell him the truth.* Tatiana silently implored the universe to hear her pleas. Her mind once again on Jaden. Exiting the station at her stop, she walked out and headed down the street three blocks to her destination.

Arriving, Tatiana steeled her resolve, opened the door, and walked inside. Garlan spotted her first, not believing his eyes. *Tatiana?* His daughter entered Christian Cathedral for the first time in seven years. Sylvia caught movement out of the corner of her eye and turned to see the usher seating the young woman on the second row, immediately at her right side. *What is she doing here?* Mixed emotions of joy and suspicion swirled in her mind. She turned her attention back to the pulpit where Samuel was engrossed in conversation with one of their associate ministers. Watching him until he ended the conversation and turned his attention once again to the congregation, she waited for his reaction when he saw Tatiana.

Virginia cut her eyes at her daughter, taking in her attire. *She looks like a total slut.* Jealousy flared. She hated how pretty Tatiana was. The figure she possessed. The way she made every man she passed look at her. Virginia wanted her youth, her beauty, and her desirability. *Why is she even here?* The lunch with Sylvia came to mind once again. *I guess she invited her.* Virginia turned her attention once more to the service, completely ignoring the young woman sitting across the aisle from her.

Samuel caught his breath as he saw the love of his life sitting on the second row. He fought hard to stop the smile that was threatening to break out as he spotted her. *She looks stunning.* The simple cerulean blue dress hugged her curves just right, accentuating every sexy angle she beheld. Samuel absolutely loved it. *She makes me look good.* His ego internally boosted twenty measures of the beautiful woman being on his arm. Tatiana looked up at that moment. Their eyes met. He couldn't help the love that shone through as he looked at her. She immediately averted her eyes. Samuel smiled slightly before turning away, feeling eyes on him. His gaze instantaneously met Sylvia's own intense stare. He gave her a loving smile, hoping to continue the farce just a while longer. Christopher called him the other day telling him almost everything was ready and in order. *Just a little while longer you needy bitch.* Samuel's mind strategized behind the smile. His baby was here today, and these people should get used to seeing her. Samuel wasn't going to waste any time. Once his divorce was final he was going to marry Tatiana immediately.

Tatiana somehow made it through the service. She smiled greeting the many hugs and hellos received now that everything was over.

"I am so glad you came," one of the mothers told her.

"Thank you."

Garlan came to her, hugging her tightly.

"What are you doing?"

Giving her a look, he kept his voice low.

"I had to come, daddy. I have to force his hand, or this will never end."

Garlan grunted faintly but acquiesced and allowed her to complete her mission. Virginia walked up as they ended the conversation, looking her over scornfully.

"Nice to see you in the Lord's house again."

Tatiana held her tongue.

"Hi Mama."

The words were a struggle now knowing the truth.

"Next time however, remember you're coming to church, not going to the club."

Garlan gave her a look.

"Let it rest, Virginia."

Virginia gave him a surprised look but said nothing further as they bid Tatiana goodbye and headed home. Taking another deep breath, Tatiana spotted Samuel, walking toward him.

Sylvia saw the young woman, watching her every move as she continued to stand almost behind the huge pillar inside the main sanctuary.

"Hi Pastor Conklin."

Tatiana greeted him as he chatted with another member.

"Hello, Tatiana."

Samuel hugged her. Taking the opportunity, he whispered in her ear.

"You look beautiful. I am so glad you came."

They parted with her sizing him up afresh.

"Hmph, are you?"

Samuel was perplexed.

"Of course I am, why would you ask me that?"

"Because obviously you and your wife…"

Emphasis fell heavily on the word wife.

"Are still the loving couple."

"Things are not always what they seem Tatiana."
Samuel tried to remain calm.
"I think things are exactly as they seem. You're done playing me Samuel."
Knowing there was nothing he could do about it here, Tatiana continued to bait him.
"Don't call me, don't come to my house, don't text me."
Samuel began to breathe hard; she knew straining to keep his temper in check.
"You and your wife keep on playing house. I'm finished with the lies and the crap, and I am finished with you."
Turning on her heels, Tatiana walked out of the door.

Sylvia continued to watch Samuel after the young woman left. She could tell he was furious. *What did she say to him?* From her vantage point she could observe them, but she couldn't hear them. Whatever Tatiana said, Samuel definitely didn't like. Making her way to her husband, Sylvia reached him moments later, speaking and garnering his attention.
"Service was wonderful as usual."
Samuel nodded in agreement.
"It was really a wonderful gift from God that Tatiana showed up."
She wanted to see his reaction.
"Yes, it really was."
Samuel refused to let Sylvia see how upset he was. His mind was racing as his wife stood before him, chattering and grating his nerves. Tatiana was angry. No, she was furious, with him. *She thinks I want to stay with this bitch!* Samuel's disdain for his wife, acid behind the calm façade. *I have got to get to her, today, now, talk to her, explain.*

Sylvia spoke again.

"Are you ready to go?"

They were going to dinner and then headed to another church in the area where Samuel was the keynote speaker.

"Yes, let me go to my study for a quick minute. I'll meet you in the car."

Sylvia smiled somewhat and left him alone.

Samuel pulled out his cell as soon as he entered his office. The call went straight to voicemail.

"Baby, I know you're angry. Please, let me explain things to you, don't shut me out like this. I love you Tatiana, I'm coming by tonight and we are going to talk."

I will not let her leave me, no matter what the hell I have to do. That will not happen. The fear of loss stayed inbeded as he climbed into the Benz. Sylvia smiled making their dinner destination known.

*****

Tatiana listened to the message as she entered her house once more. *Maybe now I can get what we need out of him.* Erasing it she made herself something to eat. She had to get this monkey off her back and soon. Now that Jaden's mother was better, he told her he would only be staying another week, two at the most, before returning home. She knew without a doubt that he and Samuel would collide. The result would be disastrous. Tatiana sat and enjoyed the meal she prepared, thinking of the questions she would ask when Samuel stopped by. *What happens when he pushes for sex?* Tatiana trembled slightly. She knew Samuel wasn't above forcing her. The thought of him touching her and having his way with her again, brought the meal immediately resurging to the surface. Tatiana ran to the bathroom, barely making it in time. She tried to gather herself as she stopped retching. Looking into the mirror at the frightened reflection she began to speak.

"God, I know of all people, I have a lot of nerve, but right now I honestly need your help. I know I turned my back on you, because I thought you turned yours on me allowing Samuel to hurt me like he did…"

The tears blurred her vision.

"But then you sent me Jaden, and he's perfect."

Sobbing at this point, the words were garbled, but she endured.

"Please set me free from this hell Samuel is making me bear."

Sinking to her knees, she wept uncontrollably.

"Please."

She continued to cry until she was exhausted, finally pulling herself together and making her way to bed.

Her cell rang again. She sighed deeply looking at the I.D. Taking a deep breath, gathering every bit of strength she answered.

"What do you want?"

She heard him sigh loudly.

"Baby, please…."

"Don't call me that."

"Tatiana, honey, please listen to reason."

"Where are you?"

"I am at the church where I'm speaking."

"Hmph. Well then you should be concentrating on your sermon instead of calling me, then shouldn't you?"

"I love you baby. I swear to you I am not lying about divorcing her, I swear."

He prayed she heard and believed him.

"Mmhm, yeah."

"Do you still love me Tatiana?"

Sighing for effect. Swallowing hard. She prayed forgiveness of the lie she was about to tell.

"Yes, but I'm not going to let you string me along and hurt me anymore."

Samuel smiled hearing her admit she still loved him. He knew he still had a hard road to travel.

"Baby get some rest. I'm going to come over tonight and I promise honey, we will talk all of this out and work it out, okay?"

Tatiana loosed another loud breath before speaking.

"I don't see the point but come if you must."

Please God, let tonight be the end. Laying back onto her pillow and closing her eyes, sleep claimed her.

*****

Samuel could barely concentrate on what Gordon was telling him as they handled business. He made it through the program earlier at the sister church. Quickly dropping Sylvia off at home, he showered, changed and headed out again. They were making the usual pick up and distribution run for the week. Samuel knew he had to shake the thoughts plaguing him .Each time he thought of Tatiana, saw the anger and heard the fury in her voice, the fear threatened to overtake him. He knew Gordon would never understand just how much he loved this woman. He kept his feelings and fears to himself.

"Wassup with you and baby?"

Gordon seemingly asked the question out of the blue.

Samuel regarded him wondering where the inquiry came from before finally answering.

Gordon nodded slightly, grunting aloud.

"What's wrong, she carrying again or something?"

Samuel exhaled.

"That wouldn't be a problem."

Taking a deep breath Samuel said nothing else. Gordon, picking up on his mood, didn't press the issue.

"There he is."

Gordon pointed at the dark complexioned, dread-loc wearing, young man on the bicycle.

"Why do these kids insist on riding their little brother's bike?"

Gordon chuckled at Samuel's comment.

"That's how they make them now."

Samuel grunted and checked his .9mm. The young man, Amp as he was known on the street, was fingered by one of their dealers as part of a robbing crew terrorizing the neighborhood where Samuel and Gordon made their money. Getting out of the car, the pair meticulously made their way toward the corner store and the young man sitting by the pole on his bicycle. Samuel took in the neighborhood as they walked. Ancient buildings that perhaps once in their heyday were something to marvel about. Windows broken out, fire gutted, covered in plywood and graffiti the once proud businesses that abode within were nothing but painful memories. Looking up the block he saw the two women standing at the corner flagging down each car that stopped at the stop sign, offering companionship for the evening. Neither was young, attractive, or sexy. Samuel supposed for anyone willing to pay for their wares, none of that was as important as getting off quickly without strings or attachments.

Reeling his mind in as they stood within arm's reach of Amp, he watched as Gordon moved strategically to the young mans left. Samuel stood at his right side. Before he could react, Gordon placed the .380's muzzle flat against his temple. You could see the fear coming off the young man in waves.

"Where is the rest of your busta ass crew?"

Samuel remained quiet, simply watching his reaction.

"I don't know what you're talking about."

"Let's go talk," Samuel told him, more command than request.

Getting off his bike the young man followed Samuel as Gordon walked behind him, gun in his back. Reaching the alley once more and out of the immediate line of sight, Samuel turned quickly catching Amp with a heavy backhand slap.

"You knew enough to steal our dope and our money the other night."

He moved up close and personal to the young man's face.

"I ain't steal no dope!"

I knew messing round with Cheddar and them fools was gonna get my ass killed.

The two men continued to regard him quietly. Gordon spoke first.

"You better come up with some other answers than the shit you are giving us right now."

Sighing deeply Amp swallowed hard knowing the men with him right now were lethal.

"I might know where your stuff is."

"Let's go get it then," Samuel told him pointblank.

"I have to go by myself."

He knew if he showed up with these two, bullets were going to fly. Amp had no intention of being caught in the middle of a war.

"Do we really look that damned stupid to you?"

Gordon threw the query back, angry as hell.

"Stop playing stupid ass boy!"

Grabbing Amp in the collar, he jacked him up. Samuel smiled marginally but said nothing.

"You know what, don't even sweat it."

Samuel regarded the young man, going on to finish his thought.

"You just take this message to your crew. Tell them the streets are looking for their asses and we will find them. When we do, we are going to kill them."

Amp paid rapt attention and prayed they would let him go with the warning. He could live another day. His mind was already working ahead to meeting up with Cheddar and letting him know he was done. Amp would find some other way to make a little money. This crew robbing was far too dangerous. The blow came out of nowhere making his ears ring from the strike to his temple. Samuel relaxed on the hood of the car while Gordon beat the young man unrelentingly. Gordon hit him again and again as Amp offered no resistance. Samuel finally intervened after watching Amp flop around like a rag doll unconscious and defenseless under Gordon's carnage.

"Let's roll."

Gordon grunted, nodding, kicking Amp one final time, hard to the side.

Gordon dropped Samuel off at his Benz, threw up deuces and left the man to his own devices. Getting inside Samuel started the car, exhaling heavily as he turned on the boulevard and headed over to Lankton Avenue. The fight waiting there made the earlier altercation look like a schoolyard spat.

CHAPTER 20

SMOKE SCREEN

Sylvia was sick of Samuel lying to her. Tonight, she was going to finally confront him. Parked outside on Lankton Avenue, directly in front of Tatiana's apartment building. She saw the black Mercedes parked on the other side of the street. *I knew he was messing around on me.* A part of her wanted to go up to Tatiana's apartment and confront him, but she couldn't. While she knew the general area, she didn't know Tatiana's exact unit number or floor. *How long have they been screwing each other?* Sylvia grew angrier and more hurt by the moment. *How could Tatiana do this to me? I was so nice to her.* The tears came. *How do you know Samuel wasn't the initiator?* The tears overflowed and ran down her cheek. Sylvia looked up scanning the various units with lights still burning. Her glance falling finally to the 10th floor and the unmistakable shadow of her husband, hugging a woman.

Seeing the embrace Sylvia broke and began to sob deeply. The hurt and pain of Samuel's deception driven home by the irrefutable evidence of his treachery. "I have given this bastard everything."
Her anger hit full throttle continuing to sit alone in the car.
"I am going to make him pay me for all the years he has stolen from me, bastard."
She just could not believe the man she loved. The man she promised her undying devotion. Been faithful too,

saw to his every need, would betray her like this. *You see him for yourself don't you? She's younger, prettier.* Her mind continually assaulted and berated her perceived shortcomings. Sylvia could only cry and endure. Her heart felt like it would burst from all the pain she felt.

"I cannot be here."

Starting the car and adjusting her seatbelt, Sylvia forced herself to leave. She wanted to go home, gather herself, and be ready when Samuel finally came home. Tonight, Sylvia was going to stand her ground. Samuel was about to find out the true meaning of a woman scorned.

*****

Samuel watched Tatiana quietly as they continued to sit in silence. She hugged him when he first arrived but that was it. He was hoping to catch her asleep and climb into bed with her. Perhaps hold her for a while. He was disappointed to find her wide awake, fully dressed, and still angry as hell.

"Are you going to even talk to me?"

Samuel pleaded anew while Tatiana regarded him.

"I have said all I have to say."

Samuel respired quietly. *Dammit.*

"Tatiana, I love you baby. You have got to know that."

Tatiana cut her eyes at him, looking him over before speaking.

"Let me tell you what I know.

Samuel braced himself, hearing the anger.

"I know you were my first. I know that you and I created a child. That you told me you loved me. I know that you deserted me seven years ago."

Samuel tried to interject and tell her that wasn't true.

"I'm talking."

He again fell quiet.

"I know that you have come back into my life. Forced me to love you again. And have lied to me every step of the way. That's what the hell I know."

Finished, she crossed her arms in front of her giving him another look.

Samuel got up and came over to the loveseat where she sat, taking her hands into his own as he sat close to her. Speaking softly, patiently, he began to explain his view of their situation.

"Baby, I didn't dessert you. I love you Tatiana, and baby, I'm not lying to you about anything."

She said nothing.

"I have seen an attorney and he is honestly working on my divorce right now."

He hoped the admission would appease her.

"Do you still sleep with her, Samuel?"

"Baby...."

Tatiana sucked her teeth at his hedging, slapping his hand away.

"Just what I figured."

Samuel ran his hand over his face. He wasn't getting anywhere. Tatiana was moving further and further away from him.

"Where were you tonight, before you came here?"

"Why did you ask me that?"

"Why does everything have to be a damned challenge with you? It was just a question. Why the hell are you so damned secretive, especially with me?"

Tatiana needed Samuel to open up, all the way up, if this plan was going to work.

"You're right baby."
Samuel reached out and taking her hands again.
"I'm sorry."
He kissed her as Tatiana allowed it.
Samuel told her about him and Gordon handling some business earlier.
"Did you shoot someone else?"
"No."
Samuel smiled slightly from the question and her assumption of his business practices.
"That's good then. Whatever happened to that other guy?"
Samuel gave her a quizzical glance.
"You remember, the guy that was in the alley, I think."
Tatiana only feigned forgetfulness. She remembered everything about that day. She would never forget it. The violence Samuel exhibited that day scared the hell out of her.
He still couldn't grasp who or what she was talking about.
"The day I told you I was pregnant."
The pain of the memory peeked through. Tatiana hurriedly squashed it needing her game full on.
"Oh, Lucky."
Samuel finally recalled.
"Yeah, that's his name."
"He's dead."
Tatiana's hand flew to her mouth.
"He died when you shot him?"
"No baby."
Samuel chuckled lightly at her reaction.

"I only shot him in the arm and leg, nothing life threatening. He died from a heroin overdose, he was an addict."

"Oh, okay. How many other people have you, um, shot and stuff?"

She hoped Samuel wouldn't shut down on her.

Samuel regarded her for a few moments more thinking how different she was from Sylvia. He could never have imagined sitting down having a conversation like this with her, or that she would take what he said as calmly.

"I don't know baby, I don't necessarily keep count."

"I guess."

Samuel chuckled again at her response.

"Maybe six or seven."

Tatiana nodded thoughtfully.

"So you and Gordon, what do you sell?"

"This part of my life doesn't bother you?"

Samuel regarded her falling even deeper in love with her.

"No, should it?"

Samuel smiled again before answering her original question.

"We sell weed, coke, a little smack and of course that gourmet crack rock."

Tatiana chuckled.

"I don't think I have ever heard crack described like that."

Samuel smiled, pleased she sounded less angry.

"I guess I'm just trying to figure out how in the world you fell into that business, being a Pastor and all."

Samuel shrugged.

"The church part came later. I've been rolling with Gordon for years, way before I came to New York."
"Hmph, okay."
Samuel changed the subject.
"Forgive me?"
Tatiana breathed heavily for effect.
"Samuel, I'm scared."
Her response was honest. Just the why of the fear was a lie.
"Tatiana, I love you. I would never hurt you baby, ever."
Samuel kissed her deeply, holding her tightly.
He began touching her softly. His breathing growing heavier, as did his touch gradually.
"No!"
Tatiana pushed him away getting up.
"You are not making love to me until you put a ring on my finger and change my last name."
Samuel rose and walked over to her, taking her into his arms again. He couldn't be angry with her. He understood. She deserved to be legitimate.
"All right baby. We'll wait."
She smiled brightly and kissed him back.
"I have to go now baby."
She graciously allowed it.
"Sweet dreams."
"You too."
Tatiana returned the fake sentiment closing the door, leaning against it. Thankful the Universe allowed her to emerge from yet another performance unscathed.

*****

Sylvia heard him come in and steeled herself. He made his way into the bedroom, trying to be quiet she could tell. She switched on the lamp at their bedside. Samuel stopped in his tracks seeing Sylvia sitting up, fully dressed, waiting for him.

"What's wrong?"

He didn't like the look on her face.

"Why don't you tell me about your evening?"

Samuel said nothing, waiting on her to speak again.

"Or better yet, why don't I tell you about your evening?"

Samuel knew she somehow found out about him and Tatiana. His temper beginning to rise, he measured his words.

"Sylvia…"

She wasn't his baby Tatiana. His tolerance level stayed extremely low when it came to her nagging.

"I don't know what it is you think you're angry about, but I need you to calm down and rationally tell me what's on your mind."

Taking a seat on the chaise lounge contained in the bedroom, he waited.

Sylvia continued to observe him silently while she gathered her thoughts and words.

"Don't try that psychologist crap on me, Samuel! I want to know how long you've been messing around on me."

Sylvia took a breath, fury at one-thousand with his nonchalant attitude.

"How many women have there been and how long you have been screwing Tatiana?!"

Samuel purged his breath, trying hard not to slap the hell out of her.

"What are you talking about Sylvia? Why are you suddenly so insecure, this isn't like you?"

She walked over to him, putting her finger in his chest.
"Stop lying, Samuel, man up! I saw you over there, I saw you hugging her!"
Sylvia continued screaming almost hysterically.
Samuel was stunned and pissed at the same time.
"So you're following, spying on me now?"
He hoped she only followed him to Tatiana's and not to the spot earlier.
"I had to do something!"
She took a deep breath, calming slightly.
"How long Samuel? Is that why she came to church? To see you, to make your date?"
Sylvia began to rage again.
"Why Samuel?! I try to be the best wife I know how to be."
The tears and lamenting left Samuel unmoved.
"Do you want an explanation, or would you just like to berate and accuse me some more?"
Sylvia's cries diminished to slight sniffles.
"Just tell me the truth Samuel, which is all I care about."
Taking a slow breath, Samuel took the extraordinary step of moving to the bed where she sat and putting his arm around her as he spoke.
"Yes, I was at Tatiana's. I have been going by to see her almost weekly since Garlan's last hospital visit."
Sylvia quietly endured.
"I didn't tell anyone because she begged me not too."
Samuel took a quick breath as he continued to spin the lie.
"Tatiana hasn't been in church, or even held a strong faith for years, Sylvia, you know that."
He still held her close speaking calmly.

"She began wavering, seeing her father, praying with him, it awakened something in her. She came to me, because she trusted me."

Sylvia looked up at him, after a few moments of silence seeing the pain in his face and the tears in his eyes.

"I never thought you would distrust me Sylvia."

He forced the words out without laughing.

"I never thought you would turn on Tatiana like her mother has for years."

He swiftly turned away as his voice broke.

Samuel wanted to give himself an Emmy for the performance he was giving right now.

"We are supposed to be people of God. Do you know why Tatiana finally came to church Sylvia?"

His serious gazed rested on his wife.

"Because I told her that you and I would welcome her, we loved her, and we would never judge her."

Sylvia felt two inches lower than dirt.

"Samuel, I---"

He sighed deeply and rose heading toward the shower.

"I need to just meditate by myself for a little while."

Sylvia swallowed the huge lump in her throat hearing the pain in his voice. She said nothing else and let him leave her presence. She broke down once again when he closed the bathroom door.

"God please forgive my foolish sinful nature."

Sylvia cried in repentance of her suspicions and accusations.

*****

"I want you to find the people who hurt my son!"

Brandi Davis's desperation poured forth, aimed at the detective taking her statement.

"Just because we're poor and black, doesn't mean his life is worthless!"

Tears joined the melee. Her son, Amp, was fighting for his life in intensive care after a brutal beating by unknown assailants. Brandi wanted to make sure the police actually investigated and did something about it.

"Ma'am I promise your economic status or race has nothing to do with our investigation."

Detective Dennis Suave tried his best to reassure the distraught mother. He was a seasoned veteran with twenty years of service, and just as many taking jokes about his last name. He was taking her statement more as a token than anything else. Dennis learned long ago that in the hood unless someone was willing to give you up, there was very little real chance of finding out who beat the fifteen-year old within an inch of his life.

"Here is my card, Ms. Davis. If you need anything, hear anything, or just want to check on the case, please call me."

Tears momentarily abated, she took his card. Detective Suave graciously showed her the way out of the precinct.

Dennis sighed deeply feeling sorry for the woman and the pain she was suffering, knowing she truly loved her son. He headed back to his desk and sat down going over the report once more. Making a few notes here and there, he placed it in a folder to be filed. *Maybe she will turn up some leads.* He knew she had a better chance than he did. No one in the hood talked to the police. Not anyone who wanted to stay alive or maintain street credit. They had a few confidential informants, but Dennis didn't think this case was big enough to warrant using one of them. Seemed that Antonio "Amp" Davis was simply in the wrong place and ran into the wrong people. His desk phone rang. He answered, further contemplation of the victim or his mother, pushed far to the recesses of his conscious thought.

CHAPTER 21

INDECISION

J aden wrestled with trying to make decisions. Though he wasn't seeking it, a wonderful opportunity presented itself in his time here in the sunshine state. Jaden recalled the offer made by the acquaintance he encountered during his mothers' illness. Jaden met Denby Caesar one morning at the hospital heading to see his mom. They spoke and began a casual conversation with Jaden finding out the man's wife was also in the hospital with a similar pneumonia. He found out Denby was CEO for one of the large communications firms in the city. Jaden thought nothing of it when they talked simply time being passed by two strangers in the same place at the same time. He told Denby of his job in New York and his experience as they exchanged stories. He was completely blindsided when he got a call from the man two days ago offering him a very lucrative position with his company. Even offering to include his moving expenses. Jaden couldn't lie and say he wasn't flattered by the offer. The salary alone doubled what he made in New York.

Jaden sighed deeply again. He wanted to take the offer. He admitted this freely to himself. He liked New York well enough, but the warm weather he found very pleasurable during his visits. The surf, the entertainment, and people were much more inviting. There were only a couple of things holding him back and keeping the yes from bursting from his mouth. The movement and Tatiana. Jaden was pretty sure his group would be fine. They would simply put another brother in charge. Tatiana however was a different story. He searched forever for her and now that he found her, Jaden wasn't going to lose her. *Would she even entertain a move?* He was hanging out at the beach this morning finding it a great place to think and unwind. He knew it was asking a lot. He himself wasn't fully averse to a long-distance relationship for awhile if it made her feel more comfortable. Jaden honestly wanted her closer. He wanted her in his arms every night when he lay down and when he got up. They never talked about any sense of permanence between them. Neither with living together or marrying one day. Now he must seriously contemplate asking her to move away from everything and everyone she knew, just for him. Jaden freed a troubled breath wondering what he would do if she said no. Equally praying she would not.

*****

'Come visit us this Sunday,' the commercial droned on. China absently watched. She was still high and dazed from her night of drinking, tricking, and smoking. She owned a serious crack habit that she supported by prostituting herself. China wasn't always down and out. She once worked a good job with children's services. She had a nice apartment, nice clothes and shoes. Got her hair done on a regular basis and lived life. That was all before her ex-boyfriend Reggie. He introduced her to the drug as they enjoyed a basketball game together almost a year ago. China loved the euphoric high, but the drug proved to be extremely addictive. She went downhill quickly until nothing else mattered except her next high.

Turning her attention again to the television set she watched the religious program as it blared loudly. Condemnation spewed toward her and every other sinner in the world for being human.

"We are a church all about love," the pastor spoke.

China watched paying close attention now. There was something very familiar about the man speaking. She was trying to clear the drug fog to figure out what it was.

"Come as you are," he droned on.

China frowned again trying to focus on the face. *That looks like dude from the other night.* She recalled wandering down the street headed to the corner store when she saw the two men beating the kid in the darkened corridor. China quickly jumped behind a dumpster at the end of the alley, careful to avoid detection as she continued to observe. *Can't be.* She dismissed the thoughts as her gut continued to gnaw at her. *He's a damned preacher stupid girl. Can't be him.* China shook all the thoughts and rose headed out into the morning. She needed to find a trick or two and get her rock supply.

*****

Sylvia greeted Samuel calmly, unsure of his mood or state of mind.

"Good morning, honey."

She rose early and made his favorites for breakfast. He remained quiet and pensive since her accusations two days ago.

"Good morning."

Samuel sounded amiably enough in his response.

He was satisfied that Sylvia would no longer be a problem. He held out long enough to throw her off track. The silence convinced her to truly believe she was wrong in what she assumed concerning him and Tatiana.

"Food looks good."

Sylvia smiled somewhat. She brought his plate.

"Sit down and enjoy, honey."

"Thanks."

She fixed her own and joined him moments later.

"Samuel, I'm sorry. I acted like a fool the other night; I don't know what got into me."

Samuel continued to quietly contemplate her words.

"I promise honey, never again."

Samuel finished his breakfast before finally addressing her and the things spoken.

"Sylvia, how long have you been in ministry with me?"

She hung her head for a moment before looking up at him again.

"You cannot go off the deep end on me like that."

Samuel knew he made her feel worse. Finally moving in for the kill, he said the magic words.

"I forgive you. Please try and get yourself together though. I would hate for Tatiana to come to service for a second time and feel like she's not wanted."

"No, that wouldn't be the case at all. I promise Samuel."

He smiled fairly and nodded, rising from the table.

"I'm visiting the shut-in today. Would you like to come?"

"Yes, I would be happy too."

Samuel headed into the bedroom to dress as she tidied the kitchen.

As he stood in their bedroom Samuel smiled of his genius. He had Sylvia like a meek child. She would accept any direction he gave her right now. Christopher called earlier updating the divorce case. Samuel smiled recalling the good news the attorney gave him. *This bullshit will be over very soon.* He continued to smirk as his cell vibrated. The smile filled his face when he saw the text from Tatiana saying good morning and that she was thinking about him. He sent her an immediate reply saying the same thing. He added how much he loved and missed her. Thinking of her immediately aroused him. Sylvia walked into the bedroom almost simultaneously taking in his growing erection as he stood in his boxer briefs. She leered giving him a look. She wasn't Tatiana, but she would have to do for now. Samuel allowed her to caress his now hard manhood and take him in her mouth. Samuel closed his eyes and enjoyed the feel of her mouth while imagining himself inside Tatiana. He came quickly, and she swallowed without question.

"Better?"

"Yes, very much," Samuel replied honestly.

Sylvia smiled and headed into the bathroom to put on her makeup.

Samuel sighed silently becoming anxious before calming himself. Just a few more days and everything would be in place. He would take Tatiana straight to city hall and marry her. Then he would take her to the suite he was renting where he would make love to her all night long. Smiling again, Samuel called out to Sylvia that he was ready. She joined him, and they headed out the door, sick and shut-in lists in hand.

*****

Jorinda rolled her eyes reading the message after Tatiana shared it with her.

"That man is actually insane."

Tatiana nodded before responding.

"I just want this finished."

Jorinda grunted her agreement.

"I am beginning to get details from him. He trusts me more and of course he thinks I'm in love with him."

Jorinda admonished her to once again be careful.

"Does he still try and touch you?"

Tatiana sighed frowning.

"Not so much now because of what I said to him. I still have to kiss him though."

Jorinda exhaled noisily.

"Hopefully between today and tomorrow you can get all the info and we can take it to the police again."

Tatiana again agreed with the sentiment.

"How is Jaden?"

Tatiana's face lit up.

"He's fine. I miss him so much."

"It sounds like you're in love."

Tatiana giggled, but didn't refute her aunt's observation.

"How is his mother?"

"Oh, she's much better. They released her from the hospital a couple of days ago."

"Jaden will be back soon?"

Jorinda's tone showed her concern. Tatiana exhaled lightly, knowing what her aunt was alluding to.

"He's staying an extra week."

Voicing both their thoughts aloud, Tatiana spoke.

"I want it over before he comes back too. If he and Samuel collide, I know it will be a disaster."

Yet another time Jorinda nodded.

"Not to mention, I would probably lose him."

Jorinda reached over and took her hand.

"We are almost there Tatiana."

"Auntie Jo?"

"Hmm?"

"Do you believe in God?"

She could never recall her aunt attending church or having much to say about religion in general. Jorinda sighed lightly before answering the young woman.

"Yes, I believe in God. But I don't have use for his so-called messengers, and people, at all."

Bitterness tinged her voice. Tatiana assumed that like herself, Jorinda experienced hurt with religion and church. Leaving the subject alone, Tatiana began to engage her aunt in more conversation about her mother. Tatiana wanted to know everything she could about Rachael. *I wish she was here.* Jorinda told her more stories of their childhood and growing up together. Tatiana continued to smile as Jorinda continued to reminisce and time continued to pass.

*****

China increased her rhythm hoping the trick would hurry and finish, so she could go get her crack. Finally, the man reached orgasm. She hurriedly gathered herself leaving him in search of her usual dealer. China didn't have to look long. She saw him standing on the corner, 40-ounce beer in his hand. She approached him.

"Let me get one."

The man regarded her.

"Ten dollars."

Handing him the money, he gave her two small rocks in a baggie.

"Thanks."

He grabbed her arm before she fully ensnared her prize.

"I'll give you another one if you give me head."

China almost told him to back off before remembering the two in her hand wouldn't get her through the night.

"OK, in the alley."

The dealer nodded and followed her.

Standing behind the dumpster, China went to her knees unbuckling his pants and putting him in her mouth. He held her head and guided her as he enjoyed her skill. China was growing impatient. She wanted to get high, to forget.

"Man what the fuck?"

She heard the masculine voice as she continued her work.

"Getting a nut man, shit."

Just as he spoke, China tasted his finish. Rising she wiped her mouth and took the rock he promised.

Turning to leave she saw the man speaking and almost dropped her prize. This was one of the men from the other night. Gordon looked the woman over, deciding he wanted a little relief of his own.

"Come here."

China immediately complied. She witnessed his wrath already. Gordon pulled the condom out of his pocket. He always carried one. Gordon was a man who believed in being prepared. Pushing China against the trunk of his car, he lifted her skirt, pulling her panties to the side. He entered her and began thrusting into her. China closed her eyes and endured. He was hurting her. She didn't dare cry out or object.

"Mmm."

He went even deeper hurting her more.

China felt the tears roll down her cheeks. Remaining mute she allowed Gordon to have his way. After what seemed forever in her mind he groaned deeply and stopped moving.

"Here."

He gruffly put the fifty in her hand.

Gordon didn't sweat it. He knew she would give it all back to them via the dope boys by tomorrow.

"Thanks."

"Yeah, now get the hell on."

China did as she was told, but she didn't go far. As soon as she hooked the corner she slipped back into the alley. There were several dumpsters. She simply hid beside a new one. Making sure her money and dope were secure in her bra, China waited and watched. The second man joined the first moments later as they both talked to the dealer. She saw the exchange. They took the money and gave the dealer more dope. China was waiting for the second man to turn around. She heard that Amp was still serious, though upgraded from critical. *Just a damned kid!* She didn't know his mom Brandi personally, but she saw her around the neighborhood. She was a nice enough woman who tried to keep her son on track. *Streets be calling.* The second man turned around. She stared as if in a trance taking in every nuance of the man's features. Having seen enough, China stealthily made her way from the alley.

She headed to the abandoned unit on the end of the street where all the crack heads hung out and got high.

CHAPTER 22

WELL LAID PLANS

Samuel walked into her apartment, grabbing himself a drink from the fridge. He headed toward the bedroom, finding her curled in bed, book in hand.

"Hey baby."

"Hi," Tatiana threw back cordially.

Samuel climbed in bed beside her, still dressed, resting on her pillows.

"What are you reading? Inconvenient Love. Romance?"

Tatiana chuckled.

"Sort of."

Marking her place, she closed the book. She needed to give Samuel her full attention. Tatiana was on a mission. She needed to get all the information she could tonight and take it to her aunt tomorrow. She wanted this nightmare over. Time was no longer on her side. Jaden called earlier telling her he had something very important to talk to her about. She tried to question him. Jaden gave away nothing. Tatiana didn't know what was going on, but she wasn't going to lose Jaden for any reason.

"How was your day?"

Samuel laid his head on her breasts.

"It was pretty busy."

Samuel went on to tell her about it.

"Hmph, well I'm sure Sylvia was on cloud nine."

Tatiana hoped she pulled of the feigned jealousy.

Samuel immediately took the bait.

"It was strictly business baby."

Raising his head, he gazed into her eyes.

"I don't love Sylvia."

Tatiana sighed delicately.

"I don't want to talk about her anymore."

Samuel again lay his head down.

"Do you know anything about that young boy that was beaten the other night?"

Samuel exhaled and pulled her closer.

"Don't let the age fool you baby. Some of those kids will kill you just as soon as look at you."

Tatiana frowned.

"I guess. Still, he was only fifteen."

"Business still has to be handled honey."

Tatiana finally figured out he did indeed know about the beating. Either he or Gordon was involved.

"Why not kill him then?"

She fished trying to find out which scenario rang true.

Samuel sighed deeply, kissing her hand as he held it.

"We weren't out to kill him, just teaching him a lesson."

"Did you even know him, know his name?"

"Ant, Amp, some street crap like that."

Samuel rattled the information off condescendingly without care.

"Doesn't really matter. He was a thief and he got caught."

"Hmph."

"Baby, don't be upset. This is why I didn't want you to know the details of what I do."

He returned to her eyes now.

"Sometimes I have to do things that are going to upset you, and I never want to do that to you."
Samuel kissed Tatiana as she smiled somewhat.
"I want to know about it, to share everything with you Samuel."
He smiled again and kissed her soulfully.
"Baby, I want you so much."
"You promised."
Tatiana's reminder elicited a loud sigh from him.
"Can I taste you?"
She was immediately repulsed by the idea, but she had to keep him talking and from hurting her.
"That's all."
"I promise baby."
They began to kiss. Samuel began touching her, arousing her, headed for her center.

*****

Dennis ran into his friend and fellow detective, Larry Monroe as he headed to the men's room.
"What's going on, Larry?"
"Same old drama man."
"I hear you."
They were passing the communication center when one of the tip line operators called out to Dennis.
"Yeah, what you got?"
Larry stood with Dennis as the operator began telling them about the tip just received.
"She swears it was this guy."
It was concerning the beating case of Antonio Davis. He frowned marginally.
Finding the information vaguely curious, Larry interrupted.

"Did anyone run a check on him?"

"The guy doesn't have a record. And...."

Both detectives paid rapt attention.

"He is a pastor, one of the largest churches in the Bronx."

Dennis frowned again.

"Sounds like someone has an axe to grind."

He was about to dismiss the tip when Larry finally spoke again.

"Dennis let's go to my cube. I've got some stuff I want to show and tell you."

Dennis shrugged, thanked the operator and followed Larry.

"Sit down."

He searched his desk, finally finding the folder he wanted.

"A couple of weeks ago, this lady comes in with this wild story."

Dennis continued to regard him.

"I just kind of blew her off, you know?"

After giving Dennis specifics, Larry continued.

"But with this tip coming in, I'm thinking maybe we should at least check it out."

Dennis nodded absently.

"Wouldn't be the first guy to get drunk with power and think he was above the law," Dennis threw out. "Who is the woman?"

"Name is Jorinda Abbey."

Dennis grunted again.

"I think we should go see Ms. Abbey tomorrow morning and find out just how much she does and doesn't know."

Larry quickly agreed with his fellow detective.

Finally making it to their original destination, both detectives relieved their calls of nature as their minds raced and they prepared for the morning.

*****

Samuel sighed deeply. He hated these moments. He couldn't wait until this divorce was final and he never had to leave her bed again. Tatiana slept peacefully. She drifted off right after he brought her to multiple orgasms. *So beautiful.* Samuel gently brushed her hair from her forehead kissing it. The thought of lying next to this beautiful woman every night, for the rest of his life, filled him with a deep sense of contentment. He thought back to their first time and how scared she was. He smiled again recalling the night of her sixteenth birthday. The night she conceived their child. Thinking about her pregnancy brought anger as well as sadness. *That bitch, Virginia.* Samuel watched the woman abuse Tatiana for years, all because of her jealous hatred.

Tatiana shifted, moving closer to him. Samuel gently stroked her shoulder, sighing again. He knew she wanted him here with her. Holding her at night and protecting her. *I need to call Christopher later this morning.* His mind went back to his original thought. Samuel remembered walking in on them. Both looking like deer in headlights as they stared wordlessly at their Pastor. He discreetly walked out and left them alone, knowing one or both of them would come to him later. True to his assumption, Virginia materialized almost thirty minutes later. *"This is definitely not the place for that,"* Samuel told her frankly. *Virginia continued to regard him silently. She was beyond doubt a hard case, but Samuel knew he held her in a vice. One thing Virginia coveted was her image. He had the power to destroy that in the palm of his hand. "What do you want," she asked frankly. Samuel sighed. "Tatiana." Virginia grunted. "Why?" Samuel continued to regard her silently. "What do you think Sharelle would do with the knowledge of what I saw today," he asked, alluding to Richard's wife. He was the deacon Virginia was screwing when he walked into the small auxiliary room unannounced. "You won't hurt her will you?" "Of course not," Samuel answered immediately. "How?" Virginia acquiescing to his demand queried. "She needs counseling." Virginia again nodded. They talked for the next forty minutes setting everything in place. Satisfied, Samuel dismissed Virginia from his presence, assuring her the secret was safe as long as she never crossed him.*

Tatiana stretched and opened her eyes, breaking his thought.

"Are you leaving?"

"I have to go baby."

Samuel absolutely did not want to.

Sucking her teeth softly, again in character, Tatiana replied.

"Yeah, whatever."

"Baby don't be like this."

He had to push Christopher when he talked to him. Tatiana was about at her end. Samuel felt her pulling away from him.

"Just go home to your wife Samuel."

"I am with my wife."

Kissing her ear, hoping to dispel the irritation he heard, Samuel turned her to face him again.

"This is almost over honey, I promise with all that is in me."

"Are you going to have sex with her when you get home?"

Tatiana held his gaze.

"No."

Samuel lied. Frankly, he was horny as hell. He couldn't sleep with Tatiana. He was about to burst.

"Promise?"

"Yes baby, I promise."

Samuel asked silent forgiveness for lying to her another time.

"OK."

"Go back to sleep."

Covering her once more he kissed the bridge of her nose.

"I love you."

"Mmm, you too."

Tatiana feigned sleep.

She heard the door close and lock moments later. The single tear rolled onto her pillow. *Please God, let them finally believe us tomorrow.* She had to have enough to at least warrant investigation. If nothing else, she had his confession to the assault on the young boy. *I really need to know you hear me this time God.* Tatiana hoped for the best a final time before closing her eyes and sleep reclaimed her.

*****

Samuel decided to swing by the spot before going home. He spotted Gordon immediately. Greeting him, he parked the Benz and got into the Pontiac with his partner.

"I thought you would be home asleep."

Samuel smiled a little.

"I was sleeping, but I couldn't stay, unfortunately."

Gordon immediately knew where he was.

"How is everything? You and baby back on track?"

"Yeah, for now."

Samuel explained a little further.

"Stay on his ass man."

Gordon offered the advice concerning the attorney.

"I'm horny as hell right now."

Gordon chuckled.

"Shit man, we can remedy that."

Cranking the car, they headed to the spot.

Cruising the street, Gordon's eyes searched until he found what he was looking for. Pulling up beside the woman as she walked, he rolled down Samuel's window, speaking through it.

"Hey!"

The woman stopped walking and turned to his voice.

China's breath caught in her throat as she regarded the car and the two men contained. *Shit!* She internally freaked out, recalling her earlier phone call. She struggled long and hard with the decision to call the tip line finally doing it almost seven hours later.

"Meet us in that alley, right now!"

China jumped slightly from the command of his voice. Turning on her heels and doing as she was told, her heart raced with every step.

"You got a rubber?"

Samuel shook his head no.

Gordon grunted and flipped his glovebox open, revealing the stash of Magnum's he kept.

"Damn, you do this much screwing?"

"Like the boy scouts say, always be prepared."
They both laughed at Gordon's statement.

Parking in the darkness, Gordon got out just as China approached the car.
"Got another fifty dollars for you."
Pulling her toward the back of the car China again said nothing, waiting on further direction. The passenger door opened. Samuel got out, walking to the trunk as well.
"Get your tension release."
Gordon chuckled walking away.
"I'm going to smoke one."
Getting back into the drivers' side, he began rolling his blunt.
Samuel wordlessly looked the woman over, deciding she would do and turned her around. *These muthafucka's like it from the back don't they?* China felt Samuel rip her panties from her, roughly entering her. She bit her lip. The flashback of Gordon returned to her consciousness. He was as big as the other one and hurt her as much. China couldn't help the tears as they again flowed. Samuel pushed her legs further apart, pushing himself deeply into her. China dug her nails into the palms of her hands. *Please let him finish, oh my god, please.* Samuel continued to assail her.

He slowed his pace and China thought the carnage was over.
"Relax, lay on the trunk."
China laid her body completely prone as he requested.
"Mm, that's better."
She had never been hurt like this. Samuel was so deeply inside her China thought he should have felt himself

hitting the car's trunk. His rhythm increased to warp speed. She knew that finally he would arrive. He finished moments later, breathing hard, calling some woman's name and releasing her.

"Here."

China struggled to stand up.

He handed her the fifty as well as another twenty and told her to go. China moved as quickly as she could, leaving them alone. Cursing him she prayed the police took her tip seriously, arresting him quickly.

PUZZLE PIECES

Samuel hoped he would get good news today. Christopher called earlier and told him he needed to see him. *Please don't let there be any issues.* He was far more than ready to end his marriage to Sylvia and be with Tatiana. He already bought the ring. He was going to give it to her as soon as the judge signed his divorce decree. Samuel smiled thinking of the beautiful woman he was in love with. He silently thanked God she still loved him. Everyone spent years trying to keep them apart and poison her mind against him. *Why can't people ever let you be happy?* Samuel arrived once again at the attorney's office, finding a park, getting out. He entered the opulent building and headed for the elevators. He pressed fifteen and waited. His mind traveled in a thousand different directions. Ideally, Samuel wanted Christopher to tell him the divorce was final. He was a free man. The soft ding of the elevator once again broke his thought as Samuel waited for the doors to open.

"Good Morning," the receptionist greeted him anew.

Samuel returned the greeting, accepting the coffee that was offered as he took a seat. The receptionist informed him Christopher was running a little behind. Court took longer than he originally planned, but he was on his way. Smiling at her, Samuel tried to quell the anxiety starting to rise. Tatiana's patience was growing thin and he knew it. *I will not lose her.* He sipped the steaming black elixir. His cell vibrated. He pulled it from his pocket, reading the text message and frowning. *Relax, this is almost over.* Samuel erased Sylvia's wishes for a good day. It vibrated again. He impatiently looked at it once more. This message from Gordon. 'Meet me, streets rumbling.' Samuel frowned again. This wasn't good. *What the hell could be going on now?* He hoped and prayed Christopher would show up, so they could get this meeting done. He needed to see about his business.

Samuel sent a quick text back to Gordon letting him know where he was and what was up. Gordon texted back letting Samuel know he could handle things until they met, but that they had to meet. Satisfied that much was taken care of Samuel dismissed it. The receptionist called out to him, alerting him Christopher was back and ready to see him. Walking back to the now familiar office, Samuel greeted the attorney and took the seat offered.

"Things are almost complete, Samuel. We go in front of Judge Kibbins, at 3:00 today."

Christopher concentrated, looking over the file in front of him.

The smile came to Samuel's face.

"He'll grant the divorce then?"

"More than likely yes. The fact that your wife doesn't show up will definitely lean in your favor."

The attorney frankly thought it very tacky of the Pastor to so unceremoniously dismiss his marriage, but they paid him to take care of business.

"That is excellent news, Christopher."

Samuel felt a weight lift from him.

"Thanks so much. I'll be there this afternoon."

The attorney nodded, shook his hand and watched him walk out of his office. Shrugging he returned to his other cases and continued his day.

*****

Jorinda and Garlan were enjoying a well overdue visit as he caught her up to speed on his plans. She did the same concerning Tatiana and Samuel.

"I want this shit over."

Garlan growled into his coffee as Jorinda sighed deeply at the utterance.

"Yes, so do I. Tatiana is about at her end."

Garlan nodded thoughtfully.

"Every time I think of that dog touching my baby, I want to rip his throat out."

Jorinda commiserated with him.

"The part that hurts so much Jo, I could have prevented it, stopped it, long ago."

The pain of his guilt shone evident.

Jorinda breathed silently and patted his hand soothingly.

"No time for regrets, Garlan. We have to concentrate on now and helping Tatiana get rid of this demon."

The forceful knock came to her door just as she completed her sentence. *What the hell?* Jorinda jumped, a bit unsettled by the sound, rising to see who it was.

"Yes?"

Jorinda eyed the two men at her door cautiously.

"Ms. Abbey?"

Jorinda nodded, seeing Larry, recognizing him.

He was the detective they saw almost two months ago with their story. He halfheartedly listened and just as quickly shut them down dismissing them. *So what does he want now?* Larry re-introduced himself and Dennis as well.

"Hmph, well come in."

They entered and found Garlan seated already.

"This is my brother, Garlan."

Jorinda didn't elaborate further.

"Nice to meet you sir."

Dennis gave his name as Larry did the same.

"Ms. Abbey, there have been some developments with a case Detective Suave is handling, that I believe may be directly or indirectly linked to the information you gave me a few months ago."

Larry got right to the point.

Jorinda continued to regard them quietly. Garlan's mind was spinning. *What gives?* His subconscious raced behind the calm exterior.

"OK."

"Ms. Abbey a young man was brutally beaten almost two weeks ago."

Jorinda and Garlan paid rapt attention.

"We have a witness who identifies the man as Samuel Conklin."

Jorinda's hand flew to her mouth. She gasped audibly.

Larry began to speak now, telling Jorinda how the name brought recollection and he pulled the file he began during her visit.

"Ms. Abbey, you told me then you had proof this man was dangerous."

Contritely embarrassed he never moved on her original complaint, Larry swallowed the ego and spat his request.

"We're here today to ask if you still have that proof."

Jorinda sighed silently and cast a quick glance at Garlan who nodded.

"Yes, but…."

Larry and Dennis gave her their full attention.

Another knock disturbed the morning as Garlan rose this time and answered.

"Hi Chip!"

Tatiana returned the smile that greeted her.

"Hi daddy. I didn't know you were here."

Walking into the living room stopping in her tracks, she regarded the two strangers and her Aunt.

"I am sorry Auntie Jo. I didn't know you had company."

Jorinda smiled a fraction.

"Your timing is actually perfect."

After telling Tatiana to sit down, and making quick introductions, Jorinda went back to her original thought.

"In exchange for what we have I want my niece protected."

Frowning quizzically, Larry spoke.

"Protection from what?"

Taking a new breath, she turned to Tatiana and spoke.

"I think you need to tell these gentlemen your story, from the beginning."

Tatiana swallowed hard, sighing heavily. She remained quiet a few moments more before lastly starting to speak in a quiet voice. Haltingly at first, she grew more confident as Garlan put his arms around her. Larry and Dennis were stunned when she finished.

"He's still threatening you," Larry asked, furious.

He had a daughter Tatiana's age. If someone did to her the things she said Samuel Conklin had, Larry knew without a doubt he would be serving time in prison.

"He's very subtle with it," Tatiana replied. "He admitted beating that boy a couple weeks ago."

Dennis leaned forward listening with interest.

"Can you prove that?"

Nodding Tatiana told them about the recorded conversations. She told them about all the visits and that she recorded each one without his knowledge.

"We thought that was the best way to get the information."

Jorinda added the tidbit as Dennis nodded.

"That's a good start. Tatiana."

The young woman regarded him.

He could see the fatigue in her face. *This guy is wearing this poor girl out.* He smiled marginally at her before speaking.

"We need to set up a sting for this guy. The recordings you have are good, but we need a little more."

Dennis went on as everyone listened silently.

"Would you be willing to let us wire your apartment?"

"He'll hurt me if he finds out I helped you."

Needing her help and wanting to reassure her, Dennis responded to her statement.

"He will never know about that evidence until the trial."

Looking at her father and her aunt to get their opinion, Tatiana finally agreed.

"Thank you, Tatiana," Larry told her. "I know this has got to be hard as hell for you."

Tatiana looked up, tears in her eyes, and quietly responded.

"I just want my life back."
Garlan pulled her close, holding her tightly as the first one fell.

Dennis and Larry made calls while at Jorinda's, setting everything in place.

"By tonight, if everything goes right, Samuel Conklin will be calling a jail cell home," Dennis assured Tatiana.

She nodded her understanding. The two detectives began giving her the list of things she needed to get Samuel to admit in order for it to hold up in court and be admissible.

"If you feel threatened Tatiana, in any way," Larry began. "Say the safe words and we are in there."

She confirmed her understanding as they continued to lay out the plan.

"When we storm in, we are going to make it look totally random."

Samuel wouldn't be any the wiser Tatiana knew the police were anywhere near. Dennis addressed her anew.

"I promise you Tatiana, if you get us what we need, this guy will never bother you again."

"I'm counting on that."

After assuring themselves everyone knew their role, Larry and Dennis rose to leave. Thanking Jorinda, Tatiana, and Garlan for their help another time, they left. Jorinda closed the door behind them. Returning to her living room, the three of them joined hands and prayed everything went according to plan.

*****

Samuel found Gordon at the coffee shop enjoying his lunch as he joined him.

"Wassup man?"

Gordon returned the greeting.

"What's going on?"

"Been a lot of heat on the street, asking questions, shaking down the boys."

Samuel sighed loudly hearing Gordon's explanation.

"About?"

Gordon gave him a look.

"Somebody is talking too much."

Samuel instantly understood.

"What did they find out?"

Gordon chuckled, answering right after the waitress set his food down.

"From what I can tell, not a damned thing."

Samuel smiled too. He was glad to hear that. The one thing they didn't need was unnecessary heat and friction to interfere with their business.

"I think everything should be said and done today with the divorce."

Gordon regarded Samuel again for a few moments as he internally processed the words.

He knew Sylvia, finding her to be quite pleasant. He really didn't understand why Samuel almost hated the woman. *Guess Tatiana cast that spell on him.* Gordon internally processed his friend's obsession with the young woman. He himself liked them younger, but Tatiana was jailbait when Samuel had sex with her. *Lucky his ass wasn't in lockdown.*

"Then what?"

Gordon wanted to see exactly how far his friend would go in his pursuit.

"Once I get that signed decree, I'm grabbing some movers and heading to the house. Grabbing up my clothes and a few other items I wanna take. I'm out."

"You're not going to even tell her goodbye?"

Gordon felt very sorry for the woman at the moment.

Samuel loosed an expressive breath, shrugging. "She's too emotional. That scene would be horrendous."

Gordon continued to eat without verbalization.

"I just want to move on, without drama."

Samuel finished his drink beckoning the waitress for a refill.

"Tatiana excited?"

Samuel smiled at the mention of her name.

"It's a surprise."

His friend again grunted his understanding.

That damned girl is gonna drain this fool. His friend was undoubtedly sprung, equally believing Tatiana was just another gold digger along for the ride.

"Well, I'm sure she's going to be happy as hell."

Samuel smiled again and produced the black velvet box.

"Damn man, you bought a ring and shit already?"

Gordon chuckled as he opened the top and saw the three-carat diamond contained.

"I've been waiting seven years to be with this woman permanently. Once that judge signs those papers today, there is nothing on this side of heaven that is going to keep me from her."

"Good luck man."

Gordon had a very bad feeling.

*****

Tatiana watched as the officers put all the devices in place. Her entire apartment was wired for sight and sound. *If he ever finds out.* Tatiana trembled with the thought. Both detectives assured her that once Samuel was arrested they would lobby for him not to receive bail. She already began the paperwork for the restraining order. On the off chance he did get bail, he couldn't come near her. *He won't care about that.* The more Tatiana continued to think, the more afraid she grew. Samuel was crazy. If no one else knew it, she did. Her cell rang, and she jumped. Looking at the I.D. she let go the breath she held and answered.

"Hi," she greeted Jaden cheerfully.

"Hey baby."

They began to talk, catching up with each other on the daily ins and outs of their lives.

"When are you coming home?"

There was still the matter of her telling him all about her past and Samuel's role in it.

"Well, I was wondering if we could have one more weekend?"

While he did want to enjoy another weekend with her, there were ulterior motives. Jaden reasoned if he could see Tatiana face to face, he stood a far better chance of convincing her to move to Miami with him.

"That actually sounds really good."

Thoughts of surf and sand, the tranquil breezes, shopping, food and nightlife semi relaxed her already. It was hundreds of miles away from the hellish nightmare she lived right now.

"Great," Jaden replied snapping her thoughts. "You could fly in Friday night."

She heard the desire in his voice.

"I'll find a flight."

Tatiana needed and wanted him just as much.

"OK, let me know so I can pick you up. You can meet my mother finally."

Tatiana smiled at the statement.

"Yeah, that will be nice."

"Call me later baby."

"I will."

"Love you."

"Love you too," she returned as they hung up.

Inhaling deeply Tatiana shored her resolve. This had to work. It had to work tonight. She was tired of the dark specter that was Samuel spilling into her light. *How many other girls have there been?* Tatiana wondered about the man's immediate and constant obsessions. Thinking about the past of course made her think of Virginia and her role in the entire mess. *How could she do that to me?* Virginia must have known the things Samuel was doing to her, yet she never said a word. *She has to really hate me.* She was however relieved to learn Virginia was not her birth mother. How hard would it have been to think that a woman who conceived, and carried you, for nine months could think so little of you? That she would care so less for you that she basically gave you to a monster and condoned his abuse. Tatiana pushed the thoughts away. She needed to get her mind together and ready herself for Samuel's visit tonight. He texted her a little while ago saying he was stopping by. *Wonder what this surprise is?* Turning her attention from thoughts of Samuel, she found Detective Monroe who was now standing directly in front of her.

CHAPTER 24

SHELL GAMES

Samuel relaxed waiting for Judge Kibbins to appear and start the proceedings. He glanced around the courtroom seeing several others also waiting for court to begin. *Wonder if they are all here for a divorce as well?* Christopher walked over to him.

"The clerk says the judge should be here in about seven or eight minutes."

Samuel nodded his understanding.

Leaving him to his thoughts, Christopher returned to the front row where all the other attorneys were gathered shooting the breeze with each other. *Just a few more minutes and I will finally have my life back, free to be with the woman I truly love.* The bailiff entered the courtroom. She admonished all contained to stand as Judge Kibbins made his way to the bench. Samuel looked him over. He was an older black man, grey temples, very distinguished looking. *I sure hope he's not one of those die hard save your marriage judges.* Samuel frowned with the thought. All he wanted from this man was a signature and pound of the gavel signaling the end of his union with Sylvia.

Judge Kibbins addressed the courtroom giving rules of conduct while in his presence. He then turned to the bailiff and spoke anew.

"Call the first case."

"Samuel Conklin vs Sylvia Conklin."

Samuel rose headed to the front where Christopher was waiting.

"Counsel present for Samuel Conklin," Judge Kibbins asked.

"Christopher Michaels for the plaintiff, your honor."

The judge grunted slightly and nodded.

"Counsel present for Sylvia Conklin?"

"Arick Sloane for the respondent."

Samuel's head snapped up. His eyes met the attorney, Sylvia standing to his immediate left.

What the fuck? Samuel fought hard to keep the anger and rage from his face.

Glancing at Christopher, Samuel saw the same surprise and shock registered. They both were blindsided.

"Fine, both attorneys are present, let's begin."

Christopher gathered himself and began to present Samuel's case.

Sylvia couldn't describe the crushing pain she felt sitting at this table with Arick fighting for a marriage that obviously only she wanted. Her finding out about the proceedings at all was a miracle in her estimation. The papers were sent to a long-ago address. She was sure she would have never seen them, were it not for their former neighbor. Miss Kinsey was an older woman who lived in the neighborhood for years. When they moved Sylvia left her number and they talked from time to time. She was surprised at the recent call and even more surprised at the content of the call. Sighing softly Sylvia reeled her mind in. Not only did she find out the man she loved with all her heart wanted to divorce her. He went out of his way to keep it a secret from her. *Why Samuel?* She listened to Christopher present

Samuel's case for petition. *When did our marriage become irretrievably broken in your mind?* Sylvia prayed the tears she held didn't overflow. She had to stay strong and get through this.

Christopher finished and sat down. Judge Kibbins allowed Arick to make his own statements about the petition before him. Samuel was livid as he listened to Sylvia's attorney. *How the fuck did she find out?* Samuel wanted this divorce. He wanted it right now. He leaned over in the attorney's ear.

"How is this going to affect our case?"

"Depends on how sympathetic Kibbins is feeling today." Samuel frowned somewhat. He certainly prayed the man granted him his freedom. He was done with Sylvia. It was over for years in his mind. This was simply a formality. *What about Tatiana?* If he didn't gain his freedom today, he wasn't sure how much longer she would wait. *I'll do anything to make her stay.* Arick finally finished and sat down. Judge Kibbins regarded Samuel silently for a while before turning his attention to Christopher.

"Is what Attorney Sloane stated true, counselor?"

Christopher sighed silently.

The attorney explained that the documentation was sent to the address supplied by his client. As far as he knew it was served.

"The sheriff brought back a signature, so we had no reason to believe Mrs. Conklin didn't get the petition."

Judge Kibbins grunted his understanding.

"So, Mrs. Conklin," he began now, turning his attention to Sylvia. "According to your attorney, you do not want this divorce?"

Sylvia swallowed hard trying to find her voice.

"No, your honor, I don't."

Samuel frowned severely. He was truly at his end with this entire fiasco. *Why can't this bitch just let go, damn!* Judge Kibbins nodded thoughtfully, still regarding Sylvia. He finally looked down at the paperwork in front of him, shuffling through the documents and remaining quiet. Samuel got a very bad feeling. After what seemed a stoppage in time, Judge Kibbins lifted his eyes and once again addressed the parties present.

"I am not going to grant your petition today, Reverend Conklin," he said, emphasis on the word reverend. "I'm going to order mediation and counseling for the next ninety days."

Samuel's anger hit broil.

"If at the end of the period, you, Reverend Conklin, still want this divorce, I will hear the petition again."

Judge Kibbins gave Samuel a look.

Everyone rose as the judge banged his gavel and dismissed them, calling for the next case. Christopher told Samuel they had no choice in lieu of the judges ruling. No other judge would even hear the case until the ninety days were passed. Thanking him for doing all he could, Samuel exited the courtroom running directly into Sylvia. He stopped in his tracks regarding her silently praying she didn't push his buttons. Right now, Samuel's mind was on overload. The longer he looked at her the more he hated her.

"Will you be home for dinner?"

Sylvia tried hard to control the hurt and anger she felt looking at him now.

"No."

"Are you moving out?"
She prayed he said no.
"I don't know yet."
Sylvia left him alone and turned leaving the courthouse, joined now by her attorney. Samuel stared at her back trying to figure out his next move. There was no way in the hell Tatiana was going to wait three months for him and he knew it. Samuel was desperate. Desperate times called for desperate measures. He plotted darkly as he too left the courthouse and headed for the spot.

*****

"Hi baby," Samuel greeted Tatiana as he drove.
"Hey. What's wrong?"
Samuel released a breath before answering.
"Nothing baby, just kind of a rough afternoon."
He didn't want to reveal the true crisis of his current situation.
"Oh, sorry to hear that."
"How is your day going baby?"
Samuel started to relax. Tatiana always had such a soothing effect on him.
"It's fine, same old, same old."
She sipped from her drink.
"I had a doctor's appointment this morning."
"You okay?"
She chuckled hearing the tone.
"Yeah, allergy shots."
He grunted a response.
"What time are you coming by?"
She needed to have herself together, so she could pull off the grand finale.

"I should be there around 8:00, baby."

"OK, you want dinner?"

Tatiana continued to lay the ground work.

Samuel smiled fully. This was the first time she offered to cook for him. Now he knew he had to get Sylvia off his back, and quickly.

"Sure baby, that would be great."

"Any special requests?"

"Whatever you make will be fine baby. I will see you soon honey, have a great day," he added, disconnecting.

As he got closer to the spot Samuel continued to brood about the events of the afternoon and the thing Judge Kibbins handed down.

"Bullshit."

Samuel found a parking space and pulled into it.

He dialed Gordon on his cell telling him where he was. Gordon arrived moments later.

"Wassup man," he greeted Samuel getting into the Benz.

"I am going to have to make a move with this marriage shit."

Gordon frowned confused.

"What's going on?"

Samuel ran down the ruling Judge Kibbins handed down and what it would mean to his relationship with Tatiana.

"She's not going to wait for me. She will think I've been lying to her all this time."

"What's your plan?"

Gordon had a pretty good idea but wanted to hear his friend say it from his own mouth.

"I'm going to send Sylvia's ass to a permanent sleep if she won't give me this divorce right now."

"How are you going to get her to agree? Especially with the judge basically giving the marriage a reprieve today."

Gordon was starting to see his friend come unglued. He wasn't sure what to make of his obsession with Tatiana. At first, he thought it was just a passing fancy. An older man getting a second chance at youth with a much younger woman. Now he saw something far more dark and sinister. Gordon knew without a doubt Samuel was deadly serious about taking his wife's life.

"I'm going to have a talk with her once I leave Tatiana."

Gordon continued to listen and take note.

"I'm going to honestly tell her that I don't love and will never love her. That ninety days or ninety years won't change that. So to avoid any more drama, call her attorney and say she changed her mind about holding things up."

Gordon nodded.

"And if she won't?"

"She's signed her death warrant."

There contained no trace of humor or remorse in his statement.

Shrugging Gordon changed the subject as his mind raced. He began making plans of his own to distance himself from Samuel, who in his estimation, had finally fallen over the edge.

*****

Tatiana was listening as Detectives Suave and Monroe gave her final instructions before Samuel's arrival. Garlan came by earlier assuring her she could make it through this and tonight the nightmare would finally end for her. *I sure hope so daddy.* Tatiana prayed as the detectives continued to talk.

"You don't have to talk out of your normal register," Larry told her.

He knew that a lot of people instinctively talked louder knowing the mics were in the room. That was a dead giveaway. He was pretty sure Samuel Conklin would be shrewd enough to know that.

"Try to be as normal as possible. We need him to be relaxed with you like always, so he will talk."

"Got it."

Tatiana confirmed her understanding.

"We are less than thirty seconds away Tatiana."

Dennis tried to reassure the young woman. They could tell she was scared too death.

They double checked everything once more then left Tatiana alone. Checking the oven, Tatiana ventured into her bedroom and headed for the shower. As the water cascaded over her body, Tatiana's mind was on overload. She wanted nothing more than for this to go off without a hitch. Leave this place, catch her flight, and see the man she loved tomorrow. *What happens when he finds out you set him up?* Tatiana's beleaguered mind kicked in anew. It was the only way though. If they didn't arrest Samuel she would never be rid of him. Tatiana was terrified every time he came over that he would force her to go with him. She would disappear from everyone she knew and loved. So far though God remained on her side and she was fine. *I sure pray that continues tonight.* Tatiana was surprised at her renewed faith, but she embraced it. Right now, she needed something to hold onto to get her through this chilling scenario. Dressing Tatiana combed her hair looking at her reflection in the mirror. Saying one last final prayer, she heard her front door close and Samuel call out her name.

CHAPTER 25

ALL BETS OFF

"Mmm," she moaned softly as he continued to arouse her. *This is so wrong.* Her mind tried to add a damper as her body resolutely told it to shut up.

He touched her breast with his tongue. She sighed deeply completely aroused by his touch, his taste, and his scent. It had been so long, but he still made her feel incredible. Still took her to a place that was nirvana. Kissing his way softly down her body, he parted her legs. Burying his tongue inside her, she arched her back to give him all of her.

"Yes, right there."

Make him stop, her mind piped up again, just as his tongue hit her spot once more. She came hard, trembling from the intensity. *You aren't being rational.* The pesky mind returned while he licked her treasure and she continued to purr her approval.

"Don't stop."

He looked up momentarily finding her eyes and smiling, before going back to work on her.

She forgot how good he was. How quickly he could bring her to orgasm. How absolutely satisfied he left her.

He brought her to one more mind-blowing orgasm before kissing his way back up her body. He reached her breasts taking each one in his mouth and playing with the nipple the way she loved. *Stop this, stop it right now!* He sucked her nipples while his hand slipped between her legs arousing her again. She began to flow freely for him once more. She moaned loudly reaching orgasm number three or four.

She wasn't sure, but who was really counting. He began kissing her neck. She felt the heavy breathing of his desire with each kiss.

"You are so beautiful," he told her lovingly kissing her lips.

Looking into his eyes the hesitation returned. This should not be happening.

"It's not wrong, baby," he told her softly as if reading her mind. "It's not wrong."

With the utterance she felt his hard manhood slide deeply inside her. The contact caused yet another deep guttural moan to escape her lips.

The pleasure of his movements took her to a plateau unreached for years. Opening herself to receive all of him, she heard him moan as he consumed her. *You have gone too far.* She arrived hard one last time, grabbing his butt pulling him even deeper, imploring him to give her all of him.

Hearing her cry out and feeling her body's response he did just what she asked. Groaning loudly, he released every ounce of his essence deep inside her.

As they lay in each other's arms, he caressed her face.

"I have waited so long for tonight."

She smiled finally at his words.

"I never meant to hurt you."

"I know baby, I know," he replied. "So, are you ready now?"

"Yes," Sylvia replied honestly.

She was ready to let go of Samuel and move on. He didn't love her. If she never believed it before court this afternoon, she certainly believed it after Gordon paid her a visit tonight telling her all of Samuel's plans for her. Gordon smiled at her answer as she laid her head on his chest and drifted off. He lay awake continuing to think as she slept. No one knew about the two of them. He was her first. He took her virginity years ago when they dated secretly. She was a pastor's daughter and he was a full-fledged street dealer, but he loved her. She loved him back. She proved it by giving herself to him one rainy August night as they spent time in his small efficiency apartment. Gordon wanted her to stay with him, but Sylvia told him she could not. She was only nineteen then. Gordon knew she was terrified of what her parents would say. He let her go. He said nothing when she hooked up with Samuel. Even after they began doing business together, Gordon never made anyone the wiser.

For years he sat back and loved her from afar. He knew the fire still burned inside her as well. He saw it in her eyes when she looked at him sometimes. He also knew she would never act on it. Sylvia was a good woman. She didn't cheat. He didn't consider tonight cheating though. Samuel wanted out. He left her years ago as far as Gordon was concerned. He smiled again thinking how hard it was to convince her to let him touch her. Gordon persisted. Kissing her softly, finally telling her the truth about Samuel having another woman. He was surprised that she already knew. Thankfully she never asked for a name. He knew she would give in though. If he could just get her to relax, which finally he did. Gordon closed his eyes thinking about how good she felt. Just like the first time he made love to her. He wasn't going to let Samuel hurt her or kill her because of his own selfishness. She was safe now. No one knew where this apartment was, not even Samuel. Gordon wasn't stupid. He remained in the game long enough to know you didn't tell anyone, everything. Kissing her forehead, Gordon pulled her closer allowing his mind to finally rest and sleep to find him.

*****

"Dinner was delicious baby," Samuel told her lovingly as he rose and helped her clear the table.

"I'm glad you liked it. You want some wine?"

"Yeah, that sounds good."

Leaving her in the kitchen he headed into her living room and took a seat. She brought him the glass moments later and sat down beside him.

"Tell me about this hectic day of yours."

Reaching out she caressed his face.

Samuel took her hand and kissed it. He loved being here with her. Tatiana was his solace. She calmed everything that was wrong in his world. He wouldn't let Sylvia take that away from him.

"Just some business honey."

"Oh, the stuff at the spot?"

Samuel grunted somewhat. He would prefer she think that, than know the truth.

"Sort of."

Tatiana groaned.

"So, we're back to keeping secrets again, huh?"

She began to sound irritated.

"Baby, no."

Samuel quickly explained, pulling her to him and holding her.

Garlan frowned severely as he watched the man touching his daughter. The detectives were allowing him to observe with them as they carried out the sting. *I want to kill that sonofabitch with my bare hands.* Reaching deep he willed himself to remain calm. All he wanted was for Tatiana to get what they needed and get away from the insane man. Garlan thought of all the years he believed this charlatan and his lies. The years he spent blind and mesmerized by the razzle dazzle, all while the so-called man of God was sexually abusing his daughter. *He got her pregnant.* Garlan recalled the hell Tatiana endured at Virginia's hands for that. *You didn't do a damned thing about it either.* His conscience pulled the sucker punch bringing tears to his eyes. He saw his baby girl falling down those stairs again in his mind. He remembered her tearful plea that Virginia intentionally pushed her. *Evil bitch!* Tatiana's voice broke his thought. He returned his eyes to the screen, continuing to watch and wait.

"Tell me the truth then, stop being so vague."

Tatiana looked directly into his eyes.

"Things are just kinda hectic baby."

Samuel kissed her.

"About Amp?"

Samuel frowned inquiringly.

"The boy you beat up."

"Yeah, there have been questions about that, but I think its pretty much cool."

The detectives smiled in the other room.

"What else then?"
She sipped her wine again.
"Police have been hassling our dealers and shit like that. Costing us money."
"I get it."
"Tatiana, you are so incredible."
Samuel kissed her intensely as Garlan's fist involuntarily clenched.
"You're not divorcing her, are you?"
"Baby, yes, I promise I am."
She gave him a look of disbelief.
"I thought that's what you were coming to tell me."
Tatiana feigned upset.
Samuel sighed genuinely looking at the hurt on her face.
"Baby, I bought this for you."
He could not lose her. He opened the box producing the diamond as she smiled a tad.
"Guilt offering?"
She forced the tears to her eyes, knowing it was his soft spot.

Garlan was proud of Tatiana holding her own. She just needed to get a little more information out of him and the detectives could come in to arrest him. He saw the fatigue in her demeanor and knew this whole charade was taking its toll. Garlan thought about their earlier conversation. Tatiana was terrified to tell Jaden about her past. She didn't want to lose him. She couldn't fathom in her own mind how he would or could still love her knowing the truth. Garlan tried to get Tatiana to agree to counseling in some form. The things she endured totally threw off her equilibrium emotionally. He hoped and prayed that Jaden was every bit the man she told him. Garlan was pretty sure if he were, he wouldn't leave Tatiana. He would help her, support her, and push to her to get whole once more. He another time returned his attention to the screen praying it would all be over in a matter of minutes.

"I don't want to talk about it anymore."

Tatiana moved in for the kill.

"OK, baby. Whatever you want."

She finished her wine and set the glass down.

"Tell me more about the business. From the beginning."

He supposed she wanted to take her mind of the pain she felt, thinking he was lying to her. He wasn't though. He loved Tatiana more than anything in the world. Once he left tonight he was going to prove it.

"Well, I started out almost ten years ago."

He ran down all the dope he sold, the cities he and Gordon did business, even the people he shot or killed along the way.

"Was there someone else before me?"

Tatiana wanted to know if he made any other girls life a living nightmare.

"I have never, ever, loved anyone the way I love you Tatiana."

"That's not what I asked you."

She gave him yet another look.

"There was this girl once."

"How old was she?"

Tatiana tried to keep the nausea and disgust from reaching her face.

Samuel swallowed hard before answering.

"Fourteen."

The reaction of repugnance was distributed equally among the detectives and Garlan, all letting out a collective sound of repulsion.

"This guy is a damned pedophile," Larry spat disgustedly.

Garlan and Dennis agreed.

Turning their attention back to Tatiana, they rose and began gathering themselves. It was time to bring this sordid chapter of Samuel Conklin to a close.

"What happened with her?"

Tatiana used every ounce of strength not to show her abhorrence for the animal sitting next to her.

"She started acting out, getting very possessive."

Tatiana nodded.

"You ended it?"

Samuel nodded.

"She didn't mean anything to me baby."

"I am beginning to think I don't either."

"Baby, listen to me...."

Tatiana gave him her full attention hearing the tone change.

"You mean the world to me, and I will do anything to be with you, anything."

He never took his eyes from hers.

"OK."

Samuel smiled and kissed her another time.

The pounding on the door made her jump. Samuel gave her a quizzical look. Tatiana shrugged and headed to her door.

"Yes, who is it?"

Samuel removed the gun from his pocket as he went and stood behind her.

"Tatiana Reynolds," Larry asked from the other side.

"Yes?"

She opened the door just a small crack.

"How can I help you?"

Samuel still stood behind her, out of the detective's line of sight.

"Miss Reynolds, we're looking for Samuel Conklin and have information that he resides here with you."

Tatiana swallowed hard.

"May we come in?"

Larry asked once more seeing that she wasn't moving.

He was beginning to worry. Something was wrong. Tatiana couldn't tell them Samuel was standing behind her door, gun cocked. Everything happened quickly after that. Samuel snatched her from the door. Tatiana gave a short scream. The door slammed, and the deadbolt engaged.

"Shit!"

Larry gave everyone instructions that the plan changed. They now had a hostage situation on their hands.

"Get up baby."

Samuel spoke to her as his mind raced.

"I didn't mean to hurt you."

Tatiana rose and stood trembling.

"Samuel, what's going on?"

Tatiana knew they could still see and hear everything going on in the apartment. Right now, that was her only lifeline.

CHAPTER 26

GAME ON

Get the floor cleared!" Barking orders Larry and Dennis tried to get the situation under control once more.

Garlan was beside himself. They could see from the monitor Samuel had a gun. *Don't let this animal hurt my baby.* He wanted about five good minutes alone with Samuel.

"Is SWAT set up?"

Dennis listened for the response from the radio he held.

Both detectives assured Garlan they would do everything in their power to bring this monster down and get Tatiana out unharmed.

"They have the green light," Larry told Dennis.

He nodded and relayed the message to the snipers.

Samuel was too unstable. If anyone could get a clear shot, they were instructed to take it. They cleared the tenth floor quickly. The residents were unceremoniously shuffled down the stairs when the elevator took too long. There were the usual uncooperative ones. Once threatened with arrest for obstruction of justice, they calmed down and quickly doing as they were asked.

"All clear," the officer finally reported.

Larry and Dennis acknowledged him, eyes glued to the monitor trying to counteract Samuel's next move.

"Samuel, we can't stay in here."

He continued to drink.

The wine flowed down his throat since he slammed the door. He tried calling Gordon on his cell getting no answer. *Shit, where is he?* Tatiana cried silently. He knew she was scared. He wasn't going to hurt her, but Samuel wasn't leaving her either. Some way, somehow, they were getting out of this building. "Do you have a fire escape?"

Tatiana nodded yes.

"Hmph."

He said nothing more for a few moments.

Samuel spoke walking to her and pulling her to her feet. "Tatiana, do you trust me?"

He had a plan. He needed her to trust him in order to pull it off. Tatiana didn't like the look in his eyes, but she answered his question, her mortality at stake.

"Yes, you know that."

He smiled and kissed her again.

"OK."

Larry and Dennis were frustrated. They thought about shooting tear gas into the apartment, but Samuel was far too unstable. In his state of mind, he might decide that murder-suicide was the perfect answer to the immediate problem. The detectives agreed they would never forgive themselves if something happened to the young woman who volunteered to help them. Garlan's patience absconded moments earlier. He wanted to choke the light from Samuel's eyes. Every time he kissed Tatiana, Garlan's fury rose. He could tell his baby girl was scared. It was all over her face. Still she held her own. He was proud as hell of her for that. *Make a move bastard so we can get to you!* Samuel began talking to Tatiana again, unfortunately whispering in her ear where neither the microphone's nor cameras could pick up the conversation.

"Are you sure," Tatiana asked.

Samuel kissed her.

"It will be fine."

"But --"

He once more kissed her silencing her.

"Trust me baby."

His gut told him not to speak aloud. He knew cops were shady and tricky. They probably found a way to bug the apartment or something while she wasn't home. He recalled the detective saying they had information he lived there. The only person who knew Samuel ever spent time with Tatiana was Gordon. *He sold me out, that's jacked up!* Samuel surmised the cops already arrested Gordon and either forced or bargained him into dropping dime. Tatiana's home phone rang. She jumped from the surprise of it.

"Should I answer it?"

Samuel nodded yes. He knew if she didn't the police would storm the apartment thinking something happened to her. He didn't want that right now.

"Hello."

Her voice shook with fear.

"Miss Reynolds, this is Detective Larry Monroe."

She grunted her acknowledgement.

"I need for you and Mr. Conklin to come out of the apartment with your hands up."

Samuel stood close and listened.

"Hang up."

He spoke loud enough for Larry to hear him.

"Hang up now!"

Tatiana placed the receiver back into the cradle without another word.

They were still watching the monitor. Samuel was clearly agitated. *Please protect my daughter.* Garlan sent the plea seeing the man's darkness begin to surface.

"I'm sorry."

"You didn't do anything wrong baby."

The detectives and Garlan breathed a collective sigh of relief. Samuel pulled out his cell and called Gordon again, getting his voicemail once more.

"So that's it then, I guess. You're covering your ass huh?!".

Tatiana continued to watch him warily. The detectives continued to observe.

"Payback is a bitch!"

In the next moment, the unthinkable happened.

"What the hell," Larry growled aloud as the darkness descended.

"No damned way," Dennis yelled.

The power was out. Samuel was delighted. *Perfect!* Grabbing Tatiana's hand, he hurried into the hallway. Larry and Dennis heard all the commotion and rushed to Tatiana's apartment, guns drawn, flashlights in hand. They were joined moments later by several other officers.

"Search it!"

Dennis had a bad feeling.

Samuel and Tatiana made it down the stairs and into the back alley where the door connected to the outside world. Tatiana was terrified. If Samuel made it to his car and took her, she knew she would never see her family again. Never see Jaden again. She might not even see her life for too much longer. She remained terrified while Samuel pulled her along. Tatiana heard the police yelling, movement all around them. It was pitch black outside. You couldn't see your hand in front of your face.

"Samuel, please…"

Tatiana began to cry.

"Shh, baby it's okay."

He knew she was scared.

"They're going to shoot us."

Tatiana continued crying, body trembling.

"No baby, we're almost out of here."

They made it to the street. Samuel crouched down behind a car pulling her down with him.

"Shh, calm down honey. I'm going to get us out of here, safely."

Tatiana nodded and said nothing else.

She was petrified. A part of her wanted to scream, to fight, to give away their position. The loaded gun in Samuel's hand kept her mouth shut and her feet moving. He again pulled her forward and they crossed the street. Samuel knew he would have to abandon his car. The police surely knew it. If he cranked it now in the midst of the darkness they would stand out like a sore thumb. Instead he methodically made his way down the street. He held Tatiana's hand tightly. Finally, after what seemed miles of ducking headlights, and voices in the darkness, they made it to the subway entrance. With the power remaining out he decided to chance hailing a cab. Getting in, Samuel gave the driver an address and sat back relaxing a bit. He held Tatiana in his arms, feeling her body still trembling.

"It's okay baby. We're safe now."

Now what? The thought brought despondency as Samuel held her and they rode. Her nightmare was complete. Not only had she lost Jaden and her family, life as she knew it was over. She would be Samuel's prisoner forever.

*****

"Where are those damned search lights?"

Before Dennis could garner an answer to his query the power finally reappeared.

"Fucking great timing."

Garlan was on the phone with Jorinda attempting to calm her.

"That man is crazy Garlan!"

He agreed with her sentiment.

Garlan racked his brain trying to think where he would go now that he knew the police were looking for him. *Hang on honey.* Garlan spoke telepathically to Tatiana as an idea came to mind. He quietly slipped away from the detectives. His cell rang. He checked the I.D. Taking a deep breath he answered.

"Where are you," Virginia asked curtly.

"What do you want, Virginia?"

Taken aback by his response she softened.

"I was just worried, that's all."

Garlan, really not in the mood to deal with her right now, answered abruptly.

"Hmph I'm fine."

"Are you coming home soon?"

She stayed unsure of his mood right now.

"In due time, yes."
Garlan disconnected before she could say anything else.
*****

Virginia held the dead phone in her hands frowning deeply. Garlan was extremely distant, almost hostile, lately. *What the hell is going on with him?* Richard walked into the room, finding her deep in thought.
"What's wrong?"
"Nothing of consequence."
Virginia smiled back, wrapping her arms around him, as they began to kiss.
Richard quickly undressed her as she returned the favor. Their affair continued for years with neither of them being able to stop.

Virginia had good sex and he loved indulging. Richard would never leave his wife, but she seemed oblivious to that fact as she eagerly spread for him every time he asked. Smiling internally, he continued to enjoy her.
*****

Garlan arrived at his destination and got out. Walking around he didn't see any visible signs of life. His gut told him he was right. Sighing quietly, he found a darkened spot and made himself comfortable. He saw a sight moments later that while not a surprise, did still bring some measure of hurt. Virginia got out of Richard's car, kissing him as she did. Garlan watched unobserved while she got into her own vehicle and pulled out of the grocery store parking lot. He assumed she headed toward their home. *That's why she wanted to know where you were. She needed to make sure she beat you home.* Garlan smiled. He was going to take care of

Virginia and all her treachery, but first things first. He returned his attention to his original purpose and intent, continuing to watch and wait.

*****

Samuel unlocked the door listening for any sign of movement. Satisfied they were alone; he allowed Tatiana inside and turned on a light.

"Sit down and relax baby. I'll only be a few minutes. Then we can be on our way."

"Where are we going Samuel?"

"Tonight, we'll go someplace safe and get some rest."

No further explanation accompanied his statement. Samuel saw the fear and apprehension in her face.

"Baby, I'm going to take good care of you, protect you and keep you safe."

"I know."

Reaching out, she stroked his face.

She needed him to trust her. Tatiana realized this might be her last chance to get away from him.

"I need to go to the restroom."

"Use the one down here."

It wasn't what she wanted to hear, but Tatiana willed herself to relax. There would be an opportunity and she would be ready to take it.

Samuel took the alone time to check his accounts. He transferred monies to his secret account. He had more than enough to relocate himself and Tatiana. The cash would keep them under the radar and out of harms way. He smiled thinking about her and how they were finally together. Granted it wasn't the way he ideally set about, it was still the way he wanted it. She was his and his alone. Searching some of the other drawers and boxes Samuel found what he sought. He took the keys out removing the ones he needed, placing them on the ring in his pocket. Glancing at the clock, Samuel knew they should get a move on. They were afforded the cover of darkness. They would go to the safe house and stay there until darkness fell again tomorrow. Then they would hop a bus and leave New York. Hearing the water running Samuel reined his thoughts in. Tatiana emerged moments later.

"Come on baby, let's go."

Kissing her lips once more his hand accidentally brushed her breast.

"Can we make love tonight, Tatiana?"

"I'd like that," she lied, smiling marginally.

If she had her way she would be long gone. Samuel smiled back and kissed her with passion.

Heading to the door he opened it. Tatiana screamed shortly as Samuel fell back, knocking her down in his wake. Garlan was inside and on top of him before he could recover. Tatiana managed to move as the two men fought. She was terrified for her father. Samuel had a weapon. Garlan had chronic asthma. Tatiana grabbed the phone dialing 911 before the receiver was snatched from her.

"No!"

Samuel threw her to the floor as Garlan tackled him once more.

The 9-1-1 operator repeated her request of information hearing the crashing and screams of the occupants. The operator immediately dispatched officers. Larry and Dennis heard the radio broadcast. Giving each other a look, grabbing their keys they raced to the location.

"Run Chip!"

Garlan hit Samuel hard knocking him to the floor.

Tatiana was paralyzed. She couldn't leave her father. Samuel was crazy. He would kill him.

"Run!"

Samuel gathered himself and hit her father with a hard right to the face.

Tatiana snapped out of her paralysis and turned for the door.

Samuel gained his footing and grabbed her arm.

"Hell no! Stop it Tatiana!"

He produced the gun aiming at a now wheezing Garlan.

"I will kill him!"

She immediately stopped struggling.

"No, please…"

Garlan managed to get his inhaler and stop his wheezing. Samuel regarded him hatefully, Tatiana in his arms.

"Leave us alone, let us live our lives!"

Garlan regarded him like the insane man he perceived him to be.

"You have got to be out of your mind!"

Tatiana continued to pray and endure.

"Tatiana was a baby when you raped her!"

"I didn't rape her! Tatiana was in love with me, just like I was in love with her."

Garlan continued to regard him incredulously.

"You cannot possibly believe that. She was fifteen years old for fuck's sake."

Samuel scoffed.

"Tatiana was a woman, with a woman's feelings and needs!"

The police stealthily made their way to the illuminated room and loud voices.

"I made love to her because we both wanted it."

Samuel's voice began to take on an eerie cold monotone.

"That's not true," Garlan countered.

Samuel sighed cavernously again.

"You, and people like you, have made my baby feel guilty all these years for wanting me."

Tatiana caught a glimpse of a shadow and held her breath.

"She wanted me Garlan. We love each other. She was carrying my child. Until that bitch Virginia pushed her down the stairs."

His eyes turned blood red with the recollection.

"But even then, you took that whore's word over your own daughter."

Garlan looked down guiltily.

"I'm the only one who has ever loved Tatiana, Garlan. Loved her without question, without doubt."

Samuel caressed Tatiana gently with his assertion.

"We're leaving this place, and we're going to be together. We're going to have our family that was stolen from us and live in peace."

Samuel finished speaking, rose from the desk, gun trained on Garlan.

"Say goodbye baby."

Tatiana began to cry in earnest.

"I love you daddy."

Garlan stood and began walking toward Samuel.

"Daddy, no, please!"

Samuel released the safety on the gun.

The first shot hit him in the shoulder. He screamed in pain and went down. Rising he reached out for Tatiana as the second shot hit him in the arm.

"No!"

Tatiana covered her ears as his arms encompassed her and began pulling her away. She screamed repeatedly, the horror of the night beginning to pull her over the edge. Suddenly smoke began to fill the room. All she heard was yelling, furniture crashing, sirens.

Then as quickly as it began, it was over. All she heard was silence. Looking around the room taking in the carnage, Tatiana's gaze came to rest on him. His eyes were wide open staring lifelessly at her. She looked up and saw Garlan holding the smoking gun, placed squarely against Samuel's lifeless body.

"Give us the gun Mr. Reynolds."

Larry took the weapon without incident.

They stormed the church just as Samuel prepared to shoot Garlan. The first shot to his shoulder caused him to drop the gun. Garlan promptly picked it up. Dennis reached Tatiana first pulling her away as the carnage ensued. The smoke grenades were employed to disorient Samuel and make his apprehension easier. Larry sighed deeply and released Garlan. He knew they could easily argue self defense. This was not how they envisioned ending this case. Larry and Dennis were satisfied nonetheless. Watching Garlan hug his daughter as tears streamed both their faces. The nightmare of Samuel Conklin was finally over.

EPILOGUE:

ENDINGS & RENEWALS

NAKIDA'S LIFE

The last six months were an up and down spiral for Nakida. Trying to pursue the rape charges against Rahshaun proved increasingly difficult. His lawyer, a shady trickster, pulled out all the stops. The police seemed to be doing everything possible to help his cause in her estimation. Tiffany dropped her complaint against Kenny, saying it was a big misunderstanding after a night of drinking. Nakida stuck to her story. She never gave consent to sexual intercourse with Rahshaun.

"Nakida, girl let it go."

Tiffany gave her repititious spiel for the hundredth time.

"Do you really want to go to court, sit on that witness stand in front of a bunch of strangers and tell them your business?"

She gave Nakida a knowing look.

"You already know how white folks are. Most of them on the jury will be white."

Nakida sighed lightly. She didn't want Rahshaun to get away scott free. She didn't want him to be able to rape other unsuspecting women.

"Somebody has to stand up, Tiffany."

Without hesitation, her friend fired back.

"Why does it have to be you? Rahshaun is sneaky as hell, but he's not stupid."

Tiffany tried reasoning with her again.

"You see even at work his ass only got a slap on the wrist after both you and Tisha filed a complaint against him."

Nakida grudgingly admitted Tiffany was right. Human Resources simply moved Rahshaun to another department away from the two women, where they had no contact. They didn't demote him in any way or reprimand him. Rahshaun successfully intimidated Tisha to the point she wouldn't even talk to Nakida anymore. Even when she herself saw him he would give her a leer and lewd wink as he looked her over. *I want that dog to get his so bad I can taste it.* She felt helpless, powerless against the system.

"I guess you're right."

Tiffany smiled and hugged her tightly.

"Thank you, girl. Now you can finally put your life together and move on."

"I still want that dog to get his."

Nakida grumbled angrily making the call. She spoke to the detective on her case alerting them she would no longer pursue it.

He told her he understood, again apologizing they didn't have stronger evidence. Thanking them again for all their help, Nakida disconnected. Finally, this sordid chapter in her life ended.

Nakida's wish would be granted two months later when Rahshaun was stabbed to death by another potential victim he met, drugged, and brought home from the club.

NAIMAH

A year passed. It was Naimah's birthday again. "Happy birthday baby."

Rueben softly uttered the words as they kissed. The entire church erupted into applause.

Today was their wedding day. Naimah couldn't think of a better present than the man standing in front of her who just made her his wife. Rueben was there for Naimah through her long recovery from the rape. He never turned away. Even when she tried time and again to make him leave. Her parents were somewhat leery of allowing her to marry so early. Naimah convinced them of her love for Ruben. They could, without a doubt, see his for her. He bought them a really nice starter home where they could be comfortable while she attended school. They talked and decided not to have kids until she graduated. Naimah took her pills religiously to ensure they stayed true to their decision. They may have been young, but they both knew what they wanted. To be together forever.

Ruben looked at the woman he loved smiling at how wonderfully meeting her turned out. The form fitted lace dress she wore was exquisite. Naimah, being who she was, decided against white. Instead she opted for the beautiful black dress trimmed in soft coral. He chuckled thinking of her mother's initial reaction when Naimah told her about the choice.

"You're supposed to wear white."

Her mother's lamenting lingered until Naimah modeled the dress.

Her mother fell just as deeply in love with it as she. Ruben loved how it hugged her softly, accentuating her curves. The hand beaded pearls brought a shimmery iridescence to the soft coral, making her skin glow next to it. She also took great care picking out his tux. The tie, vest, and cuffs, of his shirt matched the coral in her dress perfectly. The pictures would be wonderful. Ruben began making his way to Naimah, spotting her in the swell of well wishers and congratulators.

Naimah still thought about Pastor Padgett. He went through hell since Denzel's death. His wife immediately left him and filed for divorce. Thankfully the grand jury refused to indict him on any charge. Without the indictment the prosecution let the case go. He and Naimah spent a few afternoons talking. It helped her through her healing. She was sure his as well. He was a broken man after burying his son. Naimah didn't think he would ever recover. Last she heard of Mrs. Padgett she was dating some new pastor supposedly getting married. Today was extra special for her. She glanced in the audience and saw him in the very back of the church, smiling at her and Ruben. Naimah made her way to him after the ceremony.

"Hi. I'm so glad you came."

Daniel smiled back.

"So am I, Naimah."

Ruben joined them, extending his hand.

"How are you doing, Pastor?"

"I'm doing well, Ruben. I'm proud of you both."

Ruben smiled and put his arm around Naimah's waist.

The woman walked up and joined them as they talked.

"This is Carniece, my fiancée."

Daniel introduced the woman to them.

Naimah smiled and hugged him tightly. She spoke to Carniece repeating the gesture. Taking a moment to excuse themselves she pulled Daniel aside.

"I'm so happy for you."

"Thank you Naimah. She has made me want to live again."

He went on to tell Naimah about the new church they started together in another town almost eighty miles away.

"That's wonderful."

She giggled aloud as Daniel confided Carniece's pregnancy.

"Take care of yourself, Naimah."

Daniel rejoined Ruben and Carniece.

"I'll make sure of that," Ruben replied.

"I have no doubt of that at all."

The couple bid Ruben and Naimah goodbye. She smiled doing the same. Watching them walk away, she returned her attention to her groom. After a quick kiss, they headed for the reception awaiting them in the church's annex.

LIFE AFTER THE NIGHTMARE

Tatiana walked outside into the sunshine and put on her sunglasses. She was feeling better and better with each passing day. Her weekly sessions with Dr. Clayton were helping her slowly erode all the dark painful memories of her past abuse. They talked at length about Samuel. They discussed her feelings for him. His obsession with her. The underlying sickness that drove him to abuse and torment her. Inhaling Tatiana took in the fragrant aroma from the Cuban deli she was passing. Her stomach rumbled to remind her of the hunger. Chuckling she entered the restaurant greeting the portly owner and following him to her table.

"Hey baby."

Jaden stood pulling out her chair.

Tatiana smiled and returned his greeting, sitting down.

"How was your session?"

Tatiana smiled seeing the love contained in his gaze. She truthfully declared the productivity of her time spent with the psychologist.

As they perused the menu and ordered lunch, Tatiana's mind went back almost a year and a half ago. The day she sat down with Jaden, telling him the truth. *She asked him to come home after Samuel's death and he immediately complied. They met at Auntie Jo's. Herself, Garlan, her aunt, and Jaden, all sitting in the room together, with him anxiously awaiting her to speak. Tatiana remembered the terror she felt like it was yesterday. Taking a deep breath, she told him everything. She told him about Samuel Conklin seducing and abusing her when she was fifteen. She told him about the pregnancy and miscarriage. She told him about Samuel's obsessive paranoia and the subsequent events leading to his death. Tatiana admitted her fear of Jaden leaving her once he knew about her past. She told him how very much she loved him and how much he helped her find her way back to her faith. All the while he sat completely mute, his face expressionless. After spending herself, Tatiana stopped talking and held her breath. Garlan and Jorinda both spoke to Jaden explaining Tatiana's life, her birth, Virginia's abuse. How much they both knew she loved him. How they prayed he wouldn't turn his back on her now.*

Tatiana remembered the tears coming and rolling down her cheeks as Jaden continued to say nothing for the next few moments. He, as a final point, loosed an audible breath and turned to her. She was of course expecting the worse when he opened his mouth.

"I love you," Jaden told her simply. "I'm sorry for this happening to you baby."

He never looked away from her.

"But if you allow me, I'll be there every step of the way to help you get better."

Jaden hugged her tightly. Tatiana began to cry in earnest.

Garlan and Jorinda both smiled and left them alone. They ventured into her kitchen under the guise of making coffee for everyone.

"You need some therapy, you know that right?"

Tatiana nodded her understanding.

"I am sure we can find you a good one in Miami."

Tatiana gave him a confused look.

Tittering slightly, Jaden told her of the job offer and his original intent for having her come down again.

"So, can I get a yes out of you?"

She threw her arms around him, repeating the yes again and again. Pulling away to look into her eyes once more, Jaden spoke.

"I want you to always know Tatiana, I will always love you and be here for you."

He took another breath, stroking her cheek gently.

"And nothing that happened to you with that crazy man, was your fault."

Jaden kissed her poignantly after his point.

Tatiana smiled as Jaden's voice broke her thought. Their life together was incredible. Jaden was absolutely the best thing that ever happened to her. She glanced at the three and one-half carat diamond resting on her hand smiling again. Jaden proposed to her a month ago. They were still trying to agree on a wedding date. She recalled overhearing him and Andrew, his father, talking after a family dinner one Sunday evening. *"When are you going to marry her," Andrew asked his son point blank. "Soon dad," Jaden replied sighing lightly. "Don't wait too long," his father returned giving him a look. "Tatiana is a good woman. Trust me there are plenty of guys with their eyes on her." Jaden frowned a touch nodding his understanding.* He proposed almost exactly two weeks after that. Tatiana's life was good these days. She would be forever grateful to God for that. Her cell rang. She glanced at the I.D. seeing Garlan's name. Smiling she answered. She conveyed her plans to see him later this afternoon and disconnected, returning to lunch with her man.

GARLAND'S EMANCIPATION

Garlan smiled after disconnecting thinking how much he loved the Florida sun. Moving to Miami was the best decision he made in a while. Tatiana and Jaden both implored him to move. Not only to be closer to them, but to improve his health. They surmised the humidity would be better for his asthmatic condition. Garlan admitted he felt much better since being here. Sighing he thought about Tatiana and all she endured over the years. Garlan again berated himself for not being a better father to her and protecting her. He did however rid himself of Virginia once and for all. He chuckled at the memory sipping his cold drink. *"What is this,"* Virginia asked looking at the paperwork Garlan shoved across the breakfast table. *"Divorce papers,"* he said basically, never taking his eyes from hers. *"What are you going on about, Garlan?"* Virginia tried to sound brave, but Garlan could see the shock and surprise in her eyes.

Virginia picked up the packet and began to read the documents. "As you can see," Garlan began, garnering her attention once more. "I don't want anything," he told her, sipping his coffee. "I just want you to sign them and let me live my life." Virginia regarded him quietly for a few moments more. "Garlan, what are you trying to prove with this nonsense?" Garlan, setting his cup down regarding her once more, spoke. "You can be free to continue screwing Richard, no ties." Virginia caught her breath. "Though I don't know how available he will be now that Sharelle knows the truth and he is on both knees begging her not to leave his ass," Garlan's bitterness bubbled to the surface.

"You are a cold, heartless, bitch, Virginia," Garlan told her frankly. "For years I stood by and watched you hurt

Tatiana, abuse her," he went on growing angrier. "But none of that, nothing, compares to you serving her up on a platter to that bastard Samuel Conklin and letting him do the things he did to her!" He actually came across the table at her. Virginia jumped from her chair knocking it over in the process. "I should beat the shit outta you," Garlan growled walking toward her.

"Garlan, stop this!" Virginia cried out, terrified of the look in his eye right now. "Sign the damned papers Virginia." Garlan began to calm down becoming rational another time. "I want to get as far away from you as possible," he threw out. "Tatiana knows the truth you know," he told her smiling as the tears came to her eyes. "She knows that her real mother loved her, without hesitation." Virginia finally broke sobbing deeply. "Stop crying! The only person you feel sorry for in those tears is you." Garlan handed her a pen and the papers once more. "Sign." Virginia looked into his eyes and saw nothing. Garlan was completely devoid of emotion. Taking the pen, she shakily signed the documents. He turned on his heels walking out of her life forever.

Garlan's cell went off and interrupted his thoughts. He smiled seeing Jorinda's name. They tried to talk her into moving as well, but Jorinda loved New York. She did visit frequently so they still got a chance to spend time together. Garlan learned through her that Virginia was trying to rebuild her life. She found out with certainty from Sharelle, Richard was ending their affair. The veiled threat added, if she valued her safety she would stay away from him. Jorinda told Garlan that though Virginia did some low and evil things, she was still her sister. She still had love for her. Jorinda spent time with Virginia as the two tried to reconcile some type of relationship together. Garlan didn't hold that against her. He and Tatiana were done though. Neither wanted anything to do with the woman. One day Garlan prayed he would stop hating Virginia the way he did. Right now however the anger, rage, and hurt, were deeply imbedded in his system.

"How's Kay," Jorinda asked.

Garlan smiled.

"She's good. Might hit her up for lunch."

Kay was his new girlfriend. She was few years younger, but they clicked. She made him happier than he could recall in a long time. After chatting a while longer, Garlan bid Jorinda a great day and disconnected. His mind briefly recalled Sylvia Conklin to mind and he wondered whatever became of her, before dismissing it. Calling Kay and garnering confirmation, he rose to go pick her up.

FIRST LADY NO MORE

Sylvia smiled within as Gordon's arms embraced her from behind, kissing her neck.

"Don't you look delicious lying here like this."

He lustily took in the sexy halter mini as she sat on their chaise lounge.

His hands caressed her breasts sliding downward, resting lovingly on her protruding belly.

"You feeling okay today?"

He kissed her neck once more.

"Yes, we're fine."

Sylvia waited ten years to feel what she felt. The growth of a child in her womb. Sighing silently and closing her eyes, she allowed Gordon's touch to envelop her. She thought back to all the horrific events of a year ago when Samuel was killed. The scandal and shame that followed would have been unbearable if not for Gordon. He helped her through all the police investigations, the bad press, even persecution by the church board authority.

Sylvia buried Samuel in a small private cemetery, after an equally small and private funeral. He was completely ostracized from the church and church community after his crimes came to light. There were three other young women who came forward. All admitted molestation and rape during his various pastoral appointments. Sylvia got the opportunity to talk to Tatiana and learn the truth about the young woman's ordeal. They received the chance for much needed closure. Each woman admitting no ill will toward the other. She collected the monies from Samuel's insurance, still being legally married to him. She left New York, and her old life behind. Gordon brought her here to

Atlanta. They bought a house together. Sylvia still attended church, but not nearly as regularly as she used too. Gordon left the streets and got a real job. He held a degree in Multi-national business. He put it to good use at the Fortune 500 Company that hired him.

Still traumatized from her marriage to Samuel the inhibitions and restrictions of their sex life, Sylvia continued to meticulously take her birth control. She smiled again remembering the conversation with Gordon after he found them. *"I thought you wanted kids,"* *he asked holding the pill packet in his hand. "I do," Sylvia told* *him honestly not liking the tone or the look he was giving her.* *"So why are you still taking these damned things?" He gave* *her a hard look. Sylvia hung her head. The tear trickled down* *her cheek. "Because I didn't want you to leave me if I got* *pregnant."* *Breathing acutely Gordon came and took her into his arms,* *speaking soothingly to her. "Baby, you're not with him* *anymore." He kissed her cheek. She finally looked up at him.* *"I want to give you babies. As many babies as you want."* *Gordon honestly spoke his heart. She chuckled. "I only want* *one for now." He smiled anew at her answer. "Then throw* *these away."*

She did exactly that finding herself pregnant less than six months later. Much to her relief, Gordon's reaction reached ecstatic when she told him. Everyday Sylvia thanked God for surviving her life with Samuel. She promised never to be that blind ever again. Gordon still didn't go to church much. That didn't matter to her. He loved her, completely and without hesitation. For Sylvia that meant more than pretense of piousness and goodness when a blackened, evil, heart beat underneath.

"You're making me real hard laying here next to you."

Gordon whispered the erotic words into her ear, pressing his erection against her butt.

"What do you want to do about that?"

Sylvia teased him, sensuously sucking his index finger. Gordon turned her to him, kissing her passionately, untying the top of her dress.

Smiling as he proceeded to arouse and make love to her, Sylvia again thought to herself how good God was. She thanked him for her life. Her old new love, and the gift of their child.

Join Author KR Bankston and the new evolution of reading via Patreon.

Enjoy exclusive content. First looks. Free downloads. Discounts on merchandise, courses, events. Writing tips and one-on-one communication with the Author.

With five (5) Patron levels to choose from, KR offers inclusion for any budget. Join us today!

WWW.PATREON.COM/KRBANKSTON

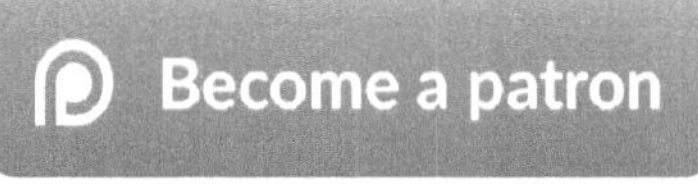